CLOUD AND WALLFISH

CLOUD
AND
WALLFISH

· Anne Nesbet ·

CANDLEWICK PRESS

Copyright © 2016 by Anne Nesbet

First paperback edition 2018

Library of Congress Catalog Card Number 2016946908
ISBN 978-0-7636-8803-5 (hardcover)
ISBN 978-1-5362-0183-3 (paperback)

18 19 20 21 22 23 BVG 10 9 8 7 6 5 4 3 2 1

Printed in Berryville, VA, U.S.A.

This book was typeset in Scala.

Candlewick Press
99 Dover Street
Somerville, Massachusetts 02144

visit us at www.candlewick.com

for Ines

· chapter one ·

GOING, GOING, GONE

Noah knew something was up the moment he saw his mother that May afternoon in fifth grade. She swooped up in a car he didn't recognize—that was the first thing. And, secondly, his father was sitting in the other front seat, and in Noah's family, picking up kids at school was a one-parent activity.

There in the back was his raggedy brown duffel, the one with the duct tape hiding a rip, perched on top of a pile of suitcases. He had to sidle in carefully if he didn't want to topple any bags.

There wasn't even an extra inch left on that whole seat for his backpack—he just swung it around and balanced it on his knees.

"Um, hi," he said to his parents. "What happened to our car? What's all the luggage about?"

"Shut that door," said his mother. "Rental car. We have to hurry. It's a sudden adventure. And hand that backpack up to your father."

The car pulled away from the curb so quickly that the tires let out a hint of a squeal (which was cool).

Noah's father turned around and gave him a reassuring smile.

"You're going to do just fine," he said as he hauled Noah's backpack into the front seat. (*Do fine?* thought Noah.) "Of course, we meant to give you a little more notice. What've you got in here, anyway?"

Apparently that wasn't a question that could wait for an answer. Before Noah could go peep, his father had given the backpack's searchlight-yellow zipper a tug, and everything inside tumbled out in a heap of pencils, erasers, and crumpled papers. Plus two books and a banana.

"Hey!" said Noah, leaning as far forward as the seat belt would allow. His mouth almost failed to make any sound at all, he was so surprised. His parents were tidy people, usually.

"Only what's essential. That's all we can take," said his dad, while his hands went picking through the debris so speedily his fingers turned into an efficient blur. He had a trash bag at his feet, it turned out, and all the papers were going right in there. Then he turned back with a wink. "What do you think—is this banana essential?"

"What are you doing?" said Noah. He didn't care about the banana. It was everything else that mattered. "Take where? Wait, don't throw *that* out—that's my math homework."

"Not anymore!" said Noah's mother. "We're getting on a plane—can't take any extra junk."

"We're getting on a *plane?*" said Noah. "Right now?"

"Yep!" said his mother. "It's that trip we've been talking about taking. Did you think those language tapes were just for fun? Hey, come on now, *German!* It's your superpower, remember? *Der-die-das-die.*"

She sang the last bit. It was true that they had been listening to language tapes at home. There was a German grammar book that came with the tapes, and they had made up songs for some of the charts. The only way Noah could get through those charts was by singing them. German has way too many consonants—and way too much grammar, his mother liked to say.

Actually, however, Noah sort of liked all that grammar. His brain was very good at patterns, and learning to understand a language is all about recognizing patterns. His mother was almost not kidding about it being Noah's superpower.

As superpowers go, though, it was a more or less

3

invisible one: Noah was a whole lot better at understanding than he was at speaking.

"But we can't go anywhere *now*," said Noah. "This isn't vacation time. Vacations happen in the *summer*."

Because it was supposed to be a vacation. That was the whole idea: they were going to go to Germany—*on vacation*—to go to the Black Forest, eat cake, poke at cuckoo clocks, and tour at least one castle.

"Plus anyway I have soccer tomorrow. I can't miss soccer. And Zach's birthday is Saturday!"

"Change of plans," said his mother. "Sorry. Couldn't be helped. And it turns out it's going to be a different Germany. Not the *usual* Germany. The other one. We have a few hours for organizing and getting our stories straight, and then we fly."

Flabbergasted. That was the word that filled Noah's head, though he kept it safely inside. Flab-ber-gas-ted.

And for the birthday party, Zach's mom was going to rent the first *Indiana Jones* movie on video. Indiana Jones! Noah opened his mouth, but before he could say one single useful, coherent thing, his father interrupted. Sometimes parents don't notice when a kid has vital things to say. Sometimes they're too busy sorting through that kid's books, papers, and candy wrappers.

"Hey, look at this!" said Noah's father. He had Noah's current book in his hands—an old edition of *Alice in*

Wonderland & Through the Looking-Glass that used to be his mother's. Noah had picked it off the shelf that very morning, because he always had to have something to read in his bag, just in case. This particular book looked battered but cheerful. It had lost its dust jacket years ago; rows of red-ink and black-ink rabbits trotted away on the cover in a diamond pattern.

Noah's father was staring at those rabbits; he looked doubtful.

"What do you think, Lisa? This okay?"

"That's not extra junk. That's my book I'm reading," said Noah, holding out his hand. He had only gotten through the first chapter or so in school today, but it was turning out to be a very weird story. Old-fashioned but weird. Noah liked it.

"No name written in it, yes? Then it's all right, I'd say," said his mother.

But as his father tossed the book back to Noah, it hit the side of the seat, and a card fell out of it, dislodged from all those pages where it must have been wedged in pretty tightly before.

"What's that?" said Noah's mother, and the car swerved a little to the right as she swung her head around to take a look.

"Don't worry," said Noah's father. "Eyes on the road. I've got this. Noah—"

But Noah was staring at the square in his hand.

"A photograph!" he said. A tiny girl stared out at him, standing very straight and upright by the knees of a large, wide-smiling man in an armchair. "Hey! Who's this kid? Who's that man?"

"Oh dear!" said his mother, and she swerved so abruptly off the highway into a rest area that Noah had to hang on to the seat in front of him. *"Oh dear!"* she said again. *"I shall be too late!"*

And the car screeched to a halt. There wasn't much to see at this rest stop. The kind of gravelly asphalt that just sits there dreaming of taking the skin off some poor kid's knees, a few sorry trees, a building with restrooms in it, and a couple of picnic tables covered with bird poop and future splinters.

Noah's hands were trembling.

"Too late for what?" he said.

"It's a quote," she said, and at that very moment Noah remembered where he had heard those words before: that's what the White Rabbit says at the beginning of *Alice in Wonderland.* Right as he leads Alice down the rabbit hole and into the world where everything's weird.

That gave Noah the strangest feeling. What were his parents up to?

"Look," said his mother cheerfully. "It's all a surprise, I

know, but the good part is, we're going somewhere where almost nobody gets to go."

"Think of it as an expedition," said his dad. His smile was conspiratorial. "If someone invites you to the South Pole, what do you do? You say yes. Right? This is like that, only not the South Pole."

Noah's mother dismissed the South Pole with a wave.

"Back to facts," she said. "It's not going to be easy, maybe, Noah, but you can do it. Hand that photo over, though, please."

Noah stretched his hand out, but slowly, giving his eyes time to see the picture first. That tiny girl—she looked familiar around the edges. She was dressed up in party clothes, with a tiara on her head and a wand in her hand, and her eyes were dark and sparkly, like she had just figured out all sorts of things other people couldn't imagine. She was maybe four years old, that little girl, and it looked like she was noticing every detail of your clothing, your hair, the nervous twitches that meant you might be trying to get away with something.

It was the look of the eyes that gave her away: this little girl was his mother. No doubt about that. There she was, four years old, maybe, and already formidable.

"Mom, it's you!" he said. He had never seen a picture of his mother as a child before. He knew that was strange, but some families don't have cameras. Or there's a fire and all the photo albums burn right up. These things do happen. "Is that your dad, then? Is that . . . Grandpa?"

A folded newspaper dangled from the man's hand— you could see about half the headline, in those big dark letters that newspapers use when they want to shout: CORONA—

Something else Noah had never seen a picture of before: any of his grandparents.

"Come on, now. Let go of that thing," said his mother. He hadn't realized he was still hanging on to it, but it was a picture filled with data, a puzzle of a picture, and Noah's mind had woken right up as he looked at it.

So as Noah put the photo into his mother's hand, he did that thing he could do with his brain: took a picture of the photograph, so he could study it later.

He used to think everyone could do this, but in second grade after his koala report, which had lasted forty minutes and contained a gazillion details, his teacher had given Noah two thumbs-up and called his memory "practically photographic." It seemed to him true and not true, both at once. A "photographic memory" sounds like it should be just like a camera, but Noah's brain was a fussy, not-so-perfectly-working camera. He couldn't take a brain-photo of everything all the time—he could still forget plenty of stuff—but when the brain-camera worked, when Noah

8

heard that tiny, secret *click,* then that picture was tucked away in his brain-file forever. His parents knew Noah had a good memory, but they didn't know the truth, that Noah's memory was *perfect*—sometimes. Imperfectly perfect. Perfect in a not-so-perfect sort of way.

That was Noah's own secret. In a family as sharp-eyed as Noah's, it was good to have some secrets even your mother didn't know.

"Well, look at that," said Noah's mother, eyeing the photo with the strangest expression on her face. "Coronation day! I was a handful and a half, even then. Thought I should be queen of the world."

"And why not?" said Noah's father.

He smiled at Noah.

"Hey, look, there's a vending machine! Why don't you go ahead and get yourself a soda?" Noah's father said. He pressed some coins into Noah's hand. "And using the restroom's a good idea, too. It's going to be a bit of a long drive from here."

Noah opened the door, but he didn't yet get out of the car.

A horrible thought had swept down out of the clear blue sky and perched itself on Noah's shoulder like a ten-ton crow. Noah turned and looked at his parents, his usually less-bizarre-acting parents, and asked, just to be sure: "You didn't murder somebody, did you? Or rob a bunch of banks?"

His parents both laughed. His mom had a laugh that was like a sharp hoot of some wild, fast-flying bird, but his father chuckled in long, rolling rumbles.

"Nah," said his father. "Nothing like that."

"An expedition," said his mother. "An urgent expedition, remember? So hurry."

Secret File #1
WHAT THE MICROPHONE WOULD HAVE TOLD YOU

An important note: If you had been listening in to Noah's family's conversation, perhaps by having left a radio-transmitting microphone in the car they were driving, which is something people sometimes do, you would not have heard it the way I just wrote it out for you above. That is not only because conversations in real life are always jerkier and messier and more mumbly than the ones in books, but also in this case because everything Noah said always came out in shards and pieces, and that is very hard to portray in words. I have written down what he meant to say, and what his parents (who had years of practice understanding him) knew he was trying to say, but not what you yourself or your hidden microphone would have heard him saying.

Noah stuttered. Not just a cute hiccup around a "Denver" or

a "dictionary," either. Any number of sounds could just knock him right down.

For Noah, talking was like riding a bike with a wheel that liked to freeze up, almost out of nowhere. He would be sailing along down a sentence (so to speak), and along would come a word with a *b* or an *m* in it, something totally everyday like "bunch of books" or "mummy," and that wheel would simply stop short, like an invisible wall had suddenly sprung up in the road before him, and he and his bicycle would just bang right into that wall and stop.

When this happens over and over, it becomes very tempting to ride your bike like you wish it had training wheels: to pedal along very, very slowly and carefully. Maybe even not to ride at all.

But Noah didn't want to stay still, and he didn't want to be silent, so he kept opening his mouth and plowing on. That was the sort of person he was. He was not a training-wheels kind of kid.

"Noah never stops trying! His attitude is good! He's very persistent!" said all his teachers. "He'll surely outgrow his difficulties with time!"

But it looked like maybe not, on the outgrowing thing. Noah had peeked into the books on stuttering his mother brought home from the library, and from all those pages of tiny print he had gathered that although little tiny kids often outgrow a stutter by the time they're medium-little kids, someone who's as old as eleven may — *may* — be a stutterer all his life long.

"But there's nothing you can't do!" his mother had said to him a hundred times. "Look at all those famous actors who used to stutter! Think of them! James Earl Jones, the guy who does Darth Vader's voice — I heard *he* used to stutter."

It didn't always help, thinking of famous actors who *used to stutter*. They sure didn't seem to be stuttering now. Noah would have paid all the dimes in his dime collection to hear some famous movie actor open his mouth and get stuck. Darth Vader with a stutter! Noah would have liked to hear *that*!

Anyway, this is all just to say that much of what Noah said to his parents in the conversation in the car had a sort of explosive, machine-gun stop-and-start quality and would not necessarily have been understood by a casual bystander. But Noah and his parents understood each other, after long practice, reasonably well.

Let's be clear, though: understanding the words your parents say is not the same as understanding what they're up to when they announce out of the blue that you'll be leaving your old life behind this very minute, right now, today.

It turns out that even people who don't stutter at all can sometimes be thoroughly incomprehensible.

chapter two

BATMAN, GOOD-BYE

When Noah came out of the restroom, he found his parents gathered around a trash can in the parking lot. His father was stuffing garbage bags full of who-knows-what into the trash can, and his mother was holding a match to the corner of something in her hands. It turned out to be the very photograph Noah had just found in his mother's old book.

"Stop! What are you doing?" said Noah. Or, rather, intended to say. He was so horrified that his voice stopped, too. He made a sound that was itself a little like fire hissing, and that was all.

The only photo he had ever seen of his mother as a child, and she was burning it up?

"Don't wave your arms around like that," said his mother as she calmly watched the flames eat away at the edges of the picture and then stamped the ashes into the pavement. "There, that's better. One of those good rules for all travelers: don't draw attention to yourself, ever."

"It's just a picture," said his dad, but at least he sounded a little sad about it. None of this made sense. Then Noah caught a glimpse of a neon-yellow zipper in the garbage can.

"That's my backpack," he said. "It's *new.*"

And it had excellent Batman logos on the many pockets. It was a terrific backpack.

"Can't be helped," said his mother. "It has to go. It has your name scrawled right across the top in indelible marker."

Why was that a problem? If you didn't have your name on your backpack, you couldn't bring it on the aquarium field trip: his mom knew that. She had written that N. KELLER there herself, just last month. And now they were throwing the whole backpack out?

"It's because of where we're going," said his father. "We have to be very careful about everything. Come on, let's get back in the car."

"People can't have Batman backpacks in Germany?"

"It's not just the usual Germany we're headed to — it's

East Germany," said his father. "That's the one behind the Iron Curtain."

"East Germany?" said Noah. His mind was having trouble with the image of a curtain made out of iron. Curtains were supposed to ripple in the breeze.

"Remember the Olympics?" prompted his father.

That's right. There had been two Germanies at the Olympic Games last summer. His parents had pointed that out to him then. One Germany was friends with the United States; the other Germany was somehow connected with Russia—now also called "the Soviet Union," just to make things more complicated.

"Swimmers," said Noah. "Didn't they have a lot of swimmers?"

"You got it! East Germany—the Communist one—the German Democratic Republic. Home of some very strong swimmers! So here's the thing. You know how your mother has been studying to be a teacher?"

"Sure," said Noah. Secretly he thought she would be an excellent and terrifying teacher.

"And so she's doing research on—?"

Noah knew this part, too: "Kids who have trouble speaking," he said. "What does that have to do with swimmers, though?"

His mom hooted a little, like an amused owl.

"Nothing!" said his dad. "Stuttering, not swimming!"

"'Differential Approaches to Elementary Education for Children with Speech-Production Impediments in East and West,'" said Noah's mother. She said that title so fast it sounded like one impossible thirty-three syllable word. "Because I figured my thesis needed a comparative angle. A unique, comparative angle. Not just American schools. Schools from somewhere different, from a different system. So! Brainstorm! Bingo! *East Germany!* They're quite interested in special education there, it turns out. And it's hard to get more different than East Germany!"

They were all already back in the car. Noah's mother turned the key with gusto, and the engine roared awake again. Noah looked back at the bright-yellow strap of his Batman backpack, poking out of the garbage can, and felt very strange about everything that was happening.

None of this sounded even the slightest bit like visiting the Black Forest and eating cake.

He was sorry about the cake, but on the other hand, Noah's mother had been working on her graduate degree in special education as long as Noah could remember. Mostly that seemed to mean reading books with very plain covers and long titles, and sometimes using Noah as a guinea pig for all the various tests she had to learn how to give. Noah and his dad both took a lot of pride in being the Most Supportive Family Ever about Noah's mother's doctorate.

"There you go," said Noah's father. "It's going to be an absolutely terrific thesis. But it turns out we have to go now."

"Before schools let out there," said his mom. "And other reasons: change being in the air, the visas having come through."

"What's a visa?"

"Official permission to enter a country," said his mother. "Visas can be very hard to get for a place like East Germany. Lots of forms. And you can't just jump up and decide you want to go there. First you have to apply to get a fellowship from this outfit in Washington, D.C., called the International Research and Exchanges Board—they're the ones who fund this kind of trip. Did I mention I'm being paid? Actual money? To do research?"

"Well, it's a great topic," said Noah's father. "Right, Noah?"

"Sure," said Noah. His mind, however, was a great big tangle of swimmers and cake.

"Thanks!" said his mother. "So that's how it went. First I got the fellowship, and then the East Germans needed to think about whether to give us our visas. They dig into everything. They ask all sorts of questions. But now we've got the visas, so we can go."

"When are we coming back?" asked Noah. He didn't want to miss any more soccer practices than he had to.

"We'll have to leave the GDR in six months," said his mother, with what seemed to be regret. "That's when the visas run out."

"Six months?" said Noah. "Did you just say *six months?"*

He couldn't believe it. He could *not* believe it. It was unbelievable. He could feel his mouth hanging open, and he didn't even care.

"Now, now, think of it this way," said his father. That was one of Noah's father's favorite phrases, a signal that something over-the-top and extravagant was probably on its way. "It's kind of like a trip to fairyland, right? I mean, because almost no one gets to go there, and it's sort of sealed away behind tall walls, you know? Some people visit, sure, but almost nobody gets to live there, and certainly nobody your age from here. You are one hundred percent sure to be absolutely the only kid in the whole place who comes from Virginia."

"Fairyland?" said Noah

"Not the kind of fairyland with fairies," said Noah's dad. "More like the places Alice goes in that book you're reading. A fairyland with lots and lots and lots of rules."

"East Germany, a fairyland? Hmm!" said his mother, swerving back onto the highway and making a beeline for the fast lane.

"It will be fun!" said his father. "It's all about attitude, people; we just have to learn to think about things a little differently."

Noah's mother winked at him via the rearview mirror. Noah's own attitude was feeling a little battered and bedraggled just at that moment, to be honest.

"More than just merely fun," said Noah's mother. "Even those scientists going to the South Pole that your father's so fond of don't head off that way just because it's *fun*. A trip like this to *the other Germany* is guaranteed to be better than fun: it'll be *highly educational*."

Better than fun?

Noah was highly dubious.

Secret File #2
"TWO GERMANIES? WHY?"

When Noah asked this question, which had been simmering in his brain ever since he had heard he was going to the *"other* Germany" instead of the *"usual* Germany," his father told him the following story:

Once upon a time there was a very terrible war. . . .

In 1939 the Germans invaded Poland, and that was the beginning of the Second World War. Germany looked pretty unstoppable at first, as it pushed on through Europe, occu-pying country after country, terrorizing and murdering those people who didn't fit into Hitler's warped ideas about "racial purity."

But once the Soviets and the Americans joined the war against Germany in 1941, the tide began to turn. Slowly the Soviets pressed the Germans back out of Russia and Ukraine and then back through Poland toward the German capital, Berlin. The Allies on the Western Front — the Americans, the British, and the Canadians — pushed east through France, which had been occupied by the Germans since 1940. In March 1945 the Allies crossed the Rhine River, which marks a stretch of the border between France and Germany. In late April the Soviet army reached Berlin from the east.

Germany surrendered on May 8, 1945.

In Soviet Russia and in the United States — and in many other places around the world — people rejoiced.

Then things almost immediately got complicated again.

With Germany destroyed, the U.S. and the USSR (short for the Union of Soviet Socialist Republics) became the world's two great superpowers: the most powerful countries left standing. You might think that the Americans and the Soviets would get along better than they used to, now that they had won the war together, but in fact the tensions between the Soviets and the West grew and grew during the years right after the war. Russia and the United States had very different opinions about how the world should be run. The U.S. believed in capitalism, in letting people's drive to make money push the economy forward, while the USSR was the world's leading Communist country, supporting state ownership of factories and industries as part of a "planned economy"—which just means everything's decided in advance by the government: how many cars and tractors to build this year; how many dentists the country will need three years from now; how many children of tractor builders, therefore, get to go to college now to study dentistry; everything. The idea was that with perfect planning, history would no longer be full of surprises, and everyone would be happy and safe.

The other countries of the world more or less lined up behind the (Soviet) Communists or the (American) capitalists. These decisions were not always made in a very democratic fashion: Hungary, Czechoslovakia, and Poland, for example, countries in the eastern part of Europe, found themselves— not by choice—on the Soviet side of the great divide. Austria and Greece fell under the influence of the Americans.

As for occupied Germany, the superpowers eventually decided to split the country into two. In 1949 the British, French, and American occupation zones in the western parts of Germany united to form the Federal Republic of Germany, and the eastern part of the country, which had been occupied by the Soviets, took the name "German Democratic Republic" and became part of the Communist group of countries known as the East Bloc.

That's how that story seemed to have ended, but the two new Germanies did not exactly live happily ever after. With time that new border between them turned into a bristling line of mines and fences and watchtowers: the Iron Curtain.

And slicing across the city of Berlin, eventually: the Wall.

· chapter three ·

THINK OF IT THIS WAY

Back in the car, Noah put his book in the boring blue knapsack (no indelible ink anywhere) that his parents had brought along as a replacement for Batman. It was already almost full: there was a jacket in there, too, and socks. Nothing that Noah could see in that new backpack, except for *Alice in Wonderland,* had any character whatsoever. Would somebody come along and notice that there was a perfectly good Batman backpack abandoned at the rest area? Somebody who wouldn't mind an N. KELLER in block print near the handle? Maybe there were other Keller families on their way somewhere; maybe they would stop at that very same rest area; maybe —

"So, Noah, the thing is," said his father, interrupting that tangled mess of thoughts, "that there turn out to be some complicating factors."

You could say that again. His parents had practically kidnapped him, had crumpled his math homework and thrown away his Batman backpack—that was definitely a lot of "complicating factors." What, in all that had just happened in the previous two hours of Noah's life, was *not* "complicated"?

"The age thing first," said Noah's mother from her confident place behind the wheel.

"Yes," said Noah's father. "See, like I said, there are many rules in this place we're off to, and one of them is that they're very fussy about people matching their papers. That means, if your birth certificate says one thing, then that's what you've got to go with. So here's the deal— it's about your birthday."

"It's going to strike you as strange, and we're really sorry about this," said his mother. "You have to believe us that there isn't another way."

"*What about my birthday?*" asked Noah. And the word "birthday" came out with all sorts of extra stops and starts, as if it had a bunch of extra joints or something.

This was all getting weirder and weirder. His birthday hadn't been that long ago—March 23. A bunch of kids from school had gone bowling with him, and there had been cake and eleven candles and presents and all the usual stuff. He didn't see how even a trip to "the other Germany" could threaten a birthday that had already safely happened.

"Well, the thing is," said his father, "to tell the truth, you were actually born in November."

"What?" said Noah. "No, I wasn't. March twenty-third. We went bowling for my eleventh birthday, don't you remember? Joey got in trouble for throwing his shoes at Larry, and we ran out of—"

Pepperoni pizza. Why was something so tasty so impossibly hard to say?

"Of course we remember the *party*," said his father. "The point is, that wasn't in fact your birthday."

"November eighteenth," said his mother briskly. "That's when your birthday actually is."

"No way," said Noah. Perhaps he just gaped from the backseat without saying anything out loud, but all of his inside mind was shouting in disbelief: NO WAY!

Birthdays are fixed dates. They do not just jump around.

"It's partly because you were such a smart young thing," said his father. "And the school had a silly super-early cut-off for kindergarten for boys. So we just worked a little documentary magic and voilà, new birthday for you."

"No way, no way. You couldn't do that. Even *you* couldn't."

"You've never seen your mother wield her extraordinary forgery talents? You've never seen her write notes in my handwriting? You've never seen her sketch ridiculously accurate-looking pictures of dollar bills when she's bored or waiting in line?"

"Oh," said Noah. Of course he had. But changing a birthday? Wasn't that illegal?

In the rearview mirror, Noah's mother smiled a satisfied, not-very-modest smile.

"Practice," she said, "makes perfect."

"Wait," said Noah. He was beginning to feel ill, and not just because his mother was taking every curve about ten miles per hour too fast and a foot or two closer to the curb than was reasonable. "Are you telling me I'm *not even eleven* yet?"

"Exactly," said his mother. "Technically, you'll be eleven in November. Lucky for us! A child coming in through the Wall to stay with a parent on a research visa has to be *young*—ten's already stretching it."

"Moreover," said his father, "there's the business about your name."

A great pool of icy numbness was swallowing up Noah's legs and arms.

"What about my name?" Noah asked.

"More paperwork," said his mother. "A graduate-school-meets-border-controls-paperwork thing."

"Here's the deal," said his father, turning to look back at Noah. "People's lives change. So, which only makes sense, their names change, too."

"They do?" said Noah.

"Sure, they do. Names change *all* the time. Some people change names when they get married. Some people write books under a pseudonym. Some people just always wanted to be called Rainbow Stormchaser, and one day they decide to make it so. Some people emerge from their wild teenage years and decide it's time to settle down to a quiet life in Oasis, Virginia, under different names entirely—"

"That would be us," said Noah's mother.

"You guys have two different names?" said Noah to his mother. "Is that what you're saying?"

"Bingo," said his mother. "We all changed our everyday names when we moved to Oasis. That was actually kind of the point of moving. To start over."

"Because you were in the picture," said Noah's father. "Look, think of it this way: a tiny sweet baby, born into a family of, um, let's say, wild adventurers—that's your mother and me. Magicians, trapeze artists, mountain climbers—"

"Trapeze artists?" said his mother. "Don't get carried away!"

She was grinning, though, Noah could see. She would be a pretty awesome figure, catapulting from a high trapeze.

"Wild adventurers," said his father again. "But let's see. When *wild adventurers* have a baby, sometimes they decide it's time to turn over a new leaf and start right over, do you understand me? To begin a brand-new life, somewhere quiet and peaceful. Because they're nice people, even if they've been wild adventurers all those years, and so they're going to do *whatever it takes* to make a nice, safe life somewhere for their sweet baby boy. Right? Am I right? They're going to do whatever it takes."

The rental car shuddered as Noah's mother overtook another truck.

"So that's what we did," said his dad. "We gave up all our old names, and we became the quiet Kellers. We picked a quiet little town. We took you to play in the quiet little park. We became super normal, quiet, ordinary people for a few years."

"Ten," said his mother, as if that had been a very, very long time. "Ten years."

"A great ten years. It's been good, living normal lives in Oasis, right? But now this amazing opportunity for your mother's research has come up! We have to grab that. The thing is, our Oasis names are lovely and useful, sure, but not technically official. So it's simple: we have to leave those Kellers behind for a while. Just until we return to Oasis, of course. Then we can be Kellers again."

"What are you saying?" said Noah, who had been stunned

into complete, total silence for the whole one minute and fifty seconds of this extraordinary speech. Now he felt his lips going dry, his heart beating fast. *Leaving themselves behind?* "What are you even saying? Are you saying we've been *hiding?* Is this like the Mafia's after us or something? Are we in *danger?* Because every day I go to school. That's the opposite of hiding."

"Well," said his father in his mild-mannered way, "going to school could be a way, actually, of blending in, if you think about it."

"The *Mafia!*" Noah's mother laughed to herself as if it were the funniest thing anyone had ever suggested in the history of suggestions.

"Point is," said Noah's dad, "we came to Oasis to start our lives over as the nice, calm Kellers. People do that. They start lives over. But to pull off this trip to East Germany, our names and our birth dates have to match up with our documents. That's just how it is. So what if the names are different from what we've gotten used to? It's a matter of wearing the appropriate costume for the occasion. Think of it this way: Does Cinderella go to the ball in her ordinary rags? Does she ride to the ball in an ordinary pumpkin? No! She puts on a special ball-going gown, and she rides in a transformed golden carriage, and every part of that outfit of hers has to be just so, so that no one looks at her and says, 'Hey! I think that's that kid Cinderella from back in Oasis!'"

"Dad!" said Noah.

"That's what we're saying: all the data we show the East Germans—the birth certificates and marriage licenses and passports and everything—it all has to match up."

Noah's father used words like "data" because he himself was a "data analyst" for some big company in Virginia that probably did things with stocks or graphs or money or something. Noah was a little vague on the details of his father's job, but it was the kind where you had to wear a tie and went early in the morning and came home when it was already a little bit dark, and to tell the truth, it was very peculiar that his father was in the car with them at this moment at all, so early on a Tuesday afternoon.

"What about your job?" asked Noah.

"I quit," said his father. "This is worth it, I figured. Once-in-a-lifetime opportunity to go live behind the Wall. Exciting! And I'm finally going to get to write my novel about mink farmers."

Wait. Wait. Noah was beginning to feel downright head-spinny. He'd heard his father joke about writing a novel before, but *mink farmers*?

"So there you have it: that's why there's all this business about the paperwork being just so," continued his father. "Everything has to line up right for the East Germans or we won't be let over the Wall."

"It's the kind of wall you climb *over*? Like with ladders?"

His parents laughed for a moment, and then both seemed to have some sudden serious thought and stopped laughing.

"Sometimes people try—from the East German side," said his father. "It's been twenty-eight years already since the Wall went up in Berlin—"

"Summer of sixty-one!" said his mother. "We couldn't believe it at first. No one could believe it."

"—and people are still trying to get out."

"Why?"

"Well, all sorts of reasons. You know, maybe they've got family on the other side. Maybe they want to be able to travel freely, not be told where they can go and who they have to be and what they have to do—"

"Ahem," said Noah, who was being dragged off by his parents to some Communist country he had basically never heard of, four days before Zach's birthday. *"GET IN THE CAR, NOAH! YOU ARE ONLY TEN! NO MORE SOCCER FOR YOU! NO CASTLES! NO CAKE!"*

The Astonishing Stutter made him sound even madder than he was, but that was okay with him.

"Hmm," said his father. "I see your point."

"Oh, nonsense!" said his mother, and there was a wicked glint in her reflected eye. "Our family is not a Communist country. Besides, like your dad said, this will be *fun*."

And when she said the word "fun," she gave the steering

wheel an extra little yank, so that the car jiggled left across the lane.

"Well, anyway," said his father, "in order to get through the Wall—to get us all through the Wall and into East Germany—you'll just have to be a good sport and play along. That means using the birthday and the name that the birth certificate we sent the East Germans says you have."

"My name is just Noah," said Noah. "I've never been anything other than Noah."

"Well, yes, of course, for us you've always been Noah. But I'm afraid officially that isn't your name at all, so we're all going to have to adjust to the change."

"It will be an adventure," said his mother. "Something different! Like putting on a new mask!"

"You'll get used to it pretty soon, I think," added his dad. "It's just like any new habit. Do it for whatever amount of days, and it becomes normal. You'll be totally adjusted to it sooner than you think. And anyway, there's a sort of nautical relationship between your real name and the one you've been using all this time; you'll see: one builds ships and the other sails in whales."

"What?" said Noah. "What what what?"

It can be hard to breathe when people who ostensibly love you pop a new mask right onto your face.

"Your actual real name, dear," said his mother as she

sped that rental car up to chase down the next tractor-trailer on the road, "is—and I do think you'll like it once you get used to the whole thing—Jonah Brown."

Secret File #3
AND THIS ISN'T NOW, EITHER

The mathematically inclined reader will already have added twenty-eight to 1961 and discovered that Noah (now Jonah) is having this conversation on the way to the airport with his parents not "now," but quite long ago, in 1989. Noah (Jonah) does not realize, however, that he is living long ago. He thinks of himself, as all of us do, as living in the present. So we will not trouble him with this added bit of confusion just at the moment.

After all, he is still thoroughly flabbergasted by the news that not only is he younger than Zach Blumberg, which is really galling and a shock, but that his name is Jonah and not Noah. That's just one extra letter and a tiny bit of rearranging's worth of difference, but you'd be surprised how disorienting an itty-bitty change like that can feel.

It made him feel sick inside, almost like someone coming down with the flu.

· chapter four ·

THE JONAH BOOK

"Look in your new backpack," said his mother as they slipped into a booth at a pizza and burger restaurant—"the most American food possible, since we're about to leave all that behind," his dad had said—on their way to the air-port. "We put a book together for you, to help. Also because it was fun."

It was buried under all those sensible socks and warm layers: a little photo album. On the cover were the words JONAH BROWN.

"What is this?" said Noah.

"Pictures," said his mother, with a touch of pride. "To help you remember who you are, with your new name and all."

"Your mother may have gotten a little carried away," said his father.

Noah opened the photo album.

Right there on the first page was a picture of a house he didn't know. A blurry family stood in front of it.

"What's that house?"

"That's Jonah's house," said his mom. "So for the next few months, that means *your* house, right? Also *Sam and Linda Brown's* house—that's us."

Could you really do that? Could you take "Mark and Lisa Keller" and turn them into people with completely different names? Noah stared at these incomprehensible photos and then up at his incomprehensible (but smiling) mother.

"House? Why do we need a different house?"

"To keep our real home in Oasis private," said his father. "To keep it safe and private, just for us, when we're done being the Browns and want to go back to being Kellers. We don't want the East Germans poking around our lives in Oasis. We don't want anybody poking around. So the Browns have their own story! Like a novel, see? Set in Roanoke, Virginia!"

"Roanoke?" said Noah aloud, but inside his brain he was sounding like Alice: *Curiouser and curiouser.*

"Lots to remember!" said Noah's father. "The names, the places, the dates. That's why we thought it might be helpful to have a Jonah Book."

"Yes, so, look: there you are as a baby," said his mother, turning the page. "Weren't you sweet?"

He thought he recognized the baby photo, but of course babies are babies.

There was a toddler edition of Noah, playing on a generic lawn.

That was fine, too.

Then things got weird.

First he saw his earliest school photo, with the hair sticking up on one side. He knew this picture by heart. But on the facing page was one of those class photographs with all the kids lined up on bleachers and the teacher standing to one side, and he didn't know anyone in that picture. The sign propped up in the photo said:

MRS. WHEELER, FIRST GRADE
JEFFERSON ELEMENTARY SCHOOL
ROANOKE, VIRGINIA
1985–1986

"That's not my school," said Noah. "Who are those people? I'm not even in this picture."

"Sure, you are," said his mother. "There you are, *Jonah Brown*. Seems a long time ago, first grade."

And she brushed her index finger against a boy in the middle row, the one whose face, as it happened, was mostly hidden behind his neighbor's.

"What?" said Noah.

His mother, utterly unruffled, turned another page in the album.

MRS. DEERBORNE, SECOND GRADE

Another group of strange kids on bleachers.

His mother pointed to one of them, who had just looked down, apparently, when all the others opened their dutiful mouths to say, "Cheese!" A generic blur of brown hair, that was all you could see.

"There you are," she said. "Jonah."

Noah didn't know what was more bizarre: this "Jonah Book" or the way his parents were behaving, as if it were completely normal to change your kid's name, to tweak your kid's age, and to make up a whole new past for him to choke on.

His father gave him a sympathetic pat.

"I know, I know! It feels sort of strange, right? But you'll get used to it. You'll learn to be careful. The book's just a reminder."

"Careful?" said Noah.

"We already had one of those rules for travelers: don't stick out," his mother said. "Well, here's another rule— and it's so important it should probably be Rule Number One: *They will always be listening.* They will *always* be listening. Indoors, we can't ever say anything that might make them suspicious. NEVER. We'll call that the second rule. And one of the things we can't say is names. No names of people, *Jonah*. Not our old ones, and not anybody else's names. And everything we say has to match our documents. I'm Linda—your dad's Sam—you are Jonah—we're the Browns, from Roanoke, Virginia. And, by the way, you *loved* Mrs. Deerborne, your second-grade teacher."

Noah thought about all of this for a moment, and it seemed like just plain too much for any one brain to have to make sense of. An avalanche, a volcanic lava flow, a tidal wave of Too Much. So he did all he could do: he took the smallest, tiniest corner of that avalanche and he chipped away at that first small thing.

"What do you mean, *'they'*?" he asked. "Who's the *they* that's always listening?"

"The secret police," said his mother. "The East German State Security agents."

"There will almost certainly be bugs in the walls," said Noah's father. "Not bugs like cockroaches! Bugs like little tiny microphones recording everything we say. They'll be listening to us, that's for sure."

"But *why*?" It seemed like so much trouble to go to, to put tiny microphones in the walls!

"Because we're Americans," said his mother, "and so they'll assume we are spies."

She could stare even better than Noah could stare—she'd

38

had a lot more practice at it. She did such a good job of staring just at this moment that Noah found it impossible to ask the next question that came to mind: *Why would they possibly think we're spies?*

He *thought* that question pretty loudly, though. Maybe his father overheard that loud thought, because he laughed and said, "We can't be too flattered, though. They think everybody's a spy. And so they spy on *everybody*. They spy on foreigners; they spy on their own people. There are probably more spies per square kilometer in East Germany than anywhere else in the world."

Noah thought someone saying something like that should sound a whole lot more worried.

"So I have to pretend to be Jonah Brown, who had these other teachers in this other town, because the East Germans are going to be thinking we're spies?"

"Exactly," said his mother.

"We don't want to look suspicious," said his father.

But really, if you thought about it, what could look more suspicious than this Jonah Book, with its blurry-headed kid messing up all the school photos? What was more suspicious than suddenly showing up for your kid in a rental car, headed to an airport for a trip he didn't know about? What was more suspicious than *throwing out that kid's new Batman backpack just because it had his name on it?*

Noah's father seemed to guess the general trend of

Noah's thoughts. He leaned forward and looked right into Noah's confused and still-flabbergasted eyes.

"The truth is, buddy, we can't do this without you," he said. "Seriously. It's a lot to ask, but it's *necessary*, and you're the smartest, best kid I know, and I know you can handle it."

It was something about the way he said "necessary" that did it: out of that crazy, confused weed patch of emotions in Noah's brain, a quiet tendril of something else was beginning to push its way toward the light. He didn't understand why this was all happening, but something rang true in his father's voice just now. Noah was needed. Noah was *necessary*.

"And now Rules One through Nine, plus milk shakes for dessert," said Noah's mother. "All coming right up!"

Secret File #4
THE RULES, AS EXPLAINED BY NOAH'S MOTHER OVER MILK SHAKES

1. They will always be listening and often be watching. Don't forget that!

2. Don't ever talk about serious things indoors; in particular, never refer to people by name. That could get you and them into a lot of trouble, because of Rule 1.

3. Don't call attention to yourself. ("That's a good one in other countries, too," said Noah's father. "Not just the ones with bugs in the walls.")

4. Smile. Be polite. Don't let your worries show.

5. If you absolutely have to talk about the past, stick to what's in the Jonah Book.

6. Never ever ever use any of our old names. The old names will be waiting for us back in Oasis.

7. If you are asked questions, say as little as possible.

8. Really. Don't talk. Think before speaking. Then, most of the time, don't speak. Because of Rule 1 again. Always Rule 1.

9. Trust us because we love you. That means don't ask awkward questions! Because of Rule 3 and always, always Rule 1.

And then Noah's father added, "Hmm, well, seems to me, as a new-minted writerperson, there should be another rule — what number are we up to now? Ten? Okay. Rule Number Ten: While you're doing all of that fine not-talking and not-frowning and not-sticking-out, also keep your eyes peeled and your ears open. It will all be new. It will all be interesting. *Notice everything.*"

chapter five

A CITY BEHIND A WALL

They were flying the last leg of the trip to Berlin on a big, fancy Pan Am plane, though not quite as big and fancy as the plane that had flown them from the United States to Frankfurt, West Germany, and Noah (now Jonah), with his nose plastered to the little airplane window, was still, it's fair to say, about one thousand percent in shock. But paying attention. Paying very close attention.

In fact, he was determined—and definitely not just because it was the tenth Rule—to *notice everything.*

Because, yes, he was going to a new and strange place, quite far away from Oasis, Virginia. And because, yes, he was supposed to be a new person, with a whole new name and a whole new life. But also—perhaps even mostly—because his parents were behaving like people who had huge secret lives he hadn't known anything about.

He was reminded of this every time his parents handed over the brand-new passports, the ones that claimed to belong to "Samuel Brown" and "Linda Brown" and, worst of all, *"Jonah Brown,"* at the counters and the check-in desks and the airport gates. All those familiar faces next to those unfamiliar names! He remembered going to the photo store to get that picture taken. His mother had said it was for his player pass for soccer. Ha. Ha ha. Ha ha ha ha ha!

So how had his parents done it, all those years? How had they disguised themselves—and Noah—as Kellers? Was it that easy to sign your kid up for school under a different name? Apparently so, if the one doing the signing-up was Noah's mother. And then he started feeling sad all over again about his Batman backpack and the soccer game and the birthday party and everything that he had left behind in Oasis, Virginia, so it was almost a relief when the pilot's voice came booming into the cabin:

"Ladies and gentlemen," said the pilot, "we have entered the airspace of the German Democratic Republic. We'll be flying along the narrow corridor permitted to Western air traffic approaching Berlin. We are not permitted to leave this corridor under any circumstances; otherwise there will be dire consequences. Fortunately, your pilot and copilot today have long years of experience and excellent navigation skills, and we are quite hopeful that we will manage not to get ourselves shot out of the sky—not today, anyway."

"Really?" whispered Noah to his father. "They could shoot us down, really?"

He got stuck on the word "shoot," perhaps because his mouth didn't want his brain thinking about things like that.

"Seems like our pilot has a sense of humor," said his father, who did not seem worried in the slightest. "But also—though don't worry, it won't happen—also, yes."

The plane made a very tight coiling turn as it landed, staying carefully inside the area that belonged to West Berlin.

Noah's father had explained it all on the Washington, D.C.–to–Frankfurt part of the journey: you couldn't fly from Frankfurt right to East Berlin; you had to fly to West Berlin and then travel through the Wall. You could get to the border a bunch of different ways: car, train, subway, the S-Bahn, which was something in between a subway and a regular train and ran on tracks above the ground, or you could even go over on foot, if you didn't have a lot of luggage.

Noah's parents had it all figured out, though as Noah

shivered a little in the cold air and lugged a suitcase up the stairs into a bus, he suspected they might not have chosen the *easiest* way: they were taking that bus to the nearest S-Bahn stop, and then riding to the Friedrichstraße Station, a place where hundreds or thousands of people crossed from West to East or East to West every day, under the tightest of controls.

"To get the full flavor of the border," said Noah's father to Noah. "You'll see. It's apparently quite astonishing. I've studied some diagrams. Used to be one ordinary railway station, and now it's the most amazing underground labyrinth. Miles of tunnels twisting and turning, sorting who can go in and who can go out."

Noah was listening with about half an ear to all this talk of tunnels, while his eyes studied the world outside the bus. This place didn't look anything at all like Oasis, Virginia. Instead of comfortable houses at the back of long green lawns, Berlin was filled with old-fashioned buildings, several stories high. The signs were all in German. He hadn't slept very much on the plane, and now he had that weird exhausted feeling in his stomach that makes it hard to believe that what is happening to you just at the moment is actually happening *in real life*.

And there was a drizzle of rain, making everything grayer and stranger.

His father did some scribbling on a piece of paper.

"See, it goes something like this," said his father, sketching the roughest of rough lines and pathways and arrows. "One of the tracks runs right through East Berlin but only carries West Berliners on it, from West Berlin stations to West Berlin stations, on a bit of the old route curling through East Berlin. And then the other track, for the trains East Berliners use, is blocked off right here, in the station. It just ends. So that's how you turn one station into *two* stations, right next to each other. Just hammer up a wall between the tracks so people can't jump from the East Berlin trains to the West Berlin trains."

"And then add a lot of tunnels," said his mother, sounding a little impatient. "Get ready to pay attention, now. Remember the Rules. All the Rules apply! And for Pete's sake, don't forget to throw out that suspicious-looking doodle of yours."

They didn't have a huge amount of luggage, but they sure had enough to stand out. People gave them a lot of polite sideways glances as they pushed themselves and their bags up a bunch of stairs and, finally, onto the S-Bahn train.

"All right. Are you ready?" said Noah's father. "Heeeere we go."

The train went past more buildings, across a gray river, through some complicated structures involving barbed wire, past more buildings —

46

"And this is already East Berlin," said his dad. He sounded more excited than Noah thought was reasonable, considering how gray and drizzly the world outside the windows was turning out to be. "See that? We're in East Berlin now, physically, but we won't be really *in* East Berlin until we've gone through the border controls. All those tunnels. Okay. This is it. Grab your stuff."

The train was pulling into a gray barn of a station.

Someone said something as they hauled their bags out onto the platform.

Noah's father made a polite and noncommittal sound in response.

"What did that man say?" asked Noah as the train pulled out of the station, leaving them on the platform.

"Don't be slowing us down with questions, now, Jonah!" said his mother, and the sharp edge of her eyes added: *Have you already forgotten the Rules? Rule Nine? And always Rule One?*

But his father smiled and said, "He said, 'Aren't you going the wrong way?' Families with lots of luggage going into East Germany—probably not something you see every day."

"Oh," said Noah. He wasn't sure how that explanation made him feel.

Then they turned to enter the Friedrichstraße labyrinth, and everything became more and more unreal. *Notice everything*, Noah reminded himself. They left the ordinary gray light filtering through the sooty glass of the S-Bahn station windows and went down a set of steps, down under the ground, where dozens of fluorescent tubes in the low ceiling cast a light that was probably actually quite bright but felt dark somehow, it was so much unlike sunlight or the sort of brightness that came from the friendly, old-fashioned lightbulbs Noah was used to. And the walls were covered in slightly glossy tiles, on the yellow side of yellow-brown, vertical rectangles everywhere, reflecting the unwarm light. It was chilly. It was like a place that didn't know what exactly it wanted to be: the basement of a hospital, maybe, or a place where creepy things might be stored on metal shelves. And everyone who had come down the steps from the train platform with them was lining up in front of doors labeled with various letters: DDR, BRD, ANDERE STAATSBÜRGER.

"That's us!" said Noah's father. "*Other nationalities*. Over here. You must be a little tired, Jonah. You look tired."

Jonah. It was meant as a reminder that he wasn't Noah anymore, not here.

Noah just looked at him and nodded. He was tired; of course he was tired. But he was also *noticing everything*. He was, in fact, despite being tired, also incredibly, intensely awake.

48

There were cameras mounted up by the ceiling, for instance.

There were men in uniforms keeping the lines in order.

The door for *Other nationalities* led into a weird little hall of a room, with blond plywood walls and a man behind glass on the other side of a high counter. The counter was high enough that Noah didn't see much of the man, just his officer's hat and his small, grim eyes. Noah held on to his father's hand, because this was a place designed to make you feel younger than you actually were, while his mother slid all the passports and papers across the counter.

There was another camera mounted up over there.

There was a mirror tilted right above their heads so that the man behind the glass window could look at the backs of Noah's family's heads, though what he expected to find back there, Noah had no idea.

The officer took what felt like forever, looking through those papers. He moved them around before him on his desk. He scrutinized every page of every passport. He asked Noah's father to look one way and then the other way, so he could see whether the sides of his head looked right. He asked a bunch of questions that Noah was too nervous to understand, and then he stood up from behind the window and peered down at Noah himself.

Noah, who had more experience being stared at than

most people his age, due to the Astonishing Stutter, had never ever been stared at quite as thoroughly as this: he felt very cold and small. And then the man's face cracked into a brief, narrow smile, and he said something else that Noah also couldn't quite follow.

The atmosphere was a little better now. Noah's mother was saying thank you, and the man was stamping their papers. *SCHWAMP SCHWAMP SCHWAMP.*

More doors to go through. More cameras eyeing them from above. More steps to go down and up.

At some point they were in a slightly larger space, with low counters for their suitcases. This was customs, where men in uniform went through all the bags, piece by piece by piece. They took away for closer inspection Noah's father's *New York Times* and a magazine and the books for his mother's dissertation and his father's empty notebooks and the two books in Noah's backpack, *Alice in Wonderland & Through the Looking-Glass* and the Jonah Book. Then they made Noah's parents make a list of everything they were bringing into the country. Everything.

"Even the curry powder?" asked Noah's mother.

Even the curry powder. The man who answered that question didn't even crack a smile.

To Noah's enormous relief, an officer reappeared from a side office with Noah's family's books in a careful pile in his hand.

The *New York Times* did not come back, however. Nor did the magazine (*Time*) his mother had been reading on the plane.

They packed everything else back into their suitcases.

"Welcome to Berlin, capital of the German Democratic Republic," said one of the border guards, and he pointed them forward, toward the steps that led back up to the outside world.

It was so good to be going outside!

But this was the "outside" that was the other side of the Wall. The East German side. And it did look different. People's clothes were different. The cars were different. The air smelled different—it was full of a strange, tangy haze. There weren't as many people in the streets. And it felt different in other ways, too, that Noah couldn't quite put his finger on.

It was like going from a color movie into one in black and white.

Noah's mother figured it out before Noah did: "First time I've ever missed billboards and ads," she said.

All the buildings were so gray over here. And the sky was gray, too, but that couldn't have had anything to do with the border.

A car was waiting for them, sent to bring them to one of the grayest and most looming buildings, which housed the Ministry of Education.

There they waited for a while, in a very large, dim hall with a squeaky wooden floor. Noah's parents talked to various officials in German. It all took forever, but eventually a woman piled their suitcases back into another car, less fancy than the first one. A few minutes later, they were pulling up in front of an apartment building, five stories high, standing next to a series of other, quite similar buildings, all looking across the gray street at "the lovely park!"—as the woman from the ministry called it.

Only at the moment the park was all fences and cement trucks and machines. Apparently there were a lot of construction projects going on in the neighborhood. And as they climbed the stairs in the building, Noah noticed that his stomach, after all of this rushing around in the backseats of cars, was beginning to feel a little wobbly.

"Just you wait until you see this. You've been assigned an apartment that reaches a very high standard," said the woman in a peculiar, square-shouldered sort of English. "The Ministry of Education just had me decorate it. Part of the current Apartment Construction Program. It's culturally equipped."

She looked at Noah as she put the key into a door on the fourth floor.

"I had the impression you would be littler, though," she said. "You'll see what I mean. There are monkeys and giraffes in your sleeping room."

Really? Monkeys and giraffes?

Maybe Noah was hallucinating by then, but for a moment he calmly considered the possibility that inside this apartment in this gray city there might be actual monkeys and actual giraffes. He did even think, *But the ceiling is too low unless it's a super-little giraffe,* and he had not the slightest awareness that his thoughts had become illogical.

"Come in and look!" said the woman from the ministry with a proud swoop of her arm. "Just imagine! I had twenty thousand marks to spend in a week!"

There was a living room with a wood-like display cabinet along one wall, and a television, and a super-fancy lamp swinging peacefully on one end of its fake silk cord, and an overstuffed sofa, and all sorts of little extras that the woman kept pointing out to them with pride: the television, with remote control! The radio! The appliances! The wall-to-wall gold-tone carpet! The three beautiful coffee-table books, one on paintings by Hieronymus Bosch, one on *Myths of Antiquity,* and one called *The GDR in Pictures!*

There were gadgets in the little kitchen. There were two bedrooms down the hall: one for Noah's parents, in which there was a safe with a combination lock—"Here's where you can put anything secret," said the woman—and another room that the woman with the keys to the apartment called the *Kinderzimmer,* the children's room, and where there really were monkeys and giraffes romping across the walls. Only pictures, however.

Noah hadn't expected to find monkeys and giraffes waiting for him in East Berlin, that was for sure. He sat down on the bed and looked up at the woman pointing out all the glories of the *Kinderzimmer*. But then she turned her head and looked at him, and it was as if all of a sudden she had caught some inkling of how tired Noah must be.

"Poor Jonah," she said.

He turned his head to see who poor Jonah might be, and found her eyes resting resolutely on him, on Noah. Because, yes, that's right, of course: *he* was poor Jonah now.

All right. He would be Jonah, since that was *necessary*. On the surface he would be Jonah. But underneath that mask—he promised himself—he would never forget he was Noah.

Because, for one thing, the animals on the walls! They made him dizzy. They made him feel like someone still on the storm-tossed ark.

Secret File #5
BROKEN BERLIN

First of all, here is something surprising: Berlin was not on the line between East Germany and West Germany. When Noah first heard about the Berlin Wall, he assumed that Berlin must have had the bad luck to be right on the border, and got split up because of that. But no. Berlin looked like a complicated island floating way in the eastern part of East Germany, closer to Poland than to West Germany.

When the Allies divided up Germany after World War II, the ruined city of Berlin, which had been the capital of Nazi Germany, was divided into four sectors, one for each of the occupying forces.

But when Germany became the Federal Republic of Germany in the west and the German Democratic Republic in the east, the city of Berlin was split like a walnut along the crack between the Soviet occupation zone and the parts occupied by the Americans, the French, and the British, into East and West.

East Berlin was named the capital of the German Democratic Republic. West Berlin remained, technically, an occupied city: not officially part of the Federal Republic of Germany but still under the watchful eyes of the Allies: France, Britain, and the United States. (Not to mention the watchful eyes of the Soviet Union.)

And Berlin stayed that way, divided, for forty years. Hard to believe, right?

In divided Berlin, the two sides caught up in what was known as the Cold War (the capitalists versus the Communists, the Western democracies against the Soviet Bloc) glared at each other over the border, and eventually over a barbed-wired, minefield-ridden, floodlit, concrete-slabbed, guard-dog-patrolled "Anti-Fascist Protection Wall."

Well, that's what the East German officials sometimes called it.

Ordinary people just called it the Wall, and they hated everything about it.

· chapter six ·

YO-YO IN BERLIN

The next time Noah opened his eyes, it was a different day entirely. It was quiet, there was no strange German woman pointing to the gold carpet and the television—had she really existed?—and he felt hungry.

He shook his head at the giraffes and the monkeys and padded across the carpeted floors to the kitchen, where he found his father drinking coffee and studying some notebook of his.

"Well, good morning, Yo-Yo!" said his father. "You had a nice long sleep."

"Yo-Yo?" said Noah.

"I just thought that up," said his father. "The Germans won't pronounce your name 'Jonah,' the way we say it, because for them a *J* sounds like a *Y*. You're going to have to be Yo-nah here. So, why not *Yo-Yo?* Has kind of a ring to it, don't you think?"

His father raised an eyebrow at him meaningfully while he said this, so Noah knew right away what was going on: all this talk about "Yo-Yo" was meant as a reminder that he wasn't supposed to be himself anymore.

He didn't much like not being himself. And whoever he was, he was hungry, so he started opening the doors of the kitchen cabinets, hoping to find a shelf that wasn't empty.

"Is there any food around here?" he asked. That seemed like a safe-enough question. "And where's Mom?"

"Your mother went off to that nice Ministry of Education again, to start setting up research visits to schools. You know how your mom likes to jump right into a task! And so I've been outlining my novel about mink farmers and waiting for you to wake up so we can go exploring. As you see, we need to find a supermarket urgently, among other things. Because we're hungry, and also because we have already been invited to a party."

"A what?" said Noah.

"A party. We've been invited to a party. By someone in charge of some big section of the library your mother is going to be using. A telegram came right to our door while you were still asleep! Kind of an official sort of party, I gather. So anyway, we need to make something tasty

58

to take along with us, don't you think? Maybe the supermarket will inspire us."

The word "party" sent Noah's brain right back to that
sore place around Zach's birthday party and the spring
soccer season and just generally everyday life in early May
in Oasis, Virginia. Nothing he was thinking could be said
aloud, however, without breaking the Rules, so he stayed
quiet and pulled on some clean clothes, and he and his
father went out to take a look at the city.

Outside it was gray, threatening to rain. Machines were
busy digging up the earth in the park across the street,
though they looked like they were in no rush about it, and
there was a strange smoggy tang hanging in the air. It
hung over the street like a cloud.

"What's that smell?" said Noah.

"Mmm, yes. Coal," said his dad. "They're burning coal
in their generators here. Haven't smelled coal like that
since I was hitchhiking through Yugoslavia."

"When did you go hitchhiking through Yugoslavia?"

"My misspent youth," said his dad with a chuckle. He
actually did say things like that.

"And are you really writing a novel about mink farmers?"

His dad laughed.

"Why not?" he said. "I think I might as well try writing
a novel about something while we're here, and won't mink
farmers be a good topic for the people listening in?"

"Maybe," said Noah. "It's different, anyway."

Raindrops began splatting lazily against the pavement around them. Noah's father opened an umbrella and made room under it for Noah.

Noah was thinking about Rule #1: *They will always be listening.* Were there really bugs in the walls of their apartment? That wasn't a very nice thought.

"You're not going to keep calling me Yo-Yo, are you?"

"You don't like it? There's a famous cellist named Yo-Yo."

"Okay, it's fine for him, but I don't want to be Yo-Yo."

His dad squeezed his shoulder.

"I was just trying to remind us both that you're Jonah now," he said. "It's not just you it's hard for, learning to be Jonah. Well, enough of that, even outdoors here."

They were walking through other streets now, and the buildings were getting larger and grayer.

"Where are we going?" said Noah. Nothing in these streets looked like a supermarket to him.

"There's something I think you'd better experience right away, so you'll understand why we need all these Rules. We're going to swing by the American embassy and pick up our mail."

"Mail!" said Noah. "We can't have letters yet! In my class they probably think I'm just out with a cold."

Then he thought some more.

"And who is ever going to write me a letter, anyway? They don't know where I've gone."

"But your mother and I might have letters waiting already. Official sorts of letters. That's possible. Anyway, you need to see how things work here. It will be educational and informative. Sooooo . . . which way now?"

And Noah's father pulled a map out of his pocket.

It was an East German map of East Berlin, so it called the city "Berlin, Capital of the German Democratic Republic." And there was a huge blank puddle to the west and south; it covered the left-hand side of the map and a lot of the lower edge.

"What's that missing bit?" said Noah. "What's wrong with the map?"

"That's West Berlin," said his dad. "It's a funny thing, but for East German maps, it officially doesn't exist."

"Oh," said Noah, sucking some of Berlin's odd-tasting coal-tinged air in through his teeth. "Oh!"

He couldn't get enough of that strange pool of blankness. But to tell the truth, Noah liked all maps. Back home in Oasis, Noah had had old *National Geographic* maps covering every inch of his bedroom wall.

His father laughed when he saw the expression that must have already taken over Noah's face.

"Okay, okay, it's yours," he said, and he tucked that map

right into Noah's hands. "Really, take it! I'll get another one somewhere around."

Now that they were walking through the streets toward an actual destination, Noah found that he was already feeling much more like himself than he had the day before. It was like the whole day of getting to Berlin had been some sort of peculiar dream, and now he was waking up again.

They crossed a little river called the Spree and found themselves on an island with buildings that must once have been very grand hidden away behind fences. "Museums being renovated slowly," said his dad. Many museums! Over on the right were the ruins of what used to be called the New Museum. It didn't look very new anymore.

On the left loomed the great round dome of an old cathedral, which in the fog that day looked like a carnivorous iron bell preparing to swoop down and feed.

On the right was a kind of mock Greek temple, behind mud and painted metal fences.

"The National Gallery," said his father, consulting Noah's helpful map. "And where they're working on the New Museum there's supposed to be a little green park."

Except, like the "little green park" across from their apartment house in the Max-Beer-Straße, this park was actually a construction site.

Peeking over the fence, Noah could see a large hollow

statue of a woman lying gracefully on her back, waiting for better days when she could stand upright again.

"Creepy," said Noah. All these huge buildings and ruined temples were beginning to weigh him down.

"Well, it's all left over from the end of the Second World War," said his father. "Makes you imagine how grim it must have been when the whole place was in ruins in 1945 —"

His father's history lecture ended prematurely, though: he tripped on a loose flagstone in the sidewalk and managed somehow to drop a bunch of little pieces of paper.

On the other side of the Museum Island, Noah and his father walked down some other grand streets, and then they turned right and went up a set of steps into a building where an American flag was waving. That was the embassy.

They had to go through a metal detector to get in, and then his father talked to someone about mail, and a couple of letters actually ended up in his father's hands, somewhat to Noah's surprise. Then his father said to him, "This next bit is the important part, so pay attention."

But the next bit was just that they went back out onto the big Berlin streets and headed back the way they had come.

"What's the important thing?" said Noah. "Knowing how to get home? Is that it?"

"You'll see," said his dad. "Let's find the supermarket

marked on your map, how about that? We need all the basic provisions. Plus possible party food."

"Okay," said Noah. He was hungry; there was no doubt about that.

Back they went down the wide streets and past those rows of large buildings, and Noah was just about to complain that there hadn't been anything worth paying much attention to that *he* could see, when suddenly, out of absolutely nowhere, a soldier popped up and raised his stern hands to stop them.

"Papers, please," he said, and Noah's dad gave Noah a comforting squeeze on the arm and then handed over their passports. The soldier opened them up and stared at the pictures in the passports, comparing them with the actual flesh-and-blood people in front of him—the same frowning stare that Noah had had to suffer through the day before. It made him want to hide somewhere very far away.

The soldier did more than merely stare. He carried on a kind of conversation with himself as he read over their papers:

"American citizens? Passport number *blablabla*, is that right? Visa seems to be in order. How long are they here for? Visa says six months."

That was strange, wasn't it? A policeman who talked to himself! But a second later, Noah realized there must have been a teeny-tiny little microphone hidden in his collar somewhere. The policeman wasn't speaking aloud for their benefit but for some other policemen, somewhere else. Maybe in that green police booth Noah had just spotted, farther down the sidewalk.

"And what is the business of your visit to the German Democratic Republic?"

"My wife is researching classes in schools for children with speech delays."

The soldier repeated something to that effect, using long German words Noah half recognized from the border guards the day before, and then seemed, finally, satisfied. He handed the passports back to Noah's father and backed away so they could keep walking.

Twenty steps later—because of Rule #1—Noah said, "Was that the important thing?"

And his father said, "Yep. You know why that just happened?"

"No, why?"

"Because we came out of the American embassy," his father said. "And they keep very close tabs on everyone who visits the American embassy."

"But that was like ages ago!"

"Not quite that long," said his dad. "But you're right: they're clever that way. They don't jump on you immediately; they give you just about seven minutes, and then they

65

jump. But they're always, always there. Always watching, always listening. That's the reason for all our Rules. Is that clearer now?"

Noah nodded. Always watching. Always listening. All right. He wouldn't forget that now. Also: it was amazing, the sorts of things his parents just seemed to know.

They walked out in the rain into a field of gray stone surrounded by city buildings all making an effort to be modern. Noah felt as small as a pigeon in all that stone. He couldn't help looking around for places to hide.

"Okay, this is the Alexanderplatz," said his father. "So where's the supermarket?"

They turned around and around, looking. Everything was huge and square. Even the decorations were gigantic: massive mosaics of children picking flowers and boys holding on to telescopes ran around the waist of one of those tall buildings.

"They wanted this part of town to be as impressive as possible. Can you tell?"

"Hmm," said Noah. He didn't think he liked enormous modern gray buildings. Over there was a tall clock sculpture with numbers and wires on it, though—that was more interesting. And behind it an enormous needle poking into the gray sky.

"That's the television tower," said Noah's dad, pointing to the needle, and he said a word that sounded like

"Fairnzaytoorm." "That's what they call it, the *Fernsehturm*. I think you can go up in it to the top; there's a restaurant or something."

The needle was huge and unsettling, but Noah liked the great big complicated clock. It looked like something a mad scientist would stick in the middle of a square.

"Over here! Over here!" said Noah's father with some delight.

It was turning out to be a very good day after all: he had found the supermarket.

Secret File #6
HERE'S LOOKING AT YOU

The Fernsehturm looked like a needle with a great big eyeball on it, staring at you, wherever you were. That made the name especially appropriate:

FERN

SEH

TURM

=

FAR-

SEEING

TOWER

chapter seven

THE PARTY PARTY

The supermarket was decorated with blue-tiled zigzags along the top of its walls and had a sausage stand outside. The rain had stopped. Noah and his dad wolfed one sausage each while they were waiting in line for a little grocery cart.

Noah had never had to wait in line to go *into* a grocery store, but that was the way it was done here. He got stared at in that line. He thought at first maybe he was eating his sausage incorrectly, or maybe you weren't supposed to eat sausages while you were waiting in line for grocery carts, but then his father said, "The kids your age are all in school today."

Oh, right: school!

"So when do I start school?" asked Noah. The thought of school in this strange place was somewhat scary, but having to sit in that apartment all day trying not to break the Rules was almost scarier.

"We'll have to wait and see," said his father. "We've asked, of course. Your mother's trying to get the scoop from the Ministry of Education."

During this not-so-very-long conversation, the stares from all those other people in line got twice or maybe even three times as intense. Noah figured he could guess the reasons why:

- He was a child who should be in school.
- He was eating a sausage in the grocery cart line.
- He and his father were speaking English.
- And of course there was the Astonishing Stutter.

Noah had had a lot of practice not minding being stared at, however. At least these people didn't have the cold, spiky eyes of policemen or border guards. They were just curious. Well, Noah was pretty curious, too!

At the moment, he was figuring out the system of the grocery store. He was very interested in figuring out systems. He had made a Hierarchical Flowchart of his fifth-grade class that showed all the layers of popularity and mobility in the class subgroups. The really popular kids, like Brian and Casey, who were also, although this might be a random variable, tall (Noah was fully aware that he probably noticed their height because he himself was so short), were listed in a cluster at the top of the chart. Then there were the groups of sporty kids and nerdy kids and the ones who were hangers-on and desperately wanted to move up the chart and the wacko smart kids with Astonishing Stutters, who sometimes hung out with one group and sometimes with another: they were what you might call free-floating, like certain electrons.

That last group was pretty small. In fact, it was a set with only one actual member: the kid who used to be known as Noah.

Noah sighed. It made his heart hurt a little, thinking about his class back in Virginia. *Stop that!* he told himself, and he went back to *noticing everything*.

Anyway, the system followed by this grocery store was apparently that you waited outside for your cart and looked at the stands nearby. If you did not have a canvas shopping bag on you, perhaps because you had just arrived from America, you might well do what Noah's father did, and dart over to the stand that sold shopping bags, returning very soon to rejoin your son in the shopping-cart line. And meanwhile, if you were that son, you made a ranked list in your head of all the different things sold in those stands. Cabbage and potatoes ranked low.

The *best* stand outside the supermarket, according to Noah's mental list, sold little doughnuts that trundled along a mechanized gangplank from the frying vat to the sugar-covered cooling board.

"On the way out," said his dad, following Noah's eyes. "I agree."

The *closest* stand sold two—exactly and only two— different kinds of cheese.

Near the entrance to the grocery store was a counter where people coming out wrapped their groceries in sheets of gray-brown paper. And then those people would put their wrapped groceries into their shopping bag and hand off their grocery cart to someone going into the store.

What was the store like? It was like a clever copy of any grocery store in Virginia. It had aisles and shelves like any grocery store, and fluorescent lights and containers of food with pictures on the outside, just like a store back home. But if you looked closely, you began to see the differences.

For one thing, the lights weren't very bright. It was dimmer here than in the shiny American stores Noah was used to, and the vegetables were limited to the not-very-colorful kinds, like potatoes and onions and cauliflower. Everything for sale in that supermarket looked edible, looked perfectly okay, looked fine, but at the same time somehow managed to look like a rough copy of the things for sale in the supermarkets of Virginia. There were pictures on the cartons, sure, but the pictures were all a little indistinct, a little fuzzy.

Noah and his father bought a box with a blurry picture of crumb cake on its cover. And rice. And a slightly dreary-looking cauliflower. And a carton of eggs. And milk in a blue-and-white-checked cardboard pyramid.

A pyramid! Full of milk!

"That's about the strangest bit of packaging I've ever seen," said Noah's dad. "Well, all right. There must be some good reason for putting milk in pyramids."

He and Noah looked at each other, and Noah's dad shrugged. They had no idea.

It was time to scoot home and make their party offering, anyway.

"What's it going to be?" said Noah's father.

Noah looked at the ingredients in their canvas bag and couldn't guess. There wasn't anything there that looked particularly party-like. Nothing fancy. But Noah's father snapped his fingers. He always, always could come up with an idea about dinner.

"Fried rice!" say Noah's father, obviously quite delighted with himself. "Curried fried rice. We can use some of our curry powder. It will be *tasty!*"

When Noah's mother came through the door later that afternoon, she looked quite surprised to find the rest of her family filling the apartment with the smell of curry powder and cooking oil.

"What's this?" she said. "You know they're sending someone to pick us up in half an hour."

"Food for the party!" said Noah's father. "Party food!"

"I'm not sure people bring fried curry rice to parties in East Berlin," said Noah's mother. "In fact, I'm pretty sure they don't."

"They do now!" said Noah's father, and then they had to rush to get ready, which basically meant putting clean shirts on and combing their hair and, in Noah's case, popping his *Alice* book into his backpack so that he would have something to read while the grown-ups sat around and talked.

"They'll be wanting to look us over, *to get to know us*," said Noah's mother. She said it with one of her warning stares, and she wiggled seven fingers at Noah for a moment, almost as if by accident, as a way of reminding Noah of that seventh Rule: *If you are asked questions, say as little as possible.* "You just stick by me, Jonah, my dear. They'll have to understand how jet-lagged and tired you are. . . ."

The car that picked them up was driven by a man with brown hair and a nervous twitch.

"Hello, hello," he said. His English didn't seem to have been used in a while. "Please take places in the car. We must not be late. What are you carrying there? Please, I hope no foods in this car will be spilt. Welcome to Berlin! We should go now, so we won't be late."

He was Somebody-or-Other from the library, and he was driving them to the apartment of Somebody-or-Other-Else, who was apparently very important at the library and who was a leader, said the driver, in the Eff-Day-Yot.

"What's the Eff-Day-Yot?" Noah asked his mother in a whisper, which meant he had temporarily forgotten Rules Eight and Nine.

"Those are letters," said his mother. "F-D-J. Stands for Freie Deutsche Jugend, which is a kind of political party for young people."

"Not a party, excuse me!" said the driver nervously. There was this anxious grin that kept flickering across his face, and Noah could see little pearly tears of sweat slipping down the back of his neck, even though it was really quite chilly that evening. "Not, accurately, a party—a voluntary mass organization! Our FDJ is the unified socialist mass organization of young people here in the German Democratic Republic! In partnership with the Socialist Unity Party of Germany, our FDJ encourages all young people to act in the spirit of socialist patriotism!"

Once the man had started, he was apparently too nervous to stop. He went on and on and on, slipping right out of his rusty English into long German sentences in which all the words seemed to have at least five syllables, and Noah's family sat in the car and listened politely as the tires bumped along the streets of East Berlin.

The man's hair was a little thin, which allowed a person riding in the backseat to appreciate the anxious sheen on his scalp.

Why is he so nervous? Noah puzzled over this question all the rest of the drive. *He's just taking us to a party!*

But of course it wasn't just a party, not for Noah's family, and even Noah knew that.

For Noah's family, it was *being looked over;* it was *the East Germans getting to know us;* it was the first test.

They climbed out of the car by an older, sooty-bricked building that actually had a tree growing in front of it. The party was in an apartment that felt darker and grander and more solid than the place they had just moved into, back in the middle of Berlin.

The important man from the library, the one who was a leader of the voluntary mass organization known as the FDJ, turned out to be named Jens, pronounced "Yens" (just as *Jonah* was pronounced "Yonah"), and he had a wife named Anke (two syllables: "An-keh"), and two boys around Noah's age. Their last name was Huppe. They must have had those boys when they were very young, because even Noah's parents, who weren't very old, didn't look quite as young as Jens and Anke Huppe.

Like the man driving the car, however, Frau Huppe had a stress wrinkle permanently engraved on her forehead. When she smiled, the top part of her face always looked like it was secretly trying to frown.

She seemed quite surprised by the fried curry rice, which Noah's father handed over in the brand-new bowl they had found on their kitchen shelf.

"But you just arrived!" she said. "And already cooking? What an odd smell! Thank you! And you are . . ."

(She took the bowl of curry rice, held it at half-arm's length for a while, trying to figure out what to do, and then put it down on a table—and it sat there, by the way, untouched, the whole evening through.)

"Jonah. I'm Jonah," said Noah as quickly as he could manage, so that his parents wouldn't tense up.

He shook the smiling-frowning Frau Huppe's hand. She was looking at him oddly. For a person who was welcoming guests to a party, she had a surprising aura of the border guard about her.

"You're the one who wants to go to school," she said.

"I hope so," said Noah in German. "Yes."

Those weren't very difficult words, but it took Noah a while to get them out anyway.

The thing about the Astonishing Stutter was that it

really liked to roar into action in awkward social situations, like being grilled in German by a woman who clearly hates the smell of curried rice but is being polite to you because you are a foreigner.

"Oh," said the woman assessingly. "Well. Ingo! Karl! Come over here!"

Those were the two boys. They were staring at Noah, so Noah stared right back and counted it as *noticing everything:* dark-blond hair on both of them, the older boy's— Karl's—one notch closer to brown. Karl was probably a couple of years older than Noah, and Ingo maybe a little younger, but those two Huppe brothers were almost the same height and looked a lot alike. They both had striped shirts on.

Noah, who had developed keen antennae for these sorts of things over the years, knew right away that he'd better be careful around the younger one. You could see from the glint in his eyes that he was the type who always wanted to take things one step too far. This was the kind of kid where you might end up hitting the blacktop hard before the end of recess even though things had started off so well at the beginning of the game.

"Hello," said Noah. Actually, since he was speaking German, what he said was *"Hallo."* There are, fortunately, some words in German that are pretty similar to English. Unfortunately, there aren't nearly enough of those.

"Remember our discussion," said the mother to the boys, in German that was, of course, nine million times more fluent than Noah's. "You will treat our visitor with respect. He has come from a place where they hear only misinformation about socialist achievements."

She actually said that! Then she shooed them off to what was apparently the boys' room down the hall. The books lined up on the shelves drew Noah's eye right away.

"We've studied America in school," said the younger boy, Ingo. "Did you just come from there?"

Noah nodded and tried to get his mouth to produce the very troublesome German word for "yesterday," which is *gestern*. It did not go well.

"All the millions of poor people," said Ingo. "All the people with no work. Is that why you came here? Why do you Americans want world war again?"

Even once he figured out the words Ingo was saying, Noah had no idea how to answer any of these questions.

"War? No!" he said. In German the word is *Krieg*, which took some time for Noah to spit out.

"Stop it, Ingo," said the older boy. "He can't really speak German yet."

"A little," said Noah, still in German. He did not add: *And I have a twisty language superpower that makes me understand about a thousand percent more than I can say. It* took him long enough to come out with the two words he did say.

"Oh," said Ingo.

"Anyway," added Karl, "it's the people running his country who want war, not the American masses."

"Is he part of the masses?" said Ingo, eyeing Noah doubtfully.

Noah, desperate to change the subject, pointed to a picture on the wall, a man with a bulky white suit on, almost like a diving outfit, smiling and waving his gloved hand.

"Who is that?" he asked. That went better. Pointing helped!

"Don't you recognize him?" said Ingo. "That's Sigmund Jähn, the cosmonaut. Everyone knows *him*."

"Oh, an *astronaut*?" said Noah. He hadn't known there were astronauts here. He used the English word because he hadn't heard the German one before.

"Cosmonaut," said Karl. "He went into space. He's a hero. Our father met him once at a Party conference."

"Yeah, yeah, and *that's* Antarctica," said Ingo, slapping his finger against another picture on the wall. "We have scientists there now. We have scientists leading in every field. What else do you want to know? Is it hard living in a place where you have to pay all your money to go see the doctor and where the working classes are so oppressed?"

Noah went back to feeling slightly stumped.

He looked over at the books on the shelf. He didn't recognize any of the titles, but he picked out one with a colorful cover and asked in his most careful German, "What—is—this—book?"

"That one's good," said Karl. "I liked it when I was younger. It's by Alexander Volkov; he's a Russian. It's called *The Wizard of the Smaragdenstadt.*"

Noah must have looked completely blank. That last word! What the heck could it possibly mean?

"Shmara . . . ?" he began.

"*Smaragd,*" repeated Karl, who was definitely nicer than his slightly younger brother. "A jewel? Very green jewel?"

"Emerald!" said Noah in English.

"I don't know. Maybe."

And *Stadt* was "city" in English; Noah knew that. So the book was about a wizard of an emerald city.

Ingo explained: "It's about a little girl in America who's very poor and goes to a magical land hidden in Kansas."

"Oh, *ja!*" said Noah. That sounded like a story he knew. "Dorothy! *The Wizard of Oz!* By, by—somebody American."

Karl and Ingo frowned at him.

"I suppose your American copied from Volkov," said Karl politely. "They don't let you hear much about Russian writers where you come from."

"And anyway, the girl's name isn't Dorothy—it's Elli!" said Ingo. He was beginning to dance from foot to foot. Getting impatient, though what he was impatient *for*, Noah had no idea. He was familiar with the ways of impatient kids, though, from the classrooms and playgrounds of Oasis. He could feel himself tense up, waiting for whatever was going to go wrong to go ahead and go wrong like it was going to—

And, sure enough, the next second Ingo had pounced on Noah's backpack, which was almost empty, of course. "What's in there?"

"Ingo!" said Karl, tugging the backpack out of his brother's hands.

They glared at each other, Karl and Ingo, and with their striped shirts they looked almost like twins. Furious twins.

"A book," said Noah, and he showed them *Alice*.

Those odd rabbits, marching away from you on the cover.

Ingo snatched the book away and started flipping through the pages, a little too roughly. "Ha!" he said a moment later, as if he'd found something he'd been looking for. Noah cricked his neck around to see what had stopped him. It was about halfway through the book, where the author had added a diagram of the chess game Alice's second adventure is sort of based on. Through the mirror, she enters another world, where flowers talk and chess pieces walk about. The chess game itself doesn't really hold together, logically — Noah and his dad had tried to figure it out on the plane. His dad had spent some time working out moves that made more sense. There were neat little notations in pencil where his dad had been trying to puzzle through everything.

"Look at this," said Ingo, waving the book around. "Look at all of this! It's a *secret code*."

"Don't be a donkey," said Karl, grabbing at the book. "Ingo, give that to me."

"Don't *you* boss me around!" said Ingo, pulling harder.

And there was a terrible sound — the sound of paper tearing. Karl was left holding Noah's book, and Ingo's hand was clenching onto one severed page of it, and they both looked rather stunned.

At that moment, the two mothers appeared at the door of the bedroom.

"What is going on here?" asked Frau Huppe. Her frown-wrinkle was dark and ominous. Ingo shrank back — Noah noticed that the hand with the page in it was behind his back now.

Noah's mother was surveying the scene, her eyes darting here, here, here, and there, taking it all in.

"Here's your book," said Karl as he handed back Noah's poor wounded *Alice*.

"Thank you," said Noah, feeling the slight tremor in his book-holding hand. He was careful not to look at Ingo.

"Why don't you come out here with us, Jonah?" said Noah's mother. "You must be exhausted."

As they walked down the hall to the living room, where the grown-ups were talking about somewhere called Kampuchea, Ingo's voice followed them, whining to his mother:

"How are we supposed to discuss things with him? He can't speak German hardly at all!"

"Oh, dear," said Noah's mother in English, putting her arm around Noah's shoulders. "It will get easier."

It had to, right?

But when Frau Huppe came back into the living room, her face had a closed, grim look to it that would worry anyone.

"You can understand we're not really equipped to scholarize someone like your son," she said to Noah's mother. "With his deficits. And his lack of German. We don't have classes for English speakers."

"Frau Huppe is in the national schools administration," said Noah's mother, smiling, to Noah. Her lips were clenched quite tensely around each of those words, which was how Noah knew she was raging inside, despite the smile. And she was using German on purpose, Noah could tell, as a way of saying-without-saying, "My son, Frau Huppe, understands quite a lot of this language of yours."

"Oh, well, now, *English* doesn't matter," said Noah's father. "Jonah doesn't need English. He wants to learn German, of course. You know how children are. They pick up languages so fast."

"*Normal* children do," said Anke Huppe.

That kind of added an icy feel to the general atmosphere.

Noah's mother drew Frau Huppe slightly to the side, so that Noah wouldn't have to sit there politely listening to his own mother argue on his behalf. And Noah's father, to defuse the tension in that room, started chatting with Jens, the father of Ingo and Karl, about world politics. "Chatting" in this case meant skillfully inviting Jens to talk about the virtues of East Germany while the rest of them listened. So they heard about full employment and free medical care and aid for young families and the housing-construction program. Noah leaned his head against his father's side and let Jens's explanations of how it was only natural that he, a leader in the FDJ, would also, of course, be a member of the governing Socialist Unity Party—because, although an American might not understand this, *unity is everything*—float above his head, somewhere way up high there, like a balloon.

"Ah," said Noah's father every now and then. "Interesting. Hmm."

(Nothing ever got Noah's father ruffled.)

At the end of the evening, the nervous man with the car took them almost all the way home, but not quite all the way, perhaps because he was in such a rush to get back to his own house, where maybe he could finally relax and stop sweating. He did offer to take them to their door, but after that painful party, Noah and his parents naturally wanted to breathe some nice, refreshing, coal-laden outdoor Berlin air. So they did not mind walking the last couple of blocks.

"Well," said Noah's mother, "that was truly *something.* Every person in that room was a Party member, I do believe. A Party party!"

She hooted with laughter, but when she looked over at Noah, that laugh turned into something else, more like a sigh.

"I'm afraid you may have to spend some more time with those boys," she said. "That mother of theirs has agreed to let you write a little essay about Berlin and how you want to be educated. She seemed to think that would help the administration decide whether to let you into the schools or not. They are going to borrow you on Monday and show you around town. I imagine they will grill you constantly. Then you write your essay and see what happens."

"Oh," said Noah. His heart had just sunk right into the ground. Nothing in that plan sounded good to him.

"They didn't like curry in their nice fried rice, either," said Noah's father sadly. He had that big bowl in his hands.

"Don't feel bad about that. We'll eat it when we get home!" said Noah's mother. "With extra spices and extra garlic! Come on, people—cheer up!"

That was a Rule. That was Rule #4. *Smile. Be polite. Don't let your worries show.*

"They're probably all writing reports on each other right this minute," said Noah's mother with relish. "On each other and on us. Think of all the nonsense they'll be having to write."

Then she looked sternly at Noah: "I say that only because we're out of doors, Jonah."

Jonah. Would he ever get used to that name? Would it always feel unfamiliar and cold?

"Well," said Noah. "If I wrote a report, I'd say . . . when they were fighting over my book, they looked like—like—like—"

His parents waited. Say what you want about Noah's parents, even if they sometimes took their child's name and birthday away and dragged him across the world to a place that smelled like coal smoke, they knew how to wait patiently for his words to appear.

"Like . . . *Tweedledum!*" he said finally, and it was an explosion. "And . . . *Tweedledee!*"

And then they all really did laugh like ordinary happy people, and went upstairs and had lots and lots of curried rice.

Secret File #7

THE WIZARD OF THE EMERALD CITY

The looking-glass cities of West and East Berlin did indeed each have a beloved children's book about a Kansas girl who goes to a magic land and meets a wizard. In West Berlin, as in West Germany, as in the United States, that book was called *The Wizard of Oz* and had L. Frank Baum's name on the cover. But in East Berlin ("Berlin, Capital of the GDR"), the book was known as *The Wizard of the Emerald City,* and the author was Alexander Volkov, a Russian.

How did this happen?

In 1939 — the same year, by the way, that *The Wizard of Oz* was turned into one of the most famous American movies ever — a Soviet professor of metallurgy named Alexander Volkov translated an old American book he had found into Russian. When he published this book in the Soviet Union with his own name on the cover, it was a huge hit. Later he even wrote a bunch of sequels. During the Cold War, these books by Volkov about the "Magic Land" were published in many of the countries on the Communist side of the Iron Curtain—Volkov proudly bragged it had been translated into thirteen languages!

West Germany, since it was solidly on the American team, published Oz books by Baum; East Germany imported Volkov's versions.

And that is how the divided city of Berlin ended up with *The Wizard of the Emerald City* on the east side of the Wall and *The Wizard of Oz* on bookshelves in the West.

chapter eight

THE SECOND TEST; ALSO THE THIRD

His parents were nice about it, but Noah knew the truth: this outing with Tweedledum and Tweedledee and their half-frowning mother was a test. A huge test. A test without hints or extra time or second chances.

Frau Huppe didn't think he should be allowed to go to school. That was enough to make Noah want to show how very ready for school, any school, school in any language, he actually was. And it wasn't just a question of his German; it was a question of how well he answered questions, maybe even questions about life back home in *Roanoke*, Virginia.

His parents tried not to show how worried they were. Noah could tell, however, because whenever they were safely outdoors together, far from whatever bugs inhabited the apartment, his parents kept dropping casual reminders into every possible conversation, about Rules 4 (*Smile*) and 5 (*Don't talk about the past!*), not to mention 7 (*When asked questions, say as little as possible!*). And when they were indoors they curled up on the couch with him and the Jonah Book, "remembering" the past that had never happened.

Sometimes Noah was tempted to say to his dear parents — ideally with that cutting lilt some of his classmates back in Oasis had already mastered, "Do you really think I'm that stupid?"

But that would have been a violation of Rule 4, right? That would not have been smiling.

And he knew his parents didn't think he was stupid. He knew that. They were just worried, that was all. Worry might not have been showing on their faces, but it was seeping out of every other seam of them.

So as much as he could, Noah kept his own worries to himself.

His father scrambled a few eggs for breakfast that morning.

"Protein!" he said. "To fortify you on your long expedition!"

They made sure he had his jacket and an extra sweater in his bag, plus his map of East Berlin and a bit of money, in the very unlikely case Frau Huppe and the young Tweedle-Huppes managed to lose him somehow. And some chocolate bars for Ingo and Karl.

Noah made a point of leaving *Alice* safely behind, though — enough lost pages.

"Jonah, your friends are here!" said Noah's parents when the Huppes arrived, even though it could hardly have been less accurate to call any of those three people at the door Noah's "friends."

The young Huppes had on track jackets over their turtlenecks. They all — the boys and their mother — looked somewhat put-upon and under stress, as if Noah himself were a great big enormous bowl of curried rice they didn't know what to do with.

"It's so kind of you to take Jonah around Berlin!" said Noah's parents, even though they knew it had very little or nothing to do with kindness.

"Our pleasure," said Frau Huppe, while the upper half of her face frowned.

"Have a lovely time, Jonah!" said Noah's parents, even though it was exactly zero percent likely that Noah — or, from the looks on their faces, any of the Huppes — would have a lovely time. Tests aren't like that.

That was the moment when Noah stood extra straight and got ready to implement his secret plan: the Turn-the-Test-Tables Plan. He had prepared that weekend because, as his mother used to say back in Oasis, where it wasn't even really necessary, "The best defense is a good offense." Noah's secret offense involved two German sentences he had practiced quite a bit, under his breath, that weekend, and they were:

1. "Could you please tell me about X?"
   and
2. "Could you please tell me more about X?"

In the Pergamon Museum, on the Museum Island, in the misty, drizzly morning hours of that long day, Noah started out bravely with "Could you please tell me about this castle?"

It was amazing: a huge blue-tiled structure right in the museum under a greenhouse roof. Just enormous! And with ceramic lions and dragons all over it and castle-like toothy battlements all along the top! But apparently it wasn't really a castle. Apparently it was a famous gate, the Ishtar Gate, the entrance to the old city of Babylon.

"Perhaps your parents have traveled to some of these old cities," said Frau Huppe at the end of her long explanation. "Have they talked about their travels with you?"

"Could you please tell me more about Babylon?" said Noah. Sometimes a sentence, even a German sentence, will just surprise you by tripping easily off your tongue. "And these lions?"

Ingo and Karl were already staring at him with astonishment. We will not say admiration; we will leave it at astonishment.

Soon enough Frau Huppe ran out of things to say about Babylon; they looked at the enormous Pergamon Altar, which is absolutely covered with statues of gods and goddesses and monsters and heroes all fighting one another.

Ingo liked the gore and the weapons, so Noah had a bit of a break from his two magical questions, but eventually Frau Huppe became impatient with Ingo and mythological battles and announced they were going next to a street called Husemannstraße, not so far away, where old buildings had been carefully preserved and renovated into a new Museum of Working-Class Life in Berlin Around 1900.

The museum was a reconstructed apartment from almost a hundred years ago. Ingo lost interest about one minute after pointing out the funny old bicycle on the wall. He had already been here on a school field trip, and he wasn't eager to do it all over again. Ingo frowned at the old-fashioned cookstove in the kitchen.

"It gives us insight into the struggle of the working people," said Frau Huppe. "Perhaps your parents, Jonah, have said something about how they feel about the working classes?"

"Oh!" said Noah, and this time he happily let the Astonishing Stutter slow him down. "Could you . . . Could you please tell me more about the working classes of Berlin?"

For lunch, they went to a restaurant in the Palast der Republik, a vast and modern building with windows that reflected the gray sky in a metallic bronze.

"This is the people's palace!" said Frau Huppe. "In it the people's parliament meets. And there are concerts."

"And good ice cream," said Ingo.

"Like your Washington, D.C., where your government works," said Frau Huppe. "Don't your parents often go to Washington, D.C., perhaps for their jobs?"

"Hmm," said Noah, looking over the menu. "Could you please tell me more about . . . *bratwurst*?"

That struck Tweedledum and Tweedledee as incredibly funny. They couldn't imagine a universe where anyone could ask questions about bratwurst, which turned out to be a kind of sausage. Lunch was followed by ice cream, and for a moment even Ingo was smiling.

After the sausage and the ice cream, however, Ingo said, "Let's take him home now."

Frau Huppe and Karl both frowned at the youngest Huppe.

"First, the Treptower Park," said Frau Huppe firmly. "Paying respect to the great Soviet sacrifice."

"Or let's go to the Pioneer Palace!" said Ingo. "Let's go see the cosmonaut exhibit!"

Frau Huppe's stress wrinkle dug deeper into her forehead.

"Not today," she said. "It's the forty-fourth anniversary of the Soviet liberation of Berlin this week, so we will go pay our respects."

Treptower turned out to be an enormous park that was also sort of a cemetery: long garden alleyways led to a small hill on which the most massive statue of a Russian soldier held a statue of a small German child in its arms.

"Please could you tell me about this . . . park?" said Noah, running out of questions — and out of nouns. A miserable thin rain began to spit down from the gray sky, and he was suddenly desperately tired.

"What does your family think about the Soviet Union?" asked Frau Huppe. She seemed tired, too. "How do they feel about socialism?"

"It's raining," said Karl and Ingo. Ingo went on to say it three or four more times; plus he pointed out that if they had gone to the cosmonaut exhibition in the Pioneer Palace, they would have been safely indoors.

So they took Noah home.

And thanks to that long day, 54 Max-Beer-Straße actually felt something like "home" now—when Noah's parents opened the door of the apartment, Noah was so glad to see them, he almost burst into tears.

"Jonah!" said his mother, and his father gave him an enormous, enormous hug. "Did you have a nice time? Say good-bye to your friends."

They weren't his friends. But they all shook hands anyway.

Frau Huppe made a brisk little speech to Noah's mother about how much there was for her office to do before the huge FDJ gathering beginning in just a few days now. And about how the schools were about to go on their middle-of-May spring vacation, too, so really nothing could be done before June. And June was practically the end of the school year. So . . .

"Your Jonah should of course write up his petition, asking to be sent to school. Why not? But we mustn't expect success."

"I thought *you* were the authority who could tell the schools what to do about a visiting child's education," said Noah's mom. That was more or less what she said, Noah guessed, but since his brain was pretty well worn out by now, some of his mother's long German words washed right over him like seawater.

"Well," said Frau Huppe, "of course, there is the

impression one has of Jonah's skills today, and the impression one had after our evening a few days ago."

There was a reasonably long silence, while Noah's family tried to figure out what this meant.

"Submit your letter to the ministry," said Frau Huppe finally. "Come on, now, Karl, Ingo."

Noah's parents had him sit right down at the table and write his little essay. "Do it while it's all still fresh in your mind," they said encouragingly. Noah wrote down two sentences about each thing they had seen that day, and he said he very much wanted to go to school, to improve his German and to get to know more about the culture of the GDR. His superpower meant he could write a pretty good letter in German, but thank goodness he didn't have to read it aloud!

"I'll take this into the ministry tomorrow," said his mother indoors that evening.

Outdoors, however, she said, "That woman had already filed her decision after the Party party. I can just tell!"

And a moment later, "Well, never mind about that. Tonight we'll make crumb cake from a mix and watch some East German television."

Secret File #8
LOOKING-GLASS TELEVISION

Almost everyone in East Germany had a television. Here were the programs offered on East German television's two channels on one weekday evening in May 1989:

CHANNEL 1

19.30 (7:30 p.m.) *Aktuelle Kamera* — the East German news. For fifteen solid minutes, the news announcer reads letters of gratitude written by international antifascists to the chairman of the Central Committee and president of the State Assembly, Erich Honecker. On the screen is a picture of Chairman Erich Honecker: he has white hair and nerdy glasses and looks pleased to be receiving all this praise and gratitude.

20.00 (8 p.m.) Obscure Austrian film.

21.45 (9:45 p.m.) "In the Name of the People"—a documentary.

22.30 (10:30 p.m.) *Aktuelle Kamera* again. More East German news. Scenes from the annual meeting of some enormous East German youth group. The newscaster reads from his notes: "A hundred thousand voices just sang their pledge of allegiance to the revolutionary roots of the youth organization of the GDR." The young people, dressed in bright-blue shirts, hold up signs saying things like WESTERN FREEDOM — NO, THANKS!

22.45 (10:45 p.m.) Yugoslavian documentary about rural life.

23.35 (11:35 p.m.) *Alles, was Recht ist* ("Everything That's Legal"). State lawyer Dr. Friedrich Wolff answers legal questions from GDR citizens: "What can I do when my neighbor won't repair his fence?"

CHANNEL 2
18.00 (6 p.m.) "You and Your Garden."

18.25 (6:25 p.m.) *Der schwarze Kanal* ("The Black Channel"). Snippets of West German television put together to make the West Germans look bad, while a man named Karl-Eduard von Schnitzler makes snide comments.

18.55 (6:55 p.m.) News headlines.

19.00 (7 p.m.) Historical program on seventeenth-century Dutch politics.

20.00 (8 p.m.) Czechoslovakian film.

21.30 (9:30 p.m.) *Aktuelle Kamera.* More news, complete with the weather report.

Not listed here, by the way, are the television programs most people *actually* watched, because those came floating over the Wall from West Berlin.

· chapter nine ·

A VOICE IN THE NIGHT

"Well, that's it, the spring holiday's over," said Noah's mother one afternoon at the end of May. "The kids are back in school, finally, and that means me, too. Can't believe how much time is being eaten out of my research by school vacations! But now my minder's going to take me around."

They were sitting on a bench in a park, because the weather was finally feeling less like winter. They had already been in East Berlin almost three weeks. Another week and it would be a month. Noah had an imaginary pencil clutched in his imaginary hand, just waiting to check off that first month on his secret imaginary calendar of How Long He Had to Be Jonah. One month down; five to go.

The hardest part about being Jonah was this: not going to school and not having any friends. Okay, that was two things. The Tweedle-Huppes—not good candidates for friendship, anyway—had completely vanished. Noah's mother had even sent them an invitation to dinner, but they had turned it down. "It would not, unfortunately, be possible," they had said. Whether it was fear of curried rice or just wanting to stay away from the dangerous Americans, Noah didn't know. By now he was so tired of being the only kid in his world, he would almost even have been glad to see Ingo.

"What's a minder?" said Noah, kicking a little at the ground beneath the bench.

"She's another one from the Ministry of Education. She'll take me to visit the various schools and make sure I don't get into any trouble during my observations."

"Like a babysitter," said Noah.

His mother hooted (quietly).

"Kind of."

"What about me going to school?"

The hoot evaporated.

"Well," said his mother, "I don't honestly know what's happening with that. The ministry's being slow. And remember that Frau Huppe wasn't exactly encouraging."

"Isn't there a law that says kids need to be in school?" he asked. "Even here? Doesn't everyone have to go to school?"

"Let's keep hoping," said Noah's mother. "Let's keep hoping. If not this spring, then maybe next fall."

"Next fall" might have been two of the most depressing words Noah had ever heard. He tried very hard not to think about them.

The next morning, he woke up to the nutty-sweet smell of something cooking.

"Good morning, Yo-Yo!" said his father when Noah appeared in the kitchen. "Ready for some pancakes? I got a little carried away this morning. I was just lying around, thinking about pancake ingredients, and then I realized that since I found the little envelopes of Baking Joy, which seems to be baking powder, yesterday at the Kaufhalle, I mean *the store*, we now have everything, absolutely everything, you need to make pancakes, and pretty much two minutes after I realized that, I was in here mixing batter together. How are they?"

"So good!" said Noah. "Yum."

Noah's mom looked at her watch.

"Five minutes before the minder arrives! And we know she won't be late, because for one thing people seem to run things on time here, and for another thing I learned *she lives in this very building.*"

"How extremely convenient!" said Noah's father. "What a coincidence!"

He said all that using his special camouflage tone of voice, the one that gave you no clue whether he was joking or being perfectly serious.

"The babysitter lives here?" said Noah. He hadn't seen anyone who looked even slightly like a babysitter in the stairwell.

"*Minder,*" said his mother, shooting him a significant look. "I guess we live in a pretty high-toned building. People from ministries everywhere. Of course, they keep to themselves. And then there's us."

The doorbell rang.

"And that's her now!" said Noah's mother, jumping up.

The minder turned out to be a medium-small woman with gray-brown hair. If Noah had ever seen her before, he didn't remember it.

"Renate März," she said.

Noah's mother organized all the necessary polite introductions. The woman looked at Noah with particular interest.

"Hello, young man," she said in German. "You must be Jonah."

Noah's mother gave him a gentle prod in the back that meant *This is when you prove you're a polite person who wasn't raised by wolves.*

"Glad to meet you," said Noah. He was nervous, and the bicycle of his speech ran into wall after wall. It wasn't really that being nervous made the stutter worse. It just made it harder for him to recover when he hit a wall or a bump, and *that* made the stutter worse.

As usual, in Noah's long experience, the woman's face changed while he was talking.

She shook Noah's hand and said to Noah's mother, "I see. He must inspire your work. It's not easy, to have a child with such a defect."

Noah bristled, but the Rules meant he couldn't say anything even the slightest bit sarcastic. Why, though, should it be hard for his parents to have a kid who stutters? It wasn't hard for *him,* particularly, to be the kid who actually did stutter; he just kept moving along and moving along, and eventually everything that needed saying got itself said. What was so hard about that?

But he noticed that the woman's tone of voice had changed. It was as if she had been testing them, and they had passed the test.

"And your husband is here to take care of the boy," she said. "Yes, I see."

It sounded like she was filling out a form in her mind as she spoke to them.

"Sam is also working on his novel while we're here," said Noah's mother, and Noah's father made a modest little sound from over in the kitchen. Noah noticed that neither she nor his father went on to mention that the novel was about mink farmers, however.

Frau März didn't seem to want to hear about the novel.

"Well, children are the future!" she said in a bright tone of voice, and in the stiffest English Noah had ever heard, she added: "I think you'll see that we do everything we can here to promote the Well-Being of the Child."

"Yes," said Noah's father, coming in with a dish towel in his hand. "Of course. I'm sure you do."

Noah's mother was gathering up her notebooks and pens. She tucked them into a bag and waved good-bye, and then off she went with the minder to visit programs for children with speech deficits in whatever East Berlin schools the minder was willing to show her.

Noah and his father looked at each other.

"Maybe I could go play in the park for a while?" said Noah. That was his place for being outside and alone when being inside and alone seemed particularly unbearable.

"Don't bother those construction crews," said his father,

as he always did. "Promise to stay out of their way and out of trouble?"

Yes yes yes yes.

He always stayed a million miles out of trouble.

So he went down to the construction site and watched holes being dug for a while. Noah had a high basic tolerance for construction, because when buildings were going up, you could see the way they were put together, and he always liked knowing the way things were put together. But here they were still just digging holes, not building things up from those holes, so when watching them dig became too boring for words, he walked around the park that wasn't really a park and kicked at weeds and twigs.

There were some interesting little nooks and crannies created by the extra fences up around the construction site, and Noah liked to seek out places to sit that were out of sight of workers and apartment windows.

He needed to think.

Something about the conversation with that minder had really gotten under his skin. She had softened so distinctly when Noah had opened his mouth and the Astonishing Stutter had popped right out and started showing off. Why was that?

And that made Noah realize that it could be useful, under certain circumstances, to have a kid with a bad stutter. Of course, it could be inconvenient, too, if you were trying to convince people to let the kid go to German-speaking schools! But if, say, you wanted to convince people that you had a good reason to be studying speech defects in the German Democratic Republic, then having a child with a stutter might be useful evidence. And that thought led to other ideas that troubled Noah's brain. He wasn't sure he wanted to be *useful,* not in that way.

That night Noah had trouble sleeping. And even once he fell asleep, it wasn't for long. Sometime late, late that night, he found himself lying in his narrow bed, looking up at the ceiling, while his heart thumped away.

A breeze had wandered in through his bedroom window—it had been so warm and summer-like that they had started opening some windows at night—and was gently swelling the folds of his curtains.

An argument was coming in with the breeze, from somewhere not too far away.

He got out of bed and walked to his window to listen harder, and it seemed to him that the sound must be coming up from another opened window somewhere nearby.

That was interesting, because one of those voices arguing belonged to a kid. The kid, whoever it was, sounded lonely and sad.

Noah shivered a little and went back to bed, pulling the not-very-soft pillow up over his head so that he wouldn't hear anything from outside that window anymore. Other people's arguments feel like something you shouldn't be listening in on, especially if you can't do much about whatever it is that's making them so upset.

He forgot about having been awake in the middle of the night during the next few hours of sleep and woke up with his mind all muddled by some fussy dream about running after balloons that kept dancing out of reach and then drifting away.

What a silly dream to have! Really, at least he should be able to have interesting and exciting *dreams*!

After breakfast he did three or four pages from a math workbook, but real numbers interrupted his work and distracted him. Namely, the number forty. Forty was a special number here this year. You saw it all over the place. That was because 1989 was the fortieth anniversary of the German Democratic Republic officially becoming a separate state. They were going to celebrate the heck out of that anniversary in October, but for now you could already see signs here and there, and of course headlines in the newspaper.

Forty is a square-cornered number, though not technically a square. Four times ten. Twenty times two. Or you could take the five out of hiding and call it five times eight. Hmm. That added some oddness to the square. Noah had always been fond of the number forty, but it was everywhere in Berlin. That might be too much of a good thing.

Then he took his mental arithmetic outside, something to think about while he wandered the construction site that was supposed to be a park.

He was feeling lonely. He was sort of a loner by nature, but this way of life was extreme. No classmates! No school! No soccer! Nothing!

In his sudden flood of self-pity, he stumbled over a small pile of sticks near the back fence.

"Watch your big galumphy feet!" said a voice nearby. Perhaps those weren't the exact words, since the voice was speaking German, but that was certainly the general meaning.

Noah jumped about three feet in the air before he saw the person the voice had come from: a girl with short blond hair and jeans. She looked like she was just about Noah's age, or maybe a little younger.

"You just broke my twig house!" the girl said.

"I'm sorry," said Noah in German: *"Es tut mir Leid."* The way you say "I'm sorry" in German is "It gives me pain." Since in German that phrase is basically just designed to stop stutterers in their tracks, suffering really was involved.

The girl gave him a long, hard look.

"You talk funny," she said in German. Or something to that effect.

"*Ja,*" said Noah.

"Are you from outer space?"

"*Nein,*" said Noah.

The girl slapped her grimy knee as if she had just figured something important out.

"*Dann musst du'n Wechselbalg sein, wie ich,*" she said.

By now—despite his lonely days—Noah could understand German sentences pretty well, and still the word at the center of this one felt like an incomprehensible mouthful.

"You must be a *Wechselbalg,* like me"—but what was a *Wechselbalg?*

"I don't know what that means, but I'm sorry about the twig house," he said, and then he remembered to start at the beginning, and added, "My name is *No—Jonah.* What is your name?"

One of the advantages of the Astonishing Stutter was that it covered up all sorts of other errors, like almost using the wrong name for yourself. The girl stared at him so intently he felt his ears beginning to pink up from embarrassment.

"Hello, *Wechselbalg,* called *Nojonah,*" she said. He

definitely needed to look that word up: *Wechselbalg*. "I'm Claudia."

Her name sounded like "Cloudia." Noah said that a few times to himself in his mind: *Cloudia, Cloudia, Cloud-ee-ya*. It was a really nice name.

She stared at him another moment and then shrugged and got to work rebuilding the house Noah had tripped over. Noah felt bad about having knocked down the first twig house, so he helped.

When the twigs were in place, Noah pointed to the building behind them.

"That's where I live," he said.

"Ja," said Claudia. "Me, too. That's where I live now."

He thought about that for a moment.

"You live *there*?" he said. "Really? I've never seen you."

"But I've seen you," said the girl. She squinted through a pretend peephole made with her fingers, to show him what she meant. "And I hear you, too. Loud feet."

So she must be downstairs — and then he remembered the arguing he'd overheard in the night. Still, it seemed strange that he wouldn't have seen her in the stairwell. On the other hand, it was the kind of stairwell that didn't invite lingering. He almost never saw *anyone* on those stairs.

"I'm not staying long," said the girl. "I don't belong here,

111

not really. I'm just visiting my grandmother while my parents are away on vacation."

"I don't belong here, either," said Noah.

The girl Claudia nodded, a short, sharp nick of her head. *"Wechselbalg!"* she said again. That word!

And then his father called his new name from the other side of the little park, and Noah waved good-bye and ran upstairs to figure out from the German-English dictionary what *Wechselbalg* meant.

Secret File #9
WECHSELBALG

What the girl Cloud-Claudia had said (according to the dictionary) was this: "Then you must be, like me, a *changeling*."

She was absolutely right, of course.

A changeling may look like a normal human child, but it's not. It's a fairy or a goblin or something else along those lines, swapped for a human baby at a tender age.

It's a creature from one world forced to live in another world.

Noah sat looking at the dictionary for a long time, in wonder.

That's what's the matter with me. I'm a changeling. I always belong somewhere else.

That struck him as an important fact to have learned early on. It was so obvious, he was surprised he had never figured it out before.

Why would Cloud-Claudia call herself a changeling, though? An East German girl living in East Berlin — what did changelings have to do with *her*?

About that, Noah had no idea.

chapter ten

CLOUD AND CHANGELING

All that evening Noah puzzled over that thing the blond girl had said out there in the muddy non-park. She had said, "a changeling, like me." Why would she call herself a changeling? And, for that matter, why was an East German kid out of school on a weekday? Noah knew from his mother that the East German schools were in session right through June.

The only children of reasonable size that Noah had seen outside of school during school hours were Tweedledum and Tweedledee, the Huppe brothers, and they, of course, had been part of a mission at the time—the tiresome mission of Testing Noah.

The next day, he went back to the non-park to see if she was there, but she wasn't.

Time went by. He looked for her in the stairwell and listened for her at his window, but there was no Cloud-Claudia. She had vanished again, just as surely as if she had really come from another world.

He was getting better acquainted with East Berlin, however. His father took him on a lot of expeditions, looking for interesting buildings or parks or doughnut stands. Mostly people tried to ignore them, but every now and then someone would stare. After almost two months in East Berlin, they must still have stuck out like a pair of sore thumbs — even when Noah wasn't talking.

On one of those expeditions, a strange thing happened. Noah's father had paused to tie his shoe. Then two minutes later, a policeman came hurrying up behind them, even though they hadn't been anywhere near the embassy at all!

"You dropped this," said the policeman, and he handed Noah's father a little piece of paper that did indeed look like the sort of thing that sometimes spilled out of Noah's father's pockets.

Noah's father looked at it. (So did Noah.) It was blank.

"Oh," said Noah's father. "Thanks!"

And he put the blank little piece of paper into his wallet, at which point the policeman did what all those policemen seemed always to do, and asked for their identification papers so he could recite their statistics to his hidden microphone.

Noah's father offered no explanation, either. The whole thing was, thought Noah, rather strange.

The next day, Noah was hiding in the non-park, studying his map of Berlin, when a medium-small hand reached out from beside him and tapped the paper. The hand had long, fragile fingers that came from a different world.

"Cloud!" said Noah. His voice fractured that one syllable into many happy ones.

She was smiling.

"Show me that map you're holding, Nojonah," she said to him, pulling gently at the map.

He let her take it. He was too busy trying to remember all the urgent questions he had been going to ask her if he ever saw her again.

"So why aren't you in school?" he said. "Isn't this the last week or something? Before summer?"

He knew that from his mother.

"School?" said Cloud.

She made a face and gagged a little and shrugged.

"I was sick for a long time. Lung sick. Then I got better, but not better enough to go on vacation. So they left me with my grandmother. My parents left me. I'm better now."

Cloud-Claudia certainly didn't look sick. Somewhat pale, yes, but healthy.

Noah asked the question that had been waiting in him for days and days:

"And why did you say you're a *Wechselbalg*?"

She looked at him and put her finger to her lips and whispered from behind that finger.

"I told you: I don't belong here," she said. "I've never belonged."

And then she went back to studying the map.

"Where have you been all these weeks?" said Noah. "I looked and looked for you."

"The *Oma* doesn't want me to talk to you," the girl said. An *Oma* was a grandmother.

"Why not?" asked Noah.

She shrugged.

"Maybe because changelings are dangerous," she said. "So *two* changelings together? Extra scary." And she said something else that Noah had to work to translate into English in his head. In English it made almost a rhyme:

Changelings change things.

Noah wasn't sure about that. There was so much in the

world that was built of concrete and barbed wire and rules. How could anyone ever hope to change any of it?

"So, when are your parents coming back?" he asked, to shift the subject in a different direction. Claudia stared at him. He tried again.

"Where did they go, your parents? *Mutter, Vater?*"

"*Ungarn,*" said Cloud with another shrug.

"*Ungarn,*" Noah repeated. That didn't sound like any place Noah had ever heard of.

But when he said that word—*Ungarn*—he had accidentally shrugged, just like her. He felt himself doing it. He hadn't meant to mimic her, but that's how it came out. Cloud's face crinkled into a grin.

"*Ha!*" she said. "*Nojonah!*"

That was, however, the exact moment when someone stormed around the corner of the fence and grabbed Cloud's arm, pouring angry German words all over her—and all over Noah, too, who stood there like a fool. It took him a few seconds to recollect himself well enough to recognize her: it was Frau März, his mother's minder.

And she was very, very, very angry.

Sometimes she paused in her long scolding of Cloud to shake a fist at Noah, too. Apparently he had done something wrong by simply being in the non-park with Cloud, who had gone limp in the hands of Frau März and was only just barely standing now, with her head hanging down, all the spirit gone from her.

And while Noah stared in horror, the woman dragged poor Cloud back toward the door of their apartment building, pausing now and then to glare back at Noah so that he wouldn't follow them. Except of course he did have to follow them eventually, because he lived in that building, too, didn't he?

He gave them a few minutes to get into their apartment and then tiptoed up the stairs to the fourth floor, passing two men with briefcases coming down from upstairs. It was a busy day in that stairwell!

It was only when he opened the door of his own front hall and went inside that he realized Cloud had gone off with his map of Berlin.

Secret File #10
CHANGE IN THE AIR

It might have been hard to notice, if you were just a kid rushing through the hazy streets of Berlin or talking to your maybe-new-friend in the non-park across the street from your apartment building, but change *was* in the air in 1989. Not just in Berlin but all over the Soviet side of the Iron Curtain dividing East and West.

The leader of the Soviet Union, Gorbachev, had started talking about change, for instance. He called it "perestroika." And at the beginning of May, the Hungarians — a couple countries south of East Germany but on the Soviet side of the Iron Curtain — had decided not to be so particular about enforcing the border between Hungary and Austria.

That plays a big role in our story.

But Noah doesn't know that yet.

chapter eleven

RAPUNZEL

Cloud's grandmother must have been watching her like a hawk, because Noah didn't see her again all that week.

She came up during a dinner conversation, however. Noah's mother was happily talking about her research and about how well it was going.

"School's ending, but I got so much data these last few weeks!" she said. "Enough to keep me happily busy all summer. And now I know the school people, so I'll have a running start on round two in the fall when the schools start up again."

"School? School? When do I get to go to school?"

His mother looked at him with those bright, sympathetic eyes of hers.

"Oh, dear," she said. "I'm so sorry about that. I've put lots of requests through, you know. I've told them it will not reflect well on socialism if you die of boredom. Everyone's just worried about what someone somewhere will think. I've been meaning to take it up with Frau März again — she's the one my official requests are supposed to trickle through. Although this whole week I haven't seen her. She's been ill, apparently. I've had to do this final round of schools on my own. Means I've triumphed over the Berlin bus and S-Bahn system, though."

"She's sick, Frau März?"

"That's what they told me. Haven't seen her in the stairwell recently, either, but I don't want to trouble her by knocking on the door. That seems too forward."

"She has a kid living with her, you know," Noah said. "Her granddaughter."

"Really?" she said. She was so surprised, she almost broke her own rules — Noah could see her swallowing her next question. "How — nice! Someone for you to play with."

Noah waited until he and his mother were walking to the supermarket to buy more cardboard pyramids filled with milk before bringing up Frau März and Cloud-Claudia again. Then he unfolded his theory, such as it was.

"I think Frau März is holding Cloud prisoner. Locked up, like in the Rapunzel story. Maybe Frau März isn't really her grandmother. Maybe she's more like an evil step-grandmother."

"Holy moly, now you're exaggerating!" said his mother. "And did you say her name is Cloud?"

"Cloud-ee-ya," said Noah, letting the syllables do whatever they wanted. "Her parents left her here while they went on vacation. We were talking outside, and Frau März saw and got mad and pounced on her and dragged her away. Poor Cloud! Frau März for a grandmother!"

His mother thought about things for a moment.

"Well, maybe I'll have to knock on her door after all," she said. "If Frau März is really sick with the flu or something, and trying to take care of a child, she might actually need some help."

Noah could tell she was making up her mind all through those sentences. Noah's mother didn't like interfering in other people's business, just as she didn't like other people interfering in her business. But on the other hand, once she had decided something needed to be done, she left doubt behind. Just set it down like a package and did what needed to be done.

So on their way back up the apartment stairs, Noah's mother shifted the grocery bag into her other hand and said to Noah, "Here goes!"

And pushed the buzzer beside Frau März's door.

By the time Noah had caught his breath, the door had already opened, and here was Frau März.

Oh, she must really be sick, after all! thought Noah, angling himself a little behind his mother.

When Frau März had come storming out to the non-park to drag Cloud away, all Noah had been able to see was her anger. But now he saw that this Frau März was a far cry from the tidy, in-control, carefully dressed minder who had shown up at their door some weeks ago to pick up his mother. She was frazzled. Strands of hair, half gray, half brown, were spilling loose from the bun on top of her head, and her eyes were puffy and red.

"Frau März!" said Noah's mother. "I'm so sorry to bother you! I heard you were sick—"

"You should not be here," said Frau März, but she said it not in an angry way, or not *only* in an angry way, but with flat despair as well.

Noah shrank farther behind his mother.

"And bringing the boy," said Frau März. "Bringing the boy. What do they know, at that age?"

"I'm so sorry," said Noah's mother. "I just wanted to say, if we can help—bring you soup, or take care of the child for you. Jonah said there was a child—"

"Yes, a child. The child is mine," said Frau März, as if that were a very bitter thing indeed. "All mine now."

And there was a strange whistling sound from a little farther down the hall, the faint sob of a shadow.

"If we can help . . ." said Noah's mother, but you could tell she was beginning to feel they might be out of their depth. "Frau März, you have a fever, I think. You need rest. Let us take the child upstairs to our place for a while. She and Jonah can play, we'll feed them supper, and you can rest."

"Rest won't help," said Frau März. "Have you ever lost any children? My only daughter is gone."

"Oh, no," said Noah's mother, and Noah could see the tremor of shock running through her. "Oh, I'm sorry. The child's mother—"

"And her father," said Frau März. "Mother and father. Car accident, in Hungary. *They were on vacation.*"

Cloud's shadow fled down the hall and into a room.

"I am so very sorry," said Noah's mother. She put down her shopping sack and reached out as if to take Frau März's hands, but those hands stayed put, on the frame of the door and on the doorknob, and there was no taking them. "Oh, I'm sorry. I had no idea. I wouldn't have troubled you, but I thought you were ill and we might be of use. My husband will be very sorry, too, to hear this. If there is anything we can do, we would be glad to help. And the child—"

"Cloud," said Noah in a whisper from behind her back, a whisper with a thousand stops and starts to it. He hadn't meant to speak at all, but he wanted the shadow in the hall to have a name.

"Yes, Claudia," said his mother. "Claudia is welcome upstairs, anytime you need some rest. Come now, Jonah."

Frau März closed the door without saying any of the usual polite phrases: she just let go with her hands and it swung shut.

Noah had never seen his mother unable to speak, but for a moment, she just stood there, silent and still, in front of that door, her arms sagging.

Then she picked up the grocery bag and marched upstairs, with Noah behind her.

"The poor little girl," she said to Noah's father, many times over. And also, "The poor woman. She looked like she had been through the wars. They must have been holed up in that apartment for days, grieving. Think how awful."

Noah's father was if anything even more shaken by the news than his mother.

"We can't do much, but I'll certainly make them soup," he said finally. "They may not have been eating properly. It was a good idea, offering to have the girl up here sometimes. Maybe she'll rethink that. I'll ask when I take the soup down."

And Noah just felt that terrible awkwardness that blankets everything when bad things, really bad things, happen. At least his parents seemed to have some idea of what to do. But Noah could do nothing. He thought about what it would mean to have your parents swallowed up by something horrible like a car accident, and his mind went numb.

It was like being a changeling.

It was like being dragged from one world into another, different one, where everything was colder and lonelier.

Two months ago, he wouldn't have been able even to imagine it.

But now, changeling that he was, and having lost *some* things — like his birthday, his name, and Oasis, Virginia — he could feel a flicker, only a flicker, of what it might mean to lose *everything*, and it made him feel sick inside, as if the ground under his feet had gone all wobbly.

His father chopped meat and vegetables, simmered things in the apartment's largest pot, and then, when it was ready, hours later, went with Noah's mother downstairs to deliver supper. Thank goodness neither of them suggested Noah should come along. The terrible awkwardness made him want to hide up here, out of view of Frau März and the Cloud shadow.

He sat at the table, looking at books, hoping his parents would forget to ask about Cloud coming upstairs with them for a visit, and of course feeling bad about wishing for something so selfish and immature.

But when he looked up from the table, there they were in the doorway: his mother, his father, and the thin, pale, indoors version of Cloud-Claudia, her eyes like shadows hiding down a long, dark hall.

Secret File #11
HUNGARY

Hungary—*Ungarn*—where Claudia's parents had gone on vacation, was another country, on the Soviet side of the Iron Curtain, like Czechoslovakia and Romania and Bulgaria and Poland. Those were the places East German tourists could go on vacation, and there were interesting things to see and do in all of them. (If you were an East German tourist who wanted to go to, say, Austria, Switzerland, Italy, France, or any other country on the western side of the Iron Curtain—including, of course, West Germany—you were almost certainly out of luck. The East German government was afraid that something bad might happen to you if you visited the West—you might, for instance, decide not to come back. Not only would that set a bad example for other East Germans, but the money the government had spent on your education would have been wasted before you had finished helping make East Germany a better place to live.) Anyway, that is why Cloud-Claudia's parents had ended up in Hungary: it wasn't just a really beautiful and interesting place; it was a place they were *allowed to go.*

Hungary is well worth visiting. It has great food, including the famous goulash, and the capital, Budapest, has a huge river running through it called the Danube. Claudia had wanted to go to Hungary with her parents for their vacation. She had wanted, of course, to eat goulash with them and listen to Hungarian musicians play the violin and hear the strange sounds of the Hungarian language, which is quite unlike most other European languages. And see the Danube River! Claudia had very much wanted to see the Danube. But she had come down with a badly timed case of bronchitis and couldn't go with her parents after all. Had been packed off to stay with her grandmother. Poor Claudia!

That gave Noah a funny feeling when he thought about it: if Claudia hadn't been a little sick, if they hadn't left her behind — which had made her feel so bad at the time — then would she have been in the car, too? She also wouldn't be alive anymore? But she seemed so very much alive to Noah now. It was a thought that made him squirm to get away from it. People who are so alive shouldn't just die. They shouldn't just vanish.

But, of course, it happens all the time.

chapter twelve

THE MERE GHOST OF CLOUD-CLAUDIA

When Cloud-Claudia was shepherded in through the door by Noah's parents, Noah's first, heartfelt, shameful reaction was to wish he could run away and hide. What could he say to her that wouldn't be stupid? He had never known anyone who had lost her parents in a car accident.

"Hallo," he said, looking mostly at his parents' shoes.

"Claudia's having supper with us and staying a little while," said his mother firmly. "You two go look at books or something in the living room while your dad and I get supper finished. Or do a puzzle. Here, have some cookies to tide you over."

"Okay," said Noah, and then he found enough courage to raise his head and look at Cloud-Claudia.

She had her mouth scrunched tight and her chin pointing forward. You could tell she was trying to be so haughty and grand that no one would dare make fun of her or pity her too much. Or pat her on her bristly blond head.

"Come in," he said to Claudia, and he pointed to the coffee table in the living room. They had to move the three coffee-table books, the big one filled with GDR photographs, and the other two, about mythology and the paintings of Hieronymus Bosch, but Claudia started looking at the Bosch paintings, her fingers trembling.

"Pictures of other places," she said. They were worlds filled with demons and goblins and strange tormented creatures. The worlds were beautiful and dreadful and interesting, all at once.

"Yes," said Noah. "Not ours, though."

She stared at them for a long time and then pushed the book away.

Noah took one of the cookies — Hansa Keks, said the box — and nibbled it, so that it would seem normal for him not to be talking. The cookie wasn't bad; it tingled in the mouth a little with the suggestion of molasses.

Not knowing what else to do, he took a puzzle, which his parents had brought all the way from Virginia, and dumped the pieces out onto the table. It was a puzzle made from an old painting of the Tower of Babel, which turned out to be a good subject for a jigsaw puzzle, because of all the little people laying bricks or climbing up ramps or greeting the ships bringing more supplies for the tower, which was rising splendidly into the heavens. Every inch of that jigsaw puzzle contained a whole story, a whole world, in miniature, and that makes for a satisfying puzzle— unless you're the type of person who loves pure white puzzles with a million pieces and no picture at all. There are such people.

Noah got to work. He desperately wanted to be putting little pieces together, bit by bit. After a few minutes, Cloud-Claudia leaned forward in her chair and started helping him. They didn't talk. They just sorted pieces that had one straight edge over to the sides and started putting together the most obvious sections of the frame, like the part where the ships coming into the harbor had long masts that ran as thin lines from piece to piece, or the rooftops of the distant town on the left-hand side.

At dinner the fact that Cloud-Claudia wasn't speaking became more obvious. She moved spoonfuls of soup from the bowl to her mouth with a kind of dogged determination. Noah wasn't going to say anything, faced with that degree of not-wanting-to-talk, but at a certain point his mother put down her spoon and said, just to make a dent in that silence, "What, Claudia, is your favorite subject in school?"

Cloud-Claudia froze, her spoon hovering just a millimeter above the surface of the soup.

"None," she said. In German that word has extra edges: *keines*. It bristled. It wanted everyone at the table to back off and stay away. Underneath the bristles, Noah could tell, lurked a squishy heap of misery.

Noah's mother was not the sort of person to be frightened of bristles, though.

"Outside of school, maybe? There must be something you especially like to do."

Cloud-Claudia put down her spoon.

"I like to be asleep in a tent when it's raining," she said.

"Oh," said Noah and his parents, a quiet chorus of ohs. They put down their spoons, too. That silence was different from the one that had come before it. It was warmer. With fewer prickles. You didn't want to interrupt it, but you didn't want the warmth to wear off, unappreciated, either.

"I like a roof overhead, myself," said Noah's father after a moment. "Less wet and less chilly."

"No," said Cloud-Claudia with conviction. She was looking at her soup, and the words started to spill out of her, fast and quiet, first a trickle, and then a soft torrent of them: "A tent is the best, if it isn't leaking. If there are blankets and you have spent the whole day climbing up the crazy rock castles by the Elbe River and stopping to draw pictures of them because you can't imagine how much they look like

133

magicians carved them and then later you eat sausages and crawl into the tent and have the every-evening picture-judging contest to see who drew the best rocks that day, which is not a fair contest says Papa, because his pictures are photographs so he can't show them to us yet and ours always win, Mama's drawings and mine, but that's how it goes and you sing one more hiking song and then roll up in the blankets to sleep better and if then the rain comes, but not all at once, just *pat-pitter-pat* like it's whispering something, then that's the best."

It was the longest group of words any of them had ever heard Cloud-Claudia say. They all tried not to gape at her. There was a lot of friendly staring at spoons.

"Yes," said Noah's father finally. "Oh, yes. I see your point. It sounds lovely."

"Last summer my stupid lungs were all fine, one hundred percent super, and we went to the Little Switzerland in Saxony," said Cloud-Claudia. "That's when I found out what I like doing most: I like climbing rocks, and drawing things, and sleeping in tents. There. It was wonderful, until the tent started leaking."

There was a pause.

"It's so stupid. Nothing ever lasts. The tent *always* leaks," she said, all fierce again, and then she sprang up from the table as if it had bitten her or something and went back to the jigsaw puzzle in the other room, and worked with

Noah in silence for another half hour, until they had the whole frame put together, the top and the bottom and both sides, something to hold a small part of the chaos of the universe at bay, like a tent built well enough not to leak.

Secret File #12
A TIP FOR UNSPEAKABLY TERRIBLE TIMES

Working on jigsaw puzzles together is the perfect way to spend otherwise awkward hours, or to bridge the kinds of silences that rise up when something literally unspeakably horrible has happened: so bad that you don't know what to say. It is much more comfortable to have a project that keeps your hands busy. Best of all, something you can do together. So: cooking, making quilts, building something, jigsaw puzzles.

I hope nothing unspeakably terrible ever happens to you or to people you love. But if it does, remember about puzzles.

· chapter thirteen ·

BRAVE NEW WORLD

Cloud-Claudia came back the next day, with a ragged enve-lope in her hands. She pulled a bunch of black-and-white photographs out of it and slapped them down on the coffee table, on top of the puzzle pieces.

"See?" she said, as if she was defying Noah to say there hadn't been actual photographs in that envelope.

There was a miraculous tower of wild rock, like one of those tall, bulbous mountains in a Chinese scroll, and there was Cloud-Claudia holding on to the sides of a rickety-looking iron bridge that seemed to run between boulders. And then came a picture of a light-haired woman with her arms around Cloud-Claudia in front of a landscape that was all hills and rocks and trees, two smiles that crooked up at the right side of the mouth with the same question mark of a dimple, one large and one small.

And another photo of a picnic next to some bicycles: that must have been from some other trip. And a very young Cloud-Claudia, her hair a puff of brightness, feeding the ducks in a lake. And then a blurry one of a man with a shadow across his eyes, looking up from a book.

"My mother took that," said Cloud-Claudia. "Because it's not fair, she says, if all the pictures are of the people who don't know about cameras."

"No," said Noah, agreeing.

It was hard to make himself remember that the people in these photographs were now really truly gone from the world—the people, that is, who were not Cloud-Claudia, who was very much right here right now, and trembling slightly as she put the photos back into their envelope.

"So that's it," she said, like a drawer slipping shut, when the photos had gone away. What else was there to say?

The puzzle was still waiting there, where the photos had been.

So they worked on that puzzle some more.

Certain people like to do jigsaw puzzles by sorting pieces out by shape. Others like to sort by color and picture—all the sky pieces over here, all the pieces with little people quarrying blocks of marble over there. Both Noah and

Cloud-Claudia belonged to the latter category. Noah liked also to take a piece, any piece, and then study it and the picture on the box until he found just that particular splotch of white with a little yellow dot in the corner. Perhaps this was cheating, but every time he figured out where a particular piece belonged, he felt like order was being made in his soul. A little, tiny, puzzle-piece-size bit of order.

They weren't completely silent this time. Sometimes Claudia commented on what the little people in the picture were doing, and sometimes Noah said something. They understood each other better and better. It always helps to have a picture to point to.

For example, Noah pointed to the tippy-top of the tower (on the cover of the puzzle box—they weren't yet far enough along with the puzzle itself to be examining the tops of any towers), where the narrow circle of those uppermost walls vanished for a moment behind a small white cloud, as a way to point out how high that tower was already getting.

"Cloud!" he said in English. "Like you! Cloud-Claudia."

"I am a cloud?" said Cloud-Claudia. First she used the German word, *Wolke,* which sounds like "vol-keh," because German *w*'s all sound like *v*'s. Then she tried out the English word, which came out sounding extremely German. Extremely like her own name—which, of course, it was.

That made her smile and reach for the mythology book, with all its lavish illustrations.

"And I saw you in here yesterday," she said.

Cloud-Claudia must have been just about the first person ever to look carefully at that particular book. (Noah's father liked to say the decorator probably chose it just because its cover matched the gold-tone carpet, and because it had so much *heft*. "Heft is a good thing in a book!" he had said. "That's what I want my mink-farming novel to have: heft!" So Noah thought he'd better ask what "heft" meant. "Solid bones," his father had said. "Strong plot, tricky characters, and enough pages that when you pick it up to throw it at the wall, you pretty much need both hands.")

Cloud-Claudia had found the picture she wanted there: a mythological whale in a bright-blue mythological ocean.

Noah just blinked at her for a moment. Was there a Noah's ark hiding in that picture that he wasn't seeing?"

"*Jonah*," she said. "It says there was a Jonah in a whale!"

The German for whale is *Walfisch:* whale-fish. Even though whales are not actually fish at all.

"Oh!" said Noah. "Oh, right!"

He was remembering the story of Jonah now, or remembering having once heard a story about Jonah. More important, he was remembering all over again that he wasn't named Noah anymore, not here. Here, he was one hundred percent Jonah. Whale-fish! Whale-fish! Whale-fish!

But then his mind tinkered with the sound of that word a little; he said it aloud, "Wallfish," with the *w* turned into a changeling American sound, almost not a consonant at all—and thought about a special kind of fish that might especially like to swim in walls.

"Ja?" said Cloud-Claudia, raising an eyebrow at him, since she couldn't read his mind.

He realized he was making funny shapes with his lips, thinking about *w*, and snapped his mouth safely shut.

"Why don't you show Claudia the Jonah Book?" said Noah's father, who had suddenly appeared in the room with his notebooks and his tea.

"Um," said Noah. He was reluctant. The Jonah Book made him feel creepy inside, like he was a character in a novel someone else was writing. But he couldn't get out of it. Claudia looked politely at the blurry photos in the Jonah Book for a moment and handed it back.

"Your pictures are in color" was all she said. She did not ask him, thank goodness, how he had liked having *Mrs. Deerborne* as his *second-grade teacher* in *Roanoke, Virginia.*

When Cloud-Claudia was leaving at the end of that day, she pulled something out of her jacket pocket and handed it to Noah.

"Your map," she said. "I enjoyed it. Thank you." And she looked at him with her intensely brown eyes, as if there were a message there for him that she was worried he wouldn't understand.

"*Danke,*" said Noah.

As soon as he had taken it into his hands, however, he realized that he should have just told her to keep the map. After all, he was pretty sure his parents could find another one. But by the time he had those thoughts, it was too late.

Later that evening, he spread out the map of Berlin to look at it, smoothing out the fold lines with his palm. That was when he saw it—a doodle on the map.

No, not a doodle.

Tiny little pictures, filling one corner of the large blank section of the map, the part where West Berlin had been erased from official consciousness.

Noah looked closer. These weren't real monuments of West Berlin. There were tiny little buildings, and parks, and schools, and a playground, yes, but also a small castle, and a forest running around the castle, and trees on which apples and clocks and candy canes grew. You could see that Cloud-Claudia really did like to draw. And that she liked small, precise things. That made Noah very happy, because miniatures and pictures with tons of tiny detail, anything that made you want to reach for a magnifying glass, all those things made him very glad, too. It was much of the reason he liked that Tower of Babel puzzle so much.

She had even labeled the parts of her extra map: in tiny capital letters, very clear, though small, and boxed to set the words apart, she had given the place a name: *Im Land der Wechselbälger*. The Land of the Changelings!

And little gates, here and there, between East Berlin and the Changelings' Land, gates and bridges and doors. To keep people out or to let them in?

It was done with such care, so perfectly and so tinily, that the imaginary world took up only a quarter or so, so far, of the blank splotch on the map.

He looked at it for a long time, thinking.

It seemed like an invitation. It must be an invitation! Anyway, he couldn't resist.

He got a couple of pens and tried them out until he found the one with the finest tip, and then he bent over the map and looked for the right place to begin.

What did he want there to be in the Land of the Changelings? He thought about it. A river, he decided, with islands in it and some icebergs for a polar bear or two. Drawing icebergs was highly satisfying, and he thought the tiny bear came out pretty well, too. And then he added more trees to Cloud-Claudia's forest, and a hill with a cave in it, and a cabin tucked into the side of the hill, with a tiny stream that emptied into the river. And then he added a fancy bridge over the river, so that you could get from the forested hills to the city proper without having to swim or go the long way around.

By the time he had finished all of that, it was very late indeed, and time for bed. He folded up the map and tucked it away under his pillow, which seemed like the safest place. Safer, for instance, than the safe.

And the next time Cloud-Claudia came over, after they had worked on the jigsaw puzzle for a while—the Tower of Babel was beginning to take shape—he handed the map back to her. She looked surprised, only for a second, and then she grinned.

"Your turn, *ja?*" said Noah.

And she nick-nodded her head and tucked the map away into her jacket.

They worked on that map for a few weeks, becoming slower and more careful and more precise in their drawings as time passed.

And they started telling each other stories about the things they had included, dropping casual little bits of information as they built the picture of the Tower of Babel together.

"There are lots of little towers in the *Wechselbalgland,* but no one big tower like this one."

"Do they speak the same language, all the changelings?"

"What?"

Noah pointed at the Tower of Babel.

"That's in the mythology book, too, I think. The tower gets knocked down and all the people start speaking different languages, so they can't understand each other and can't build it back up again."

"Oh," said Cloud-Claudia, considering. "That's sad. Well, they all have funny voices there, but they understand each other, I think, sure."

"They do puzzles sometimes—big ones, so big they would cover this whole floor."

"And they have *Wechselbalg* parties when the moon is full—they go skating on the pond and then sit under the tinselly trees and drink lemonade."

"Or hot chocolate. They really like hot chocolate, in bright mugs with tops on, so it doesn't spill on their feet."

"Especially when riding on carved wooden horses. You can't see it very well, but behind that big building in the center of the city is a merry-go-round; only about one horse's worth of it actually shows, though."

"Oh, right! Best job ever: merry-go-round engineer!"

"Your German is getting better," said Noah's mother to him one evening after Cloud-Claudia had gone home. "Have you noticed?"

No, he hadn't really noticed. But once his mother pointed it out, he did think he was a little better at speaking than he had been. The stopping-and-starting was beginning to be only at ordinary levels. It made him hope, all over again, that they would let him go to school.

For the moment, however, it was July outside the windows of the apartment building.

Simply enormous black beetles sometimes flew in through the windows when they were left open, but you couldn't shut out the warm July air. That would have been a criminal waste.

"I'm worried about Frau März," said his mother one day when they were all walking outside, through one of the local parks, because Noah's dad needed a break from writing his mink-farming novel. "I went to pick up some papers at the Ministry of Education, and I gathered she hasn't been there for ages. I'm beginning to think she won't come back. The woman in the office over there told me Frau März was probably thinking of retiring. And then she put her hand over her mouth, as if she hadn't been supposed to say any such thing. It was very peculiar. If I knew Frau März better, I could just ask her, but she never comes upstairs, and we don't really know her at all. Just her poor granddaughter."

Noah frowned a tiny bit on Cloud-Claudia's behalf.

Usually his mother could be counted on not to get overly sentimental. His father put a hand on Noah's arm, which meant he had seen that frown.

"Well, she may be a little young for retiring," he said, "but they retire younger here than in the States. And, anyway, a tragedy like that would really knock anyone off her feet, wouldn't it?"

Secret File #13
MINKS AND SAFES

Noah's father's mink-farming novel wasn't really all about mink farmers. It did, however, have a main character who ran a mink farm near Vancouver, and who was at the same time a pepper-tongued, sharp-eyed amateur sleuth ("like Agatha Christie's Miss Marple, only brinier," said Noah's father), a philosophical poet, and the producer of better strawberry jam than anyone else in the universe. The novel was apparently very cheery and heartwarming, despite all that talk about *heft,* and Noah's father said he was going to publish it someday under some comfy pseudonym and retire to a big house in the country.

Every night Noah's dad took his great pile of notebooks and draft pages and shuffled them into a more square-cornered heap, and then he made a big show of locking them safely into the safe in the closet in Noah's parents' bedroom, along with some of Noah's mom's notes for her thesis on speech impediments.

"Yes," said Noah's mother when he first did that. "Absolutely ideal."

His parents grinned at each other.

Because of the Rules, they had to wait until they were outside to explain the joke to Noah.

"The private safe has to be the least private place in the whole apartment," they said. "They pretend it's private, and we pretend to put private stuff into it. It's all part of the game."

A strange game!

chapter fourteen

OTHER TOWERS

When Cloud-Claudia wasn't there, Noah didn't touch the jigsaw puzzle, so the building of the Tower of Babel stretched out over a number of weeks. Cloud-Claudia couldn't come over every day. Some days Noah's parents were too busy, and some days they went on expeditions to other cities, even as far as Dresden, with its church tower still in skeletal ruins and the art museum filled with pictures from long-ago centuries, or as far as the city of Leipzig, in the south, where there was an enormous dark ziggurat of a monument left over from 1913.

It was Noah's dad who used the word *ziggurat*. A ziggurat was apparently a kind of Mesopotamian pyramid built up from square-cornered layers. "Think of it like the tower in your puzzle," said Noah's dad. "Only squarer." This particular ziggurat was German, not Mesopotamian, of course. It was called the Völkerschlachtdenkmal, which was a very long word meaning "Monument to the Battle of the Nations," and had been built, all those years ago, to commemorate the 1813 Battle of Leipzig.

Of course, it's not like Noah had ever heard of the Battle of Leipzig before. He inched his way through the informative displays in the little glass house and concluded that it had had something to do with Napoleon.

The Völkerschlachtdenkmal rose up, high and high and high and black and black and black, and you could climb up the dark staircases as if you were processing toward some sort of terrible sacrifice or a battle with orcs or both. In the little glass house at the side were old photos of youth groups using the place for ceremonies: the people back in 1913, and the Nazis during the thirties, and the Free German Youth in the decades after the Second World War. Apparently they all liked to parade up the five hundred steps, holding flaming torches.

Noah looked up and up and thought, with a satisfying chilly shiver, of the Tower of Babel.

When they got back from Leipzig, Cloud-Claudia came over to visit again, and they went back to work on the puzzle. It was August already.

"How's your grandmother doing?" asked Noah's mother.

"She's getting better, but she's very tired, thank you," said Cloud-Claudia in that flat and automatic voice she used only with grown-ups. Her eyes, which were full of life and never flat, flickered away from Noah's mother's face, down toward the table where the puzzle was.

"And there's no summer camp or something you could go to, somewhere that might be more fun for you?"

"They wanted me to go, but I screamed and carried on," she said, still in her quiet, flat, careful voice.

"Oh," said Noah's mother.

They put some more pieces into the tower.

After supper, Cloud-Claudia handed over the map of Berlin and the Changelings' Land.

"There's a problem, you know," she said. "When people cross that bridge over the river, when they go from one world to the other, their memories start to fade. They start to lose the names of things, all the names of the people they used to care about in the other world. Every day even their own names fade, and their pasts fade, and they forget about us a little more. But they don't even know it's happening. They're just going about their normal lives in the *Wechselbalgland*, but everything they do makes us fade in their minds."

"But were we in their minds in the first place?" asked Noah.

"Of course!" said Cloud-Claudia with the emphasis of someone who can't believe you're asking such a stupid question. "I'm talking about the people who start here and go get themselves lost in the other world, the Changelings' Land. They get lost there because it's so nice, and they don't notice how they're forgetting who they used to be. And the people they used to care about. They forget all the names of everyone."

"Like the river," said Noah. "There's a river like that in the mythology book. Look, here —"

He knew the coffee-table books very, very well by now, since there were only those three of them.

"See!" he said. "The river called Lethe, on the border of the land of the dead. The water makes everyone forget."

Cloud-Claudia squinted at the picture in the book and ran her finger along the lines on the page beside it; then she shook her head.

"No. Doesn't look the same," she said. "Where's the bridge? There should be a bridge. And why's everything so gray in that picture? That's not the Changelings' Land. Anyway, this is an emergency. We've got to get their names to them, somehow. If they could just remember what those names used to be, they could remember everything else, too, maybe."

"How's that?" Noah asked.

"Names are like codes, yes? Like magic codes. They have

everything that ever happened to you squeezed tightly inside them."

Noah twitched in his chair. For a moment he felt like someone whose life has been squeezed tightly into one name-shaped container after another. And he wasn't sure whether you could talk out loud about codes that way. Not indoors!

But Cloud-Claudia had already pulled out a strip of paper and started furiously writing names—a strange sort of list, Noah saw. *Sonja Bauer Sonja Bauer Sonja Bauer Sonja Bauer* went the first four names on the paper. And then *Matthias Bauer Matthias Bauer Matthias Bauer Matthias Bauer.* And some *Claudias,* too.

"*She* doesn't want me to worry about them forgetting," she said, pausing mid-list to point with her finger downstairs. "*She* wants us all to forget, and to let them forget. Then they really will be all gone."

Noah didn't know what to say.

Cloud-Claudia leaned forward and whispered:

"I know something strange happened to them in Hungary. Some bad magic. Not just a car accident! Something *worse*. She's not telling the truth. I can tell."

And that was perhaps the least Rules-following thing anyone had ever said in that apartment.

. . .

That evening, when they dropped off Cloud-Claudia at her grandmother's, the person who opened the door was not her grandmother but a youngish man with glasses on.

"*Hallo,* Claudia," he said, in crisp, official German. "I've been chatting with your grandmother, who's a colleague of mine. And may I ask who all of you are? Samuel and Linda and Jonah Brown? From the United States? How kind of you to invite Claudia to supper."

"It was our pleasure, I'm sure," said Noah's mother. "Good-bye, Claudia."

Cloud-Claudia looked a little lost, standing there clutching the map of Berlin in her hands—it was her turn to have it—but it couldn't be helped. They had to leave her behind now and go upstairs, where their rooms felt empty and quiet.

They stood there, each thinking about what had just happened, in silence for about ten seconds.

"Oh, dear," said his mother to his father, but it wasn't entirely clear to Noah what she meant by that. His father squeezed his mother's hand.

The little hairs on the back of Noah's neck had reacted right away to that man, even though he had done nothing terrible. The little hairs on the back of Noah's neck thought there was something scary about him. Noah considered the problem and decided it was the way the man spoke, almost like one of those soldier-policemen popping up on the sidewalks of East Berlin to check your papers. There was just the slightest hint of machinery about that man who had opened the door downstairs.

As he lay in bed later, trying to fall asleep, he found himself fretting about that man who had reminded him, oh so slightly, of a machine: wasn't that just the kind of thing—thought Noah—that a *merry-go-round engineer* might start constructing, late at night in his workshop where nobody could see? Putting mechanisms together that would look just like human beings when you turned the clock key in the back? Who would protect the Changelings' Land from *them?*

And then he realized that even his thoughts were now filled with Cloud-Claudia's particular off-kilter way of seeing the world, and that made him feel sad and worried about her all over again.

Secret File #14
CODES, CODES, CODES

Codes and walls, codes and walls. In places surrounded by walls, codes spring up like mushrooms after a rain. When the Wall went up overnight in 1961, families that had been separated so suddenly and so brutally would gather on either side of the Wall and convey life's news to one another through signals and signs and hand gestures. The Wall kept growing, though, and simple signals became harder to convey.

There were other codes in the air, too. Every night at about six p.m., for example, a radio station would start broadcasting, beginning with a series of clock bells chiming. Then a strange voice — half female, half artificial machine — would start spitting out groups of five numbers: 70869 70869 50217 50217. These were secret messages for East German spies in the West.

The Berlin air was thick, thick as gravy, with codes!

chapter fifteen

THE WALL GOES HORIZONTAL

The next day, when Noah and his mother stopped by Cloud-Claudia's door, it was opened not by Claudia, and not by the strange man, but by Frau März, who looked even worse than she had when Noah had last seen her.

She glared at them through the six-inch distance she had opened up between door and doorway.

"Haven't you done enough harm?" she said.

Noah blinked in surprise. Then he blinked again, because his mother did not seem so surprised: sad, maybe, but not surprised.

"It has been brought home to me that it can't be healthy for Claudia, who must adjust to a new way of life, to be spending so much time with a child who comes from such a different background," said Frau März, the poison in her voice easing. Now she sounded both very formal and very ill at ease. "Though of course we thank you for having her visit, and thank you for the soups you have brought me during my illness. But I'm better now, and we will not need your aid anymore."

"You should know we will be very glad to have Claudia over again anytime," said Noah's mother. "She has been a very good guest, and it is so lovely for Jonah to have a friend."

"I'm afraid she has a great deal of work to do, to catch up with the curriculum before the new school year begins," said Frau März firmly. "You will be doing us all a great favor if you just *stay away*. Stay away, please. Good-bye."

And the door swung shut.

Noah jumped a little when it shut, from surprise and discombobulatedness more than from the noise. Frau März hadn't exactly slammed the door: she had just moved her hands and let it fall closed. But if Noah's toes had been a little closer to the inside of Frau März's hallway, they would have been stubbed.

"Oh, no," said Noah's mother. She could probably see some sign of the steaming, unhappy pressure that was beginning to build up in Noah's head. "Come outside with me for a moment—you can help me lug some grapefruit juice home."

They had discovered little glass bottles of grapefruit juice from Cuba. So good! "I love Cuban vitamins!" Noah's father had said. "First the lovely bell peppers and then grapefruit juice!" North Korea provided their soy sauce, which was also a fine thing to have, but it tasted just slightly off compared to the soy sauces found in Virginia. The Cuban grapefruit juice, however, was bright and sweet and tart and perfect.

Noah waited until they were twenty steps away from the building—that was the absolute limit of his patience for the Rules at that moment—then it all burst out of him, an angry, red-faced mix of words: "See! It *is* like Rapunzel! That Frau März is keeping her there! She won't even let her out! And she's blaming me! She's saying it's all my fault! We have to rescue her! She is my only friend in this whole country! I'm not staying in this horrible place if I'm going to be one hundred percent lonely *all of the time!*"

"I know, I know, I know," said his mother. "I'm so sorry. I'm sorry for you, and I'm very, very sorry for Claudia. We were trying to help, but I'm afraid we only made things worse for her."

"So you think it's our fault, too? You're as bad as that awful Frau März! How can it be *our* fault her parents were in a car accident? And she's making Cloud-Claudia suffer for it—it's awful!"

"It is awful, but listen," said his mother. "That's what

can happen in a place like this. That's *why* we have all the Rules. Because if we're not really careful, people can end up getting hurt. Badly hurt, even."

"But we *were* careful. How were we not careful?"

"Having Claudia over all those times—that wasn't actually being as careful as we could have been. And then who knows? Maybe even the things we sometimes say to each other, even though I know we've all been good about following the Rules. Your father or I may have mentioned something accidentally about politics when she was visiting—that wouldn't have been so smart. What if Claudia went home and told her grandmother something about how we talk about Gorbachev upstairs? That could get end up getting them into trouble. Not *us,* so much, but *them.* For associating with us."

"I'm sure Cloud wouldn't say anything about us," said Noah, indignant on Cloud-Claudia's behalf.

"Of course she probably wouldn't," said his mother.

But then he remembered what Cloud had said herself yesterday about her grandmother, about names and codes, and his stomach felt like ice inside.

"Cloud said, she said—" It was like the whole idea was stuttering in his head, not just some particular sounds or syllables. Maybe because it felt like telling Cloud-Claudia's secrets somehow, and Noah was always careful about keeping other people's secrets. But if she had said it aloud in their apartment, and the bugs in the walls were listening, was it a secret anymore at all? "She said there's something strange about what happened to her parents in Hungary. She said her grandmother's not telling the truth. She thinks there was some kind of bad magic that happened. Why would she say that?"

They were walking again, toward the Kaufhalle, but Noah still felt like kicking bricks, if only there had been some loose bricks around to kick.

He could see his mother looking surprised, starting to say something—and then biting it back. What was that?

"She said that *in our apartment?*" she said instead. It was so obviously instead of that other thing she had been about to say.

"It wasn't her fault," said Noah. He felt that so strongly. It wasn't Cloud-Claudia's fault! And just to be very clear about that, he added in the slimmest of whispers, "She doesn't know the Rules."

His mother bit her lip.

"She's *upset*," said his mother. "She lost her *parents*. They'd have to see that."

Then she said, more bitterly, "Rats."

"Why rats?" whispered Noah.

"Because we blew it, that's why. Come on, keep smiling."

Noah tried to smile for whoever might be watching, but

it must have been a horrible smile, all tied up in knots the way he was feeling.

His mother was a thousand times better at the smile thing. Her face had absolutely nothing to do with the words she was saying. She looked cheerful and bouncy, but what she was saying was "I should have been more careful. I was so worried about what *we* might say, I forgot to worry about *her*. Well. I'm sorry. All we can do is back way the heck off and stay away."

"What?" said Noah. "What? Back off from Cloud-Claudia?"

"Shh," said his mother, brightening the smile a few notches. "You're getting way too loud. But yes, we have to leave her alone."

"No," said Noah. "No way. That's awful."

"For her own sake, *Jonah*," said his mother, putting some edge into her smile. "Look: *we* can leave if we get into trouble. The people we care about here can't. They live here, and they can't go anywhere else. It's not a game for them. It's their lives. Do you understand what I'm saying? Do you really understand?"

Noah nodded, but inside he was still dug in at *no way*. *No way* was he abandoning his one and only friend in this whole place. No way!

"I see you," said his mother, from whom secrets

could not be kept. "You're being all Alice. You can't be Alice here."

She was so tricky, his mother! She had caught him already, like a fish on a hook!

"What do you mean?" he asked. "What Alice?"

"The Alice-in-Wonderland Alice," said his mother. "At the end of the story, when she gets fed up because the trial's so unfair and the Queen of Hearts is so horrible, and she loses her temper and says, 'You're just a pack of cards!' Remember that? I know you remember that. But you *can't* be Alice, *Jonah*."

"I'm not," said Noah. He wanted to say, "And I'm not *Jonah*, either," but the look in his mother's eyes restrained him.

"None of us can safely be Alice," said his mother, and her lips got very thin as she said it, "when it's our friends who are cards in the deck."

Noah sort of saw the point she was making, but he was mad all over again anyway.

"There's only one single person I'm friends with here," he said. "One person! And she's being held prisoner downstairs. That Frau März is purely evil."

He did take some pleasure in spitting out those words. He enjoyed the *rat-tat-tat* his voice made of the tricky letters. At that moment, he wanted to make all his words sound as vicious as possible. And yet that wasn't the truly largest, most whale-like thought in his mind. To tell the truth, he knew that on some level he was only pretending to be furious. It was a way not to have to think about how awful it was going to be, not having Cloud-Claudia to talk to.

"Don't say things like that," said his mother. "She's not very lovey-dovey, that's true, but the woman has lost her daughter and her son-in-law. You can't know how that feels. And she has a granddaughter to take care of. And you know what I learned today at the ministry? She's lost her job, too. She's retiring early; that's the official story. But that man who was there yesterday, I'm pretty sure that's what he was there for—to tell her she was going to have to leave her job."

"Just because of *us*? Because her granddaughter was doing jigsaw puzzles upstairs with *us*?"

"It's possible," said his mother.

That was so hard to believe! But his mother looked serious. She wasn't even kidding.

That night Noah lay in bed scowling up at the shadowy images of monkeys and giraffes, and he thought that the Berlin Wall had shifted position: now it was the floor of his apartment, which was the ceiling for Cloud-Claudia. He was on one side of that horizontal Wall, and Cloud-Claudia was on the other side, and they couldn't even wave handkerchiefs at each other the way people had done in the old days right after the Wall had gone up.

He leaned over the side of his bed, looking at the floor that was really a Wall, and let his fingers drift down against its cool surface.

Cloud-Claudia was probably looking up at her ceiling right now, thinking upset thoughts in German.

That made him wonder about something. He was the Wallfish, after all. He knocked with one finger-knuckle against the floor: *tap tap tap.*

What was the quietest possible tap that a person on the other side of a horizontal Wall might be able to hear?

He tried it again: *tap tap tap.*

Then he padded over to his desk and got a pen, which he thought might tap more clearly than a knuckle.

Tap Tap Tap, said the pen against the floor, three taps for three words:

Are you there?

As he let that pen click out its question against the floor, it occurred to him that in German those three words sounded even more tappy, thanks to all the consonants:

Bist Du da?

Once or twice, just for fun, he let the pen have a temporary, not-so-astonishing stutter of its own:

Tu-tap, tu-tap, tu-tap.

He tapped on the horizontal Wall a bunch of times,

and then thought how terrible it would be if Frau März happened to barge into Cloud-Claudia's room just at the very moment some mysterious wallfish upstairs (himself, Noah) was tapping away on the ceiling, and he put the pen down and waited.

At first: nothing.

Maybe it hadn't been loud enough, the pen? He considered going into the kitchen to get a spoon, as the next step up in tapping material, but then he realized that if he left the room, he couldn't be listening properly to his floor, so he curled up on his side in his bed and waited.

And almost dozed off.

And then woke up with a start when the floor suddenly spoke to him after all:

Tup! Tup! Tup!

Wow! It sounded like she might have hefted a chair over her head or something, to tap out that very solid pattern, but of course, it's a lot harder to reach a ceiling than a floor.

Noah *tu-tapped* quickly back, but just once.

You're there!

And then, despite all the misery of that day, he smiled himself to sleep.

Secret File #15

TUNNELS AND WIRES

Berlin wasn't just thick with codes. Berlin was thick with people intercepting those codes. After all, as Noah's dad liked to say, in Berlin there were probably more secret messages per square meter than anywhere else on the planet.

Everyone was listening to everyone else.

The East Germans were spying on the West Germans, and the West Germans were spying on the East Germans. The Soviets were spying on the West Germans and on the Americans, and the Americans, French, and British were spying on the Soviets — not to mention, as it turned out, on one another.

And of course the people who lived on either side of the Wall had their own messages they wanted to convey: *I love you. I miss you. How are the parents and cousins doing?*

In 1955, even before the Wall went up but after the city had been divided into pieces, the United States and Great Britain dug a tunnel from West Berlin right into the Soviet zone so that they could tap into the Soviet army's phone lines. This tunnel cost millions of dollars and was in operation for almost a year.

Thirty-four years later, upstairs in Noah and Claudia's building was an apartment where two men with briefcases seemed to spend a great deal of time. They almost certainly were listening to what was going on in the rooms below, so that there could be a proper record made of the things Noah's father said about the quality of East German rice when he was cooking, and of Noah's mother's hooting laugh . . . and, of course, of the Astonishing Stutter. Who knows what they made of that?

Noah liked to think the Astonishing Stutter might just fry any technological apparatus that was trying to record it.

Ts-ts-ts-ts-ts-ts-TSAP! End of that wire! Ha ha!

· chapter sixteen ·

CLOUD IN THE WINDOW

Noah wanted to protest the injustice of everything that had happened to Cloud-Claudia, and the especially great unfairness of saying she could never come visit upstairs again. When he looked at the puzzle, which had finally been taking shape there on the coffee table, the sheer awfulness of it all rose up and threatened to capsize him.

He was not the sort of person who just gives up when things become difficult. Noah was used to finding a way around barriers and obstacles . . . including, when necessary, certain consonants. He thought about Berlin, the city of secret messages, and he decided that he was not going to abandon Cloud-Claudia, not now when she had had pretty much the most horrible thing you could think of happen to her, not now when she had lost her parents. And was even being held like Rapunzel in the apartment of the awful Frau März!

He had about twenty ideas for things he could do to help Cloud-Claudia or to see her, and each of those ideas was based on some ridiculous assumption or hope that made no sense at all when you looked more closely at the problem. It was not until the twenty-*first* idea that Noah thought he might have come up with something that could serve as an actual plan, a way to make sure she knew he hadn't forgotten about her. And even then, it was probably silly.

But Noah didn't care one single whit about seeming silly.

He found a sheet of paper. He found the scissors.

And he cut out a puffy white-gray cloud, and he stuck it up in his window. He figured it would go just fine with the monkeys and giraffes. Already they thought he was a little kid who wanted to sleep in a room with zoo animals on the walls, so how could they fuss about him hanging a puffy paper cloud in his window?

His parents saw the cloud hanging in his window but said nothing about it. He wasn't sure whether they understood it was a message or not. Of course, it would be part of the Rules that you didn't point at something and say, *Hey, is that a secret encoded message? Because it looks kind of cool!*

Then he started the really difficult part of sending any secret message, which is the having to wait patiently, maybe for a long time, maybe even *forever*, to find out whether someone has received your message, whether that someone ever successfully decoded it, and whether when they got the message, they went, "Aha!" and smiled in satisfaction—assuming it was the sort of message that would make a person smile, which was probably not the case for many secret messages in Berlin.

Noah's parents had told him—when they were well outside the apartment, looking at bears in the East Berlin zoo—that in West Berlin there was a place where you could climb up to a small platform from which you could look over the Wall into East Berlin, where at the far end of the street people seemed to be walking around, going about their ordinary lives. That made Noah feel a little queasy.

"Looking in at us like we're looking at the bears?" he said to his parents.

"Not so much looking at *us*," said his mother with surprise. "Looking at East Berliners. I've been up on that platform myself, years and years ago."

"But we're inside now," said Noah. "No, wait."

He had just remembered the map of Berlin.

"The Wall goes all around *West* Berlin," he said.

"It does," said his mother.

"So even though they feel like they're peeking in at East Berlin from outside, the West Berliners are inside, and *we're* outside," said Noah. "Right? If I were standing over there, looking in here, would I be outside looking in or inside looking out?"

The bears had no comment. His parents gave each other looks.

"Complicated mind you have there," said his father, and he scritched the back of Noah's neck. "Guess it depends on how you look at it."

Inside Noah's complicated mind, he was saying to himself, *The way I look at it is, I belong to both places. What I am is a wallfish. I swim through the stone wall in the middle of inside and outside.*

He liked the idea of being a border fish, a wallfish, a stone creature swimming through stone.

And the next day when he was wandering around the fence of the non-park, he found a small picture of a whale drawn in chalk on the bottom of the wooden fence, and that made him very glad indeed.

His message had gotten through, apparently.

That afternoon he put another cloud up in the window of his room. He began to think about making some actual cloud mobiles. He was getting ambitious!

The next day there were a few tiny scraps of whale-shaped paper on the apartment stairs. He scooped them up and took them safely home in his hands.

Cloud-Claudia was like a ghost haunting his steps. He kept finding little traces of her, in chalk or as whale-shaped pieces of paper, but she herself was absent.

Secret File #16
THE ZOO AND THE ZOO

Berlin had two zoos. The old Berlin Zoological Garden, in the western part of the city and founded long, long ago in 1844, was one of the most famous zoos in Europe. Sometimes a tourist might lean a little far over the railing of the crocodile pit in the old, old reptile house of the Berlin Zoo, and those crocodiles would simply explode into action. See all the humans jump back! East Germany needed a zoo of its own, though, so in 1955 they built what was for the time a very large and modern zoo on the eastern side of the city.

One of the features of the East Berlin zoo was that many of the animals wandered across large fields and meadows.

"No cages!" said Noah, amazed, when they went there for the first time.

But then he looked closer, and he saw that there were clever ditches dug into the ground, as effective as walls of bars. The animals weren't free, not really. They just *looked* free.

"When you look at it this way," said Noah's father, eyeing those ditches, "you see that freedom is a tricky, tricky thing."

He said it very quietly, though, so that no one but Noah could hear.

· chapter seventeen ·

A BAD CASE OF FARSICKNESS

August weighed heavily on Berlin. Everyone, not just Noah, who was now stuck on one side of his building's horizontal Wall, was anxious and tense. Noah wished he had thought more about codes before coming to this country. Morse code, for instance . . . the basic code of wall-tappers! But even if he had known Morse code, Cloud-Claudia wouldn't have had a clue, and what's the point of a message that can't be read? On top of all that, tapping wasn't a safe activity, not for Cloud-Claudia, anyway, who must have been standing on her bed with a chair or a broom in her hands — risking Frau März's wrath every minute.

It wasn't just Noah feeling blocked and worried. His parents were quieter indoors — which was a sign of having things to say that could not be said inside, because of the Rules—and more puzzling and cryptic in their comments to each other when walking outside with Noah, though they kept the smiles of a happy family outing on their faces. They were both working very hard over their notebooks, his mother sorting through her research notes, and his father giggling occasionally as he heaped up clues for his mink-farming, jam-making sleuth. Noah, who wasn't writing a novel or a thesis, was lonely and bored.

Without really meaning to, he finished the Tower of Babel puzzle. He had been putting in a piece here or there but no more than that, trying hard to save the puzzle for Cloud-Claudia, but she still wasn't allowed to come over, so eventually, no matter how slowly Noah worked, he found himself putting the last two pieces into place.

Then he said to his parents, "That's it. I can't spend one single more day doing absolutely nothing. Don't we get to go on vacation? You've been working hard. It's summertime. I know where I want to go."

He had been thinking this over for a while.

"Where's that?" said his parents.

"Hungary," he said.

The parents looked at each other, changed the subject, and eventually moved that whole conversation outside, where the evening was warm and humid.

"There's a word for what you have," said his mother,

poking him. "I just learned it from someone here. You have a case of *Fernweh*."

"What's that?"

"Guess you'd translate it as *farsickness*. You want to travel. So does just about everyone in East Berlin. They want to go to places they can't."

"We can go somewhere, though," said Noah. "Can't we? Let's go to Hungary. We can find out what really happened."

"What do you mean, what really happened?" asked his father.

"*To Cloud-Claudia's parents.* Remember? She said her grandmother's been hiding something. We can go to Hungary and find out the truth."

His parents exchanged another significant glance. This one had several layers to it.

"Hungary's a big place," said his mother. "I'm sure car accidents happen there all the time."

"You'll ask people and find something out," said Noah. He had absolute confidence in his mother's ability to find things out.

"I'm curious about Hungary myself," said Noah's father, but there was something teasing in his voice that Noah didn't quite understand. "Goulash and so on. Wild music. The fading border—"

"Right," said Noah's mother, picking up the pace of her quick, determined feet. *"Goulash."*

"Wait!" said Noah. "What do you mean? How can a border fade?"

His father sighed. "Hungary's on the eastern side of the Iron Curtain; Austria's on the west, right? They're like next-door neighbors with a great big fence between them. But Hungary's new government doesn't seem to want to be shooting people trying to leave anymore. In fact, the leader of Hungary and the leader of Austria had a nice little ceremony where they snipped through some of that barbed wire at the border!"

"Unclear what it all means," said Noah's mother with a carefree smile. "But people are full of talk about it, that's for sure. Someone I know said, 'Maybe we could even sneak across the Hungarian border into Vienna for breakfast and back again without anyone noticing. Breakfast in Vienna! I hear they have fantastic pastries.'"

"Really?" said Noah.

"Really could one sneak across the border or really do the Viennese make fantastic pastries?"

"Both."

"Well, Vienna's famous for its strudels; that's a fact. The rest is less certain. The same person told me how she and her husband had been traveling in Hungary last summer, and there was a point on the road when a sign had said cruelly, 'A hundred and fifty kilometers to Vienna.' And she said she'd looked over at her husband and said to him, 'For you and for me, it will always be a hundred and fifty kilometers to Vienna.' And some people even say they may close Hungary as a place to travel to if the border rumors are true. People here vacation in Czechoslovakia, Hungary, Bulgaria, Romania, right? Those are places they are allowed to go. But have you been paying attention to the posters in the train station recently?"

She leaned closer and picked some imaginary specks of dust off his shoulder.

"Posters only mention Romania, Bulgaria, and Czechoslovakia. No Hungary. Now *that's* the sort of thing that starts rumors."

The scary thing about Noah's mother was that you always had the sense that if *she* had been put in charge of a land behind a wall, she would have run the place much more effectively than the people who were actually in power.

"Well, I think we should go to Hungary," said Noah stubbornly. "And ask questions and stuff."

"You're not smiling," said his mother, who, of course, *was* smiling, though not with her eyes. "And you need to be about four notches quieter; you know that."

Noah could see that his parents thought the discussion

was over, but he wasn't going to give up that easily. He spent the next few days working all conversations back to the question. Back to *Hungary,* where the truth about that awful car accident must be hiding. *Inside,* Noah talked about sightseeing and goulash and fiddle music. *Outside,* Noah made his case differently:

"It would be a research trip," he said. "About the kind of bad magic that causes car accidents."

"It's not bad magic that causes car accidents," said his mother. "It's bad roads or bad tires or bad luck. You know that." Noah tried so very hard to see what thoughts were lurking there behind those secret-holding eyes of hers, but the curtains — so to speak — were thick. Noah's mother did not let her inmost thoughts slip into view.

And then that very evening in the middle of dinner, someone came pounding at their door.

"Cloud!" said Noah. He could tell from the quick patter of the fist against the door. It wasn't a grown-up sound. It was the same language the back of the chair or the broom- stick spoke when it tapped against the horizontal Wall at night — only this time, Cloud-Claudia's taps were shout- ing, loud and worried.

His mother had already shot his father a lightning-fast glance and was hurrying to open the door.

Cloud-Claudia was standing there, shivering and pull- ing at the fingers of her right hand.

"Quick!" she said. "My grandmother—something's wrong—please come—"

And she turned and ran back down the steps.

"Oh, no," said Noah's mother. For a split second she stood frozen.

They were supposed to stay away. Even Noah knew that. They had been told: *Please stay away.* But if Frau März was really sick or hurt. . . . You can't *stay away* when your friend comes pounding on the door. Noah was already leaping down the stairs, following Cloud. Behind him he heard his mother speaking right into the air of their apartment, as if someone might be listening: "If you people are listening—I think they need help downstairs," she was saying, every word in the crispest and clearest German. "Something has happened to Frau März. She may have fallen down. Please send help."

Talking directly to the people who had planted those bugs in the walls! Wild!

But Noah didn't have time to think about bugs, because they were already running into Cloud-Claudia's apartment, which was exactly like Noah's, except completely different in every way.

All its furniture was older and darker than the furniture Noah's family had upstairs. There were more books on the shelves—even the complete works of Lenin. The very air smelled different down here, as if Frau März used a different set of spices when she cooked. And in the larger bedroom, right under Noah's parents' room, Frau März was resting her head on a desk.

No, not resting her head.

"She fainted!" said Cloud. "I think she fainted! I heard a sound when her head hit the desk!"

"Oh, no," said Noah. He tried to be brave, since that's what Cloud needed right now. He walked right up to Frau März, with her head flopped sideways on the desk, and said, "Um, Frau März! Hello! Wake up . . . please!"

Though maybe when you have fainted, it's not just a question of waking up, exactly?

He put his hand right out and shook her shoulder. The sweater she was wearing felt rough under his hand.

"Frau März!"

Wait—did her eyes just blink? Yes!

His relief was so great, he could feel his arms tremble. She was alive. Thank goodness, thank goodness, thank goodness.

"*Oma!*" said Cloud with a gulp. "Oma, are you all right?"

Frau März was pushing away from the desk. Noah could see that her head had been resting on a very official-looking paper of some kind, covered with the kind of typewriting that looks cold and unkind. Noah would ordinarily not be interested in a letter like that, but there, right in the middle there, staring up at him—

181

"What is going on?" Cloud's grandmother was saying, dazed. "Claudia, is that you?"

"You fainted, Oma," said Claudia with a little quaver in her voice. "Come lie down. We'll help you."

—right in the middle of that sheet of paper was a word Noah knew well:

CLAUDIA

And before he had any time to think about right and wrong or privacy or ethics or any Rules, his brain powered right up and took a picture of that letter. *Click.*

Not that he had time to examine that new brain-photo now. There was a commotion out by the apartment's front door, and he heard his parents' voices, arguing there with somebody. Several somebodies.

"I'd better go," said Noah.

"Thank you, you Wallfish, for helping us," said Cloud. "I was so scared—I couldn't help thinking—"

She did not seem to have noticed that paper.

"I know. Me, too," said Noah, and two men came into the room, men too dressed up to be doctors. Noah recognized one of them: the same young-looking man with glasses who had sent them away from this apartment a week before. They looked at Cloud's grandmother and looked around the room, and one of them said to Noah, "Out with you, now. Quick. Don't cause trouble, boy."

"He was just helping!" said Cloud. "She bumped her head, but he helped wake her up!"

"Your parents are waiting," said the man to Noah. "Time to go."

Noah and Cloud looked at each other, and their eyes said, *What can we do?*

"Bye," said Noah. In German the word is *Tschüß*, and it was a word the Astonishing Stutter turned into a whole complicated code in its own right.

Claudia made her hands clap, almost as if they were just nervously clapping on their own:

Tu-tap tu-tap.

She was very clever, Cloud-Claudia.

At the front door, Noah found a third man, who also didn't look like a doctor, busy keeping Noah's parents from coming inside.

"Jonah!" said his dad. "Everything all right in there?"

"You—don't mix yourself into places you're not wanted," said the third man. "You must go up to your own apartment now, please. Keep in mind that it is a crime to harass official representatives of the German Democratic Republic."

The man with the glasses was in the hall now, too. He gave Noah and his parents a rather nasty smile and said, "Can't you people keep from causing trouble? Go away for a few days. Let things settle. Take this boy of yours to Hungary, the way he wants. I hear the goulash is tasty this time of year."

"Just please tell me, is poor Frau März all right?" asked Noah's mother.

"She's fine. Of course she's fine. Lots of alarm here over nothing at all. She thanks you for your concern but asks you not to keep forcing your way into her apartment. Good-bye."

Noah and his parents slogged back upstairs. There was nothing they *could* say to each other and still be following the Rules.

In particular, no one said, *How did those men who didn't look much like doctors know where Noah wanted to go on vacation?*

Because they knew precisely how those men had known that. Their little bugs hiding in the apartment walls had told them—were always telling them everything. It made Noah shiver, deep inside.

There can, however, be a silver lining to having little bugs in the walls, listening greedily to everything you say. This time Noah could think of *two* silver linings:

Silver Lining #1: His mother had been able to get help for Frau März merely by speaking into the air! Almost like magic!

Silver Lining #2: Noah's parents were people who knew

how to take a hint. The men in their suits really, really wanted them to clear out of that apartment for a while. Maybe the little bugs in the walls needed cleaning. Well, then, all right!

The next day the Browns—*Sam, Linda, and Jonah Brown, of Roanoke, Virginia*—packed a couple of little bags and went to Hungary on vacation after all.

Secret File #17
HAPPY HOLIDAYS ABROAD, DEAR CITIZENS!

From the "Recreation and Leisure" chapter of *The German Democratic Republic,* a book published in 1981 by the government of the German Democratic Republic "to serve as an introduction in words and pictures to a country which, along with its allies and friends, has been following the path of peace and socialism for more than three decades":

> All the year round, the GDR travel agency arranges excursions to cultural centres and areas of great scenic beauty in the GDR and neighbouring socialist countries. . . . With every year that passes more and more GDR citizens are spending their holidays abroad. The travel agency offers more than 400,000 package tours annually to the most beautiful regions of other socialist countries.

On November 30, 1988, the government modified its rules for travel in a "Decree on Trips Abroad by Citizens of the German Democratic Republic." This decree was read very carefully by the citizens of the German Democratic Republic, you may be sure. They noted particularly Sections 6 and 7 of the decree:

>**§6.** Private trips to the People's Republic of Bulgaria, the Korean Democratic People's Republic, the Mongolian People's Republic, the People's Republic of Poland, the Socialist Republic of Romania, the Czechoslovakian Socialist Republic, the Union of Soviet Socialist Republics, and the Hungarian People's Republic may take place without presenting particular justification — *as long as it is not decided otherwise.*

>**§7. (1)** Requests for permission for private trips to foreign countries other than those named in **§6** may be submitted by grandparents, parents (including stepparents), children (including stepchildren), and siblings (including half-siblings) on the occasion of births, baptisms, naming ceremonies, school entrance celebrations, dedication ceremonies for young people, confirmations and first communions, civil marriage ceremonies and religious weddings, on the 50th, 55th, and 60th birthdays, as well as every birthday after the 60th, on the occasion of 25th, 50th, 60th,

65th, and 70th anniversaries of weddings or civil marriage; also in the case of life-threatening diseases, the need to care for another, as well as for deaths and burials.

Just because you applied for permission to travel did not, of course, mean you could be sure such permission would be granted! In the summer of 1989, travel to the People's Republics of Mongolia or Hungary was still infinitely easier than travel to a non-socialist country. But pay attention to those last words of **§6:** *"as long as it is not decided otherwise."*

That's why East Germans noticed so keenly when Hungary seemed to vanish from the tourism posters.

It might mean nothing.

Or it might mean that the government was *deciding otherwise. . . .*

chapter eighteen

PRETENDING TO BE WHAT YOU ARE

It's not just people who change their names and put on disguises, Noah was learning. Towns do it, too. On the way to Hungary, Noah and his parents spent a day in the Czech city of Karlovy Vary, which—as Noah's dad explained as they walked to dinner—used to be a German-speaking town called Karlsbad. Before the Second World War, it had been the sort of place where people went to spend time in spas, to sit in steaming baths and pools. It was the closest city outside Germany to both East Germany and West Germany, so there were a lot of Germans there, people separated by the Wall getting together for a few days for a visit, for news from home, for romance, for long discussions in which somebody would plead with some other body to please, please, please come over the Wall and join them on the other side. Noah's family got into a cheerful conversation with some of those Germans—the West German kind, sitting over there at the next table, since it wouldn't be safe for the East German Germans to chat so freely with foreigners. The biggest German guy at that table laughed and said there was a nickname for the city of Karlovy Vary: "The Czech Center for German-German Relations."

At that point in their trip they were playing a game, thought up by Noah's parents: they were pretending to be American tourists.

"But I don't get it," Noah had said. "How can we pretend to be what we *are*?"

"First of all, people are always pretending to be what they are," said his father. "That's basically a philosophical question. Part of being something is pretending to be it. When you were born, I felt like I was pretending to be a father. But I kept changing diapers and rocking you to sleep and feeding you, like a real father, and one day it didn't feel so much like I was just pretending. Haven't you ever had that feeling?"

"Well, duh!" said Noah the wallfish, who had spent the past three months pretending his name was Jonah, which perhaps it really was, and years before that pretending to be a normal elementary school student, when he hadn't been sure that that was true at all. But that seemed different

189

from letting people think they had just flown into Eastern Europe from the United States somewhere for a summertime tour.

Then they got to Budapest, in Hungary, and the game changed all over again.

"This seems a good place for us all to be inconspicuous for a few days," said his mother.

"So you can do research," said Noah, "into the bad magic that causes car accidents!"

"Who said anything about research?" said his mother. "We're here on vacation."

The curtains were tightly closed in her eyes. Not a chink of light was showing. Noah decided to hope anyway.

"So, inconspicuous!" said Noah's father. "Inconspicuous means not looking American." He smiled a little when he said that, but the look he and Noah's mother shared was serious.

"How do we do that?" said Noah.

"We keep quiet," said his mother. "And when we talk, we're careful to talk only in German."

It looked to Noah like he might not be doing very much talking of any kind here in Hungary. But at least they were somewhere new!

"Think of it this way," said his father. "It's an exciting time. There's a tang in the air—can you smell it? Can you?"

"More coal?" said Noah, but his father shook his head.

"No! Not coal!" he said. "*History!* There's just the slightest taste of history in the air! It's wild! It's like that tingle all around while the clouds are gathering and the sky's beginning to churn itself into a fever and you just know a storm's on its way—*history!* And not everybody gets to be right in the thick of actual history. Mostly history happens over there in a slightly different part of the world, or you miss it by a decade or a century. But we *just maybe* are going to be able to nose out actual history our very own selves. Keep sniffing the air; that's what I'm saying!"

He demonstrated, his nose testing the atmosphere of Budapest, the breezes coming from the west, the east, the end of the block . . .

"You have lost your last marbles," said Noah's mother, but she was grinning. "Hmm! Sniff whatever you want— but a little more *inconspicuously,* would you mind? Not like a noisy horse hoping for sugar cubes."

"Don't you worry," said Noah's father. "We'll sniff tactfully, won't we, Jonah? We'll be inconspicuous little East German tourists all day long, as quiet as mice and twice as shadowy."

Despite their having to be mice, Noah liked Budapest very much. It was a city with big grand sights, domed monuments, imposing statues on tall columns, and a very wide river crossed by an impressive bridge. He liked the food, too.

But when he looked up at the clouds in the sky, drifting freely from east to west, he remembered all over again that this was the country where Cloud-Claudia's parents had smashed up their car. And died. What was Cloud-Claudia doing this week, while Noah and his parents were eating goulash and going to museums? Was the evil Frau März well again? Was she still keeping Cloud prisoner, or now that dangerous Noah was gone for a few days, was she freer to go out to the non-park and maybe draw more whales?

Then he remembered the paper that had been on Frau März's desk when she had fainted. He looked over that letter with his inside eye, and this time he noticed the date, which was early July. Then he tried to make sense of the endlessly long German words there. It was amazing to him that he could remember a bunch of words that he didn't even understand, but he could. It was the picture of the words his brain held on to — every little stroke of every letter. Now and then he would try one of those words out on his parents:

"What does *Er-zieh-ungs-recht* mean?"

"Like custody rights," said his dad.

"How about words with the letters *h-a-f-t* in them?" he asked.

"Has to do with prison. Have you been reading something strange?"

Stranger than strange, yes! Suddenly even the squiggle at the bottom of the page came together in Noah's brain, and he recognized it as a signature: a name. *Matthias Bauer.*

Noah shivered. That was Cloud's father, who had died in Hungary.

So it made no sense, did it, that his signature should appear on something that looked like a document about custody, dated (Noah shivered again) just about a month ago, but after that horrible day when they had learned about the car accident.

How could Cloud's father be signing things if he wasn't even alive?

His mother ran some errands that first day in Budapest—though to Noah's disappointment those errands seemed to have absolutely nothing to do with car accidents or bad magic. Noah's mother reported that there were hundreds of East Germans camped outside the West German embassy.

"Families with kids—tents—imagine!" said his mother. "That's because of the possibly leaky border. They're just going to wait until something happens."

Noah's father sniffed the air and gave Noah a significant look.

"What about Cloud-Claudia's parents?" said Noah,

impatient with all this irrelevant stuff. "When are you going to find out the truth about *them*?"

"Hold your horses," said his mother. "This is vacation, remember? I've got another idea: Would you lovely people perhaps be interested in a picnic?"

"A *picnic*?" said Noah.

He was staring as hard as he could at his mother, but her expression gave absolutely nothing away.

"A very large picnic," said his mother. "A large and special one. It will be fun and exciting—though a long day for you, I'm afraid. Sorry about that. It's quite far away. Out in the country."

Noah tried to be as sneaky in his thinking as his mother always was.

"Out in the country where car accidents sometimes happen?"

And he did think—just maybe—that he saw a tiny quick shard of pride light up her eyes. But then the curtains went back down.

"And that's about the end of questions from you, young fellow," said Noah's mother with a quick grin. "Back to being inconspicuous."

"Not American," said Noah.

"Right," said his mother. "Tourists from East Germany, that's who we are. Can you handle that, Jonah?"

"Technically not a lie," Noah's father pointed out.

"True," said his mother. "But anyway, this picnic is way out in Sopron," she said. "The Pan-European Picnic, that's what they're calling it."

"History?" said Noah's father, and he sniffed the air once or twice.

"Maybe so," said Noah's mother. "In any case, *Jonah*, Advanced Rules will apply. In fact, I kind of think you perhaps shouldn't talk at all. And *you*"—she was waving a finger at Noah's dad now—"should not *sniff*!"

Noah's father just laughed at that.

Secret File #18
ACTING AND BORDERS

It wasn't just Noah and his family who sometimes had to pretend to be what they actually were. All the German-German couples meeting in Karlovy Vary were pretending to be two people in love, on vacation in Czechoslovakia. And they *were* that. But they were also sneaking around the edges of the law. The one coming from East Germany would be careful not to bring much luggage, in order to look as much as possible like someone who wasn't considering leaving the country. And much of the time he or she *wouldn't* be thinking of leaving the country. But by the time a border agent has gone through all of your stuff three times and asked you five million times,

Why are you going to Czechoslovakia? Whom will you meet there? Are you planning to attempt an illegal exit from the German Democratic Republic?—you feel like someone who is breaking the law. Even if you aren't. And it feels more and more like just *being who you are* means actually playing a role, wearing masks, spying and sneaking and hiding something.

This is true even for people who aren't crossing borders or dealing with police. Many people in middle school, for instance, are pretending to be who they actually are. A lot of bad acting is involved. That goes on way beyond middle school, because being human means sometimes feeling awkward in our skins — like we really should have learned our lines better, if only someone had shown us the script, but somehow here we are on stage, and we don't remember ever having seen whatever the words are we're supposed to be about to say.

chapter nineteen

THE PAN-EUROPEAN PICNIC

It was promising to be a warm, warm August day, perfect for a picnic, but only just *promising,* because the sun was still busy rising when the man with the car came around to the hotel to pick them up.

They had to leave Budapest very early in the morning to get all the way to the picnic Noah's mother had heard about, two-hundred-something kilometers to the west. Hungary is one of those sideways-lying countries in the middle of Europe, so distances are farther from east to west than from north to south. All Noah knew was that it was going to be a long, long drive.

A long, long, *quiet* drive, if you were Noah. He was under strict orders not to say anything. "Advanced Rules"!

That meant being part of a very small audience watching his parents give their perfect performance as a pair of visitors from the German Democratic Republic—a pair of visitors with a silent child. They had even brought appropriate costumes along: items of clothing that looked—he had to admit—almost plausibly like something you'd see on the streets of East Berlin. A tracksuit for Noah. A blouse for his mother. Different shoes all around. And then they kind of ran their hands through their hair, and it looked more German, too.

Noah was impressed. Not just by the costumes, but by the way his parents talked to the driver: in absolutely perfect German. Of course he knew they could speak German, but all this time they had been living in East Berlin, Noah had never heard his parents sound like *that*, like actual genuine Germans. That was strange, thought Noah. That meant—and this was the *really strange* part—that meant they must have been holding back their German in Berlin. Talking more like Americans than they actually needed to. So were they acting there or acting here? Or *acting, acting everywhere?* It's an odd feeling, when you realize there are all these corners to your parents that you've never been allowed to peek into. That you didn't even know existed.

"Don't you look comfortable and cozy back there!" said

his mother in absolutely perfect East German German. She was sitting up front with the driver.

The driver—the only other member of the audience, though of course he didn't *know* his car had just been turned into a theater—seemed reasonably all right, as people go: he had smiled at Noah and patted him on the head. The smile was nice, but being patted on the head is just like someone yelling right in your face: *You are small for your age and I have mistakenly assumed you must still be a very young child!* So Noah didn't care for that, but he remembered to stay quiet.

In the actually not-so-terribly-comfortable backseat of the car, next to his father, Noah spent a few hours watching fields and fields of grain go by the windows. He stopped worrying about how well his parents spoke German and went back to thinking about Cloud-Claudia. Her parents. The mystery of what had happened to them. The letter that had apparently made Cloud-Claudia's grandmother faint. One short word stuck out in his memory now, like a traffic sign: *Haft.* The word that his parents had said meant "prison."

Prison? he found himself thinking. *Really? That letter had something to do with* prison?

Prison and horrible car crashes and bad magic all tangled themselves together in his brain.

They did not get into any accidents themselves. He was glad about that.

"It's a pretty town, Sopron," said the driver at one point to his parents. "You should go back sometime and see it properly. Nice square in the middle. Nice church with a pretty tower. Don't want to stop on your way to the village?"

"Not this time, thank you," said Noah's mother in that scarily German German.

They were headed for a village in the middle of nowhere.

No, farther than that—they were headed for a field on a rolling hillside outside a village in the middle of nowhere.

"You know what's over there?" said his mother in German, but before there was any danger of Noah forgetting the Rules and replying, she supplied the answer: *Österreich.* Austria.

They had driven so far west that they were now in a part of Hungary stretching right into Austria, like a finger poking at a mound of dough.

And here's the really peculiar thing about this field in the middle of nowhere: it was absolutely filled with people. Picnics are something you do with a few people—your family, maybe, plus a couple of friends. Or at most your whole class from school. But in this pretty place, a field amid rolling hills and green, green trees, hundreds and hundreds of people—maybe even a thousand people— were milling about. Many of them, maybe most of them, were speaking German. They were flushed with excitement, talking in quick low voices among themselves. There were lots of other families with kids, and some people with little suitcases.

"This is the Pan-European Picnic!" said Noah's mother from up front, seeming quite delighted. "They were distributing leaflets about it in Budapest, to all the people holed up around the West German embassy: 'Pan-European Picnic in Sopron, at the Site of the Iron Curtain,' that's what the posters said. Right at the border here, both sides working together, Austrian and Hungarian. It's quite an adventure. They're going to open the border station itself for a few hours, so that the picnickers can mingle properly."

None of this sounded at all like a *picnic* in the usual sense. Weren't picnics about a family and a few friends and Frisbees, and spreading a tablecloth out on the grass, and ants? What kind of picnic advertised itself on posters and took place at borders? He opened his mouth, about to explode into the word *WHY*—

"Well, now, look at all those cars parked over there!" said his father just in time. Noah remembered he wasn't supposed to say a single thing and swallowed that *why*, at least for now.

They got out of the car and stretched. There were people setting up grills for barbecuing food in the field—that much was picnic-like.

But one thing Noah noticed right away about the crowds was that they were more German than Hungarian, and they were more excited than people usually ever are about picnics.

It was pretty clear that the grilled food wasn't the main thing for them at all. It would have been a very long way to come for a bite of sausage, out here in this westernmost cranny of Hungary!

A couple of boys his age ran by, walloping each other with handfuls of grass and laughing. All the kids! Noah couldn't help himself: he grinned as wide as Humpty Dumpty. One freckled boy must have caught that grin because he echoed it and cried out, "Come along, slow-poke" in German, and before the cautious, practical side of Noah's brain had any chance to sit down and consider its options, Noah was already running across the field, chasing the boys who were chasing one another—and now him. It was so great to be running! He felt like an animal that had finally gotten free from the zoo, released from bars and guard ditches and let loose on the grassy savanna!

His mother had said something when he had taken off, but Noah couldn't even make his feet stop long enough to listen to it. Anyway, he was pretty sure he knew what she must have been *meaning* with whatever she said: *Be careful! Be cautious! Remember the Rules!*

But he thought he'd heard his father begin one of his

chuckles just as Noah began running, so he didn't worry too terribly much. Let his parents scout around in their parental way! For once Noah was just going to be a kid.

It was a glorious hour. He tore up and down the field and ate a sausage in a bun that some smiling person handed him at one point. And all that time, he even managed to stick pretty closely to the Rules — because it's normal for a kid to nod and mumble when his mouth is full of sausage. And it's also normal to tear around a grassy field without talking all that much.

There were signs up in Hungarian, banners that looked like they belonged at a fair or a political parade. Noah couldn't read those — Hungarian is a very difficult language, and Noah knew pretty much only how to say "hi" and "thank you": *"szia"* and *"köszönom,"* which sounds something like "kursurnum." (That was already bad enough, but "good-bye" was hopeless. Noah's mother had written it out to show him: *viszontlátásra*. Really!)

In any case, there was so much German being spoken amid all the Hungarian that Noah didn't feel completely at sea. He sort of lost track of his parents for a while, and even that felt gloriously refreshing and freeing.

And then the crowds began to move. There was a German guy who started talking pretty loudly to the adults in the group, and pointing at some line at the edge of the woods, and the boys who had been running around with

Noah were called back to their families by anxious moth-ers. Noah couldn't see his own parents, but he knew they were here somewhere. He wasn't too worried.

He stuck near one boy's family—the kid who had freckles—and just trotted along up the hill after them, wondering where they were going and hoping, in the care-free spirit that the grassy freedom had made rise up in him, that maybe dessert might be involved. Wouldn't an ice cream bar be the perfect thing right now? Warm sum-mer day, after running around chasing people in a field for an hour? Not that he'd seen a lot of ice cream bars so far here in Hungary.

He still had bits of grass in his hair! What a great, scratchy feeling. It was the opposite, the exact opposite, of having the cloying taste of coal smoke clogging up your lungs and making you cough.

There were pretty little hills all around, a rolling green carpet of trees.

"Three p.m.—they're going to open the gate!"

"For people with papers."

"Who cares? If it's open, it's open. Why not for us, too?"

Up ahead the crowd had reached the end of the field, where there were a handful of Hungarian soldiers in uniform—white caps with dark visors, light shirts, darker pants, handguns on belts—guarding the fence. On the other side was Austria, as well as trees. This was the actual

Iron Curtain itself, Noah realized. Though here it looked more like a fancy fence. The crowd looked at the fence and at the soldiers—and past them at the soldiers in different uniforms on the other side, the side with more trees. Austria.

And over there a guard tower, a real one, like in a World War II movie.

Noah looked around for his parents and didn't see them. But he couldn't feel too worried, not yet. Although there were border guards here, they didn't seem to be very threatening. They looked concerned but not exactly hostile.

It was the middle of the afternoon, and time, apparently, for them to open the old gate in the fence, so that the people with papers—that would be the Austrians and (since very recently) the Hungarians, of course, and not the East Germans, who were not allowed to travel to Austria—could mingle happily. The soldiers discussed something among themselves, eyeing the crowd, and then two of them went over to the gate and opened it. It looked like a creaky old farm gate more than the border between two countries. Old wire holding on to weathered gray crossbeams. The gate squeaked a little as they opened it.

Some of the Hungarians went up and showed papers and wandered on through, while the crowd murmured (mostly in German) and shuffled about. Then a small group of people carrying backpacks, sacks, and children came up to the open gate and did not show anyone any papers. The guards looked at them, but they went right through the gate and then kept going.

The whole crowd held its breath. Would the guards haul them back? Would they shout? Would they shoot?

But the Germans just pushed forward, and nothing terrible happened.

A family with a tiny little girl, all blond curls, came forward. The girl tripped for a moment, and others picked her up and popped her back onto her feet: *"Weiter gehen! Weiter gehen!"* Keep going!

The little road passing through the gate was crowded with people now, all surging forward. More and more were coming, hurrying up through the field from the road where all the East German cars had been parked. Mothers holding on to their children's hands.

"What's going on?" asked the boy Noah had been running with earlier. "I want to go see!"

The crowd was moving forward, making it hard to go any other way. The freckled boy's mother was calling, "Come along, quickly!"

And then they weren't just walking forward; they were trotting. Everybody was running, even people who looked too grown up to move that fast. Noah trotted along with them, caught up in the crowd, hundreds of people running forward to that gate in the middle of nowhere.

Some of the people had white handkerchiefs in their hands; someone near Noah was saying that was what you should do, that was what you should do, so the guards would know not to shoot at you.

There was a little shouting among the guards, and then they shook their heads and turned their backs, to show all those people that they were not going to shoot.

On the other side of that gate, Noah looked around, excited and disoriented. The family he had tagged along after was hugging one another. All these people around him were hugging, shouting, crying. But of course no one was hugging Noah!

Now, as everyone around him pushed forward, farther into the Austrian side, Noah began to feel worried about his parents. Where had they gotten to? He didn't see them anywhere in this crowd.

He had been in one of the early groups to come through. So now he turned around and fought his way backward, trying to return to the creaky wooden gate, which was absolutely overwhelmed by people coming through. It was like swimming up a river that was flooding in the other direction.

He was feeling a lot worse now. How stupid had he been,

to let himself be swept along *right into a different country*? It wasn't as if he had a passport or anything. His mother had his papers tucked into a pocket of her purse.

Someone said something to him, patted him on the shoulder.

Was he lost?

"J-j-j-j-ja," said Noah. It was breaking the Rules, but it was just a single word. And the Astonishing Stutter made it sound like he was so distraught that he was sobbing, which wasn't really the case. He was worried, true, but it took more than mere worry to get Noah to the sobbing stage.

He hadn't really intended to put on an act, but here he was anyway, accidentally acting. People were taking him—the poor sobbing child—by the elbow, trying to lead him somewhere. Most were trying to lead him back in the Austrian direction, with all the flood of people. "Your family is surely already there," they kept saying. "Come with us; we'll help you find them."

But Noah shook his head and pushed on in the other direction, though people were shouting at him now not to go back.

Then he heard the strangest and yet most familiar sound: his mother's voice, fluently and urgently saying words that Noah couldn't understand.

His mother, *speaking Hungarian.*

She was talking to the guards and pointing as she explained something, back on the Hungarian side of the border.

Noah called out, not committing himself to any particular word, just shouting and waving his hand.

His mother turned.

"János!" she cried, and the guard talking to her gestured for Noah to keep coming. People scooted to the side to let him through, and some were laughing, caught up in the general excitement.

Then he was back through the gate, and his mother had him wrapped in her arms, but still she kept scolding him in her fluent, incomprehensible Hungarian. The guard took them off to one side, where he gave Noah a drink of water and called him János, like his mother had done. Noah worked hard at looking very young and very unable to talk at all.

Meanwhile, the border guard and his mother kept talking.

The tone was different now. They were speaking in quick phrases, with shadows rippling through them.

When Noah finished his glass of water, the border guard shook their hands and sent them away. And they made their way back through the field down to the road, where Noah's father was waiting for them.

"Found him!" said Noah's mother, as a report to Noah's

father. "Great success!" Considering that Noah himself had almost ended up in the wrong country, he was not sure that was the word he would have used to describe the past hour.

"You were speaking in Hungarian!" he said to his mother. It was disconcerting having a parent who had all sorts of talents you knew nothing about.

"Well, the guard didn't speak German, did he?" said his mother, as if that explained everything, and then she nodded toward the car. "Rules are about to kick in. So hush."

Thinking can still be done when you're being quiet, however. What had they been talking about, the guard and his mother? Something more than just how Noah had gotten himself lost. And then there was that other looming question: When had his mother learned Hungarian?

It had to be pretty long ago, before Noah was old enough to notice Hungarian books or Hungarian tapes hanging around. And he had never seen any such thing.

But when, then? His mother was fairly young, as mothers go. She had gone to college, and then started graduate school, and then taken time off to have Noah, and then gone back to finish her thesis, which was now on speech disorders. When was there time in that history to learn a whole language, not to mention one that was hard and rare and spoken in a country on the Soviet side of the Iron Curtain? He added up the years, and he just didn't see how it worked out.

Research! That's what his mother always said was the way to find things out. He would just have to do some research—that's all.

And in his mind he opened a new file: MOM.

And a second one, while he was at it: DAD.

Next to these new files, of course, was the older one, with a question for a title: WHATEVER HAPPENED TO CLOUD-CLAUDIA'S PARENTS?

Secret File #19
IT'S ALL TRUE

The Pan-European Picnic did actually occur, on August 19, 1989, at the border between Hungary and Austria, in the rolling hills near the little Hungarian town of Sopron.

It had been organized to demonstrate growing friendship and cooperation between Hungary and Austria. But that summer many citizens of the German Democratic Republic, hearing that the Iron Curtain was growing thinner on the Hungarian border, came to Hungary with tents and backpacks, and literally camped out, waiting for an opportunity to leave for the West. The campgrounds in western Hungary were filled with East Germans; so was the embassy of West Germany in Budapest. Young families were living in tents on the embassy grounds!

When all these desperate people heard that the border would be opened for a few hours for a ceremonial "picnic" near Sopron, Hungary, many of them decided to crash the party and try their luck getting through the gate.

Hundreds of East Germans made it across the border into Austria, thanks to that picnic.

It was one of the stranger events of that strange year.

· chapter twenty ·

THE TELLTALE TIARA

When they got back to Berlin, there was a blue paper fish dangling in the window below Noah's room. No, not a fish: a whale. And around the whale, other smaller, more complicated sea creatures, since Cloud-Claudia was better at both drawing and scissoring than Noah was, but the center of that mobile was definitely a whale.

It was like having a huge banner saying WELCOME HOME! hung up over the front door. And maybe there was a pale face at the window for a moment, when they hauled their rackety suitcases over the curb. In any case, however calm he kept his expression outside, on the inside he was grinning. Frau März must be all right if Cloud-Claudia was still living behind that decorated window!

Noah's mother went right back to her work. She sat at the table, going over her field notes and writing up preliminary versions of thesis chapters, and occasionally she went to visit the people at the Ministry of Education, to see how things looked for her research in the fall.

She wouldn't tell Noah what that conversation with the border guard had been about, however. Noah tried to wheedle hints out of her, and she just looked at him with shuttered eyes.

Noah thought again about that mysterious *h-a-f-t* that had shown up in the long words in Cloud's grandmother's letter.

"Prison," he found himself muttering out loud on the evening walk.

"What?" said his mother sharply. "What did you say? Where are you getting that?"

"It was a letter I saw, back when Cloud's grandmother fainted," said Noah. He hadn't meant to say anything out loud, but now that he had, he just kept going. "But what would prison have to do with car accidents?"

His mother gave him a look that could have cut tidy little holes in concrete.

"You need to *leave this alone,*" she said. "We're not supposed to be mixed up in any of this stuff. You need to think a little less—all right, I know that's hopeless. Think

214

if you have to, but keep your thoughts strictly to yourself. And if I need you to know something, I'll tell you."

That was irritating and frustrating, but you could not budge Noah's mother when she was intent on keeping a secret from you. At least she was almost acknowledging there *was* a secret! Noah figured that was progress.

He soon had a distraction from these thoughts he was not supposed to be thinking, however: one day his mother came back from the Ministry of Education with a smile so bright it made the August sun seem like a wimp.

"Jonah! Good news! I mean, actually, great news!"

"What? What?" said Noah, who was busy cutting out a new generation of clouds for his window.

"They are letting you go to school! I'm so happy! I kept asking and asking and asking, and they kept giving me long-winded speeches about the difficulties or about how they were waiting for some other important office to sign off on the papers, et cetera, et cetera, but suddenly they've decided you can go! Of course, it's a school way the heck away from where we live—out in the area where they've been building new apartments like crazy. A brand-new school, actually. Built this summer! Maybe that's why they can fit you in. Wait, what kind of expression is that on your face? Sam, come look at our Jonah's face—he's in shock!"

And her hooting laugh filled the apartment.

"Eep," said Noah. Or something along those lines. He was so surprised. He had to put the scissors down because his hands had started shaking. He was going to get to go to *school!* Where there were other kids! Like a halfway-normal person! Yes, it's true: he was in happy shock.

However, it's funny how quickly happiness at getting what you've been asking for—even, if we're totally honest with ourselves, *whining about*—for ages can turn a quick corner and metamorphose into a new set of worries.

For one thing, his brain had already calculated the odds of Cloud-Claudia being in the same school he was going to be in, and those odds were zero. So he still wouldn't be able to hang out with her freely, his one East German friend. In fact, that suspicious, file-opening, spy-versus-spy part of his brain he was beginning to get to know better figured that might even be the reason he was being assigned to a school that was "way the heck away" from the center of Berlin. To keep him far away from his only friend.

For another thing, although it was great to have the chance to go to school like a halfway-normal person, of course Noah did have the profound sense—shared by most of us—that he might not actually be "halfway normal."

And school would be in German, and German has all those consonants for a person to slam into and be blocked by.

"You'll do great," said his dad. "Such an opportunity, going to school in a place as different as this! Think of it this way: you'll be the first American any of them has ever met! They probably think American children are mythical creatures, like unicorns."

"Hmm," said Noah's mother, rereading the letter with her research-sharpened eyes. "There's actually a whole section in here informing us that if 'scholarization in the GDR Polytechnical Upper School' turns out to be a poor fit for you, due to behavior issues or your known speech defect or any other reason, then they will give you the boot. But I guess that was to be expected."

"Don't worry about it," said his father. "That's my advice. And consider everything you learn in this school a plus. What grade is it going to be?"

"Well, with a birthday in the fall, that puts him in the fourth class here."

"No, really?" said Noah, in some shock. At home he had been finishing up fifth grade! So his stupid new birthday *was* going to give him trouble. He had thought it would eventually.

"Don't look so glum," said his mother. "Remember, the whole system's different from the one at home. And the age kids enter the different grades is different, too. For someone turning eleven in November, the fourth class is perfect."

Well, perfect if you hadn't already secretly turned eleven back in March. But he knew better than to say any of that out loud. The "fourth class"! He would just have to be extra careful to make sure this bit of damaging information did not get out once he was finally back home, back in the sixth grade, where he belonged, with all of his friends.

"An adventure!" his mother kept saying. And it was true. An adventure, for sure.

They went shopping for the flat rectangular backpacks kids in East Germany wore to school, and they also bought pens and pencils and a ruler. For the last week of August, Noah let his parents drill him mercilessly on his German whenever they felt like it. He looked at grammar charts. He studied the public transportation out to Hohenschönhausen, where that new school he was supposed to be joining was being finished in a rush so it could be opened for actual students like him.

And all the while, in a corner of his brain that his mother and father had no idea existed, he was beginning to work on those important, strange files, "Mom" and "Dad." For some reason, it had begun to bother him, ever since that photograph had come tumbling out of *Alice in Wonderland*—and even more ever since he had seen his mother burning that one precious photo to ashes—that he knew of no living grandparents or cousins on either side. How likely was that? No grandparents or cousins anywhere at all? So he started asking very gentle questions whenever the opportunity arose (outdoors).

From "Do you remember your first day of school?" to "Did you have any pets when you were younger?" to "Why were you wearing a crown in that picture of you and Grandpa?"

That last question got a very sharp look from his mother in return.

"Was I?" she said.

She didn't realize, of course, that Noah had filed away a picture of that picture in his brain.

He took that mental photograph out of the "Mom" file now and looked it over again with his secret, interior eye.

There was his grandfather in the armchair — the newspaper shouting about some CORONA — and that small version of his dark-eyed mother. A tiara sat confidently on her head.

"Yes," said Noah. "And you had a wand in your hands."

"Scepter," corrected his mother automatically.

"What's the difference?" said Noah.

"Fairies have wands," said his mother. "*Queens* have scepters. It was my birthday, and I thought, quite reasonably, that I should be queen."

She had this sparkling, dangerous smile, still, that made her look oddly like that little girl in the picture.

Noah couldn't help smiling back.

"Weren't you young to be queen? What birthday was it?"

"Fourth," said his mother. "I was turning four. I remember—"

And then she snapped her mouth shut, as if she had almost been caught in some kind of trap.

"Remember what?" said Noah, but he knew it was hopeless. Once his mother had decided to shift gears, those gears were as good as shifted.

"We're out of milk again," she said now. That meant the subject had been officially changed. "We can't go home without milk—"

She thought that photograph was burned and gone. She didn't know that Noah was even now going back over it in his mind, paying attention to all the little clues hidden there.

He thought about it, and thought about it, and then he asked his father about another piece of the puzzle when they were running errands in Berlin.

"Was there a big star explosion or something, long ago in the month of June? In the 1950s? Like—"

Noah counted in his mind. His mother had been twenty-three when he was born. That was the family story. And Noah was born in 1978—of course he wasn't as sure about *when* in 1978 as he used to be, but he was pretty confident the year was still 1978.

"Like 1959 or so?"

His father was used to hearing oddball questions from Noah, but this one managed to make him look completely taken by surprise for a while.

"A what?" he said, laughing. "When? Did you just say 'star explosion'?"

"A *corona*," said Noah. "Isn't that something to do with stars? In the fifties."

"Good grief, where are you getting these things? Maybe a solar eclipse? I don't know when those were. I guess we can look them up in an astronomy book somewhere."

"Something big that would fill headlines — corona-something. Corona —"

"Sounds almost like you're doing a crossword puzzle," said his father.

That was helpful, actually. When they got home, Noah looked the word up in the dictionary: *corona . . . coronal . . . coronation.*

He stared at that page for a while. Hadn't his mother mentioned something about a "coronation day," way back when? Queens and crowns!

"Dad," he asked, "who's the queen now?"

"Queen of what, England? Queen Elizabeth the Second," said his dad from the kitchen. Apparently saying queens' names aloud didn't break any Rules.

"How long has she been queen? A long time already, right?"

"Yep, a long time. Nineteen fifty-two? Nineteen fifty-three?"

Noah's brain was running back and forth, jumping up and down, waving bits of paper to catch his attention.

"Nineteen fifty-three?" said Noah. "That can't be right."

"Or nineteen fifty-two, I said. We can look it up in an encyclopedia somewhere sometime, if it matters. Does it matter?"

"No," said Noah. "I was just wondering."

That was a lie, however. The truthful answer to that question would have been *YES, it really does matter!*

Why?

Because in 1953 (or maybe 1952), when that photograph had captured the very young version of Noah's mother, staring so boldly into the camera, she wasn't even supposed to be alive yet!

He checked his math all over again: 1978 minus twenty-three equals 1955. Maybe 1954, depending on when the months of everyone's birthdays fall.

A picture of Noah's mother, aged four, in June 1953, therefore, standing next to a newspaper headline about Queen Elizabeth's CORONATION, was one of those things that simply could not exist. A paradox. A puzzle.

The file folder labeled "Mom" in Noah's brain was

beginning to get thicker in the middle. Bulging with questions. Something was definitely not right.

Secret File #20
THINGS THAT HAPPENED IN 1953

The most successful movie of the year was Disney's *Peter Pan*. The hero of *Peter Pan* is a boy who, like Noah's mother, has a very ambiguous date of birth.

Joseph Stalin died. He had been the leader of the Soviet Union for decades.

Jonas Salk invented the polio vaccine.

Sir Edmund Hillary and Tenzing Norgay became the first people to climb Mount Everest.

Queen Elizabeth II was crowned in Westminster Abbey.

There was a workers' uprising in East Berlin; it was squashed violently.

And Noah's mother appeared, at the age of four, in a photograph taken two years before she was even born.

???

chapter twenty-one

NEW PLACES ON THE MAP

For days there had been little whales on the stairs for Noah to find and take home and add to the envelope he now thought of as the Folded Ocean.

Every now and then there was a *Tup! Tup! Tup!* calling up to him from his floor at night, and Noah would respond with a *tu-tap* or two, though he was worried, always worried, about Frau März catching him.

Then, one afternoon, right before school started, there was a knock on their door. Of course, there had not been any knocks on their door since the awful evening when Cloud's grandmother had fainted over that weird document with the long, long words, so they looked at one another in surprise as Noah's father moved to open the door. Noah came along to see, of course.

Outside the door was Cloud-Claudia, looking slightly scared but stubborn.

"I've brought your map back to you," she said. "Even Oma would say I should return it to you."

"How nice to see you!" said Noah's father. "Come in, come in!"

"I can't," she said. "Not allowed. But I brought the map."

"I'm going to start school tomorrow," said Noah.

Claudia grinned.

"What school?" she said.

"Out in — where is it, Dad?"

"Hohenschönhausen," said his father.

"Oh," said Claudia. "I don't know where that is. Wish it were my school."

"Ich auch," said Noah. "I do, too."

Then he had an idea after all.

"I finished the puzzle. But I want you to have a chance to finish it, too. Here —"

He darted into the living room, pulled the puzzle box off the shelf, and came running back with it.

"Good luck, Cloud," he said.

"Thanks," said Cloud-Claudia, and then she looked at him with that brave stubbornness she had, and she added, *"Bis bald."*

Which means "See you soon."

That made Noah happy, since what she meant was they shouldn't just sit in their apartments dutifully, on either side of the ceiling-floor. There was something so ridiculous about it. A bunch of adults with their hysterical political Rules. It seemed so obvious, once Cloud-Claudia broke the ice. He looked right back at her and said it with gusto—with extra gusto, even, thanks to the Astonishing Stutter:

"Bis bald!"

There were steps on the stairs.

Border patrol for the horizontal Wall, thought Noah. Frau März, stomping upstairs to see where her granddaughter had gotten to.

"Tschüß, Jonah," whispered Cloud-Claudia. "Bye."

And she was gone, clutching the puzzle to her chest, before the stomping feet had time to come around the bend in the stairs.

Noah and his father ducked back into their apartment and closed the door.

"I just hate that grandmother!" said Noah. "Is she going to take away that puzzle? And throw it out or something?"

"Surely not," said his father. Then he thought a little more. "Probably not?" There was another pause. "That is, to be honest, I sure do hope not."

. . .

It was a while before Noah could look at the map on his own, but when he did, he could hardly tear himself away from it. Every square centimeter of the blank splotch that had been West Berlin was filled in now with buildings, streets, lakes, trees, little people, dogs, camels, horses, boats . . .

They had made a whole little world together, he and Cloud-Claudia. He let his eyes wander through it, testing the various alleyways. There was no doubt that Cloud-Claudia could draw! Noah's contributions looked very basic in comparison—but precise! He was very neat with a pen.

He didn't have a lot of time to study the map just now, though, because there was school starting up the next morning.

Noah's mother was almost more excited about Noah getting to go to school than Noah was himself. She went through Noah's clothes, trying to find the pants and shirt that would blend in best with the East German crowd. She put paper and pens and pencils into his mock-leather school backpack.

"It's going to be so much more interesting than sitting around here at home," she said. "I've felt so guilty, dragging you off to a place where you've had to sit around so much. You're just a kid! You deserve to have friends and a normal life!"

She had a point. But really, who was anyone kidding? Noah was never going to blend in here, and this life in East Berlin was never going to feel "normal," and he knew it.

As they walked to the S-Bahn at what felt like dawn the next day, and was actually very, very early, since school started at 7:30 a.m. and was pretty far away, Noah voiced his deepest worry.

"When I get home, I'll still get to go into my usual grade, right? I'm not going to be left behind forever? I'll still be graduating from high school in 1996?"

He had always liked the number 1996. But mostly because it implied that his *college* class would be 2000, and only one lucky group of kids in a thousand years gets to say "Class of Something Thousand."

"Oh, goodness, *yes*," said his mother. "I mean *no*. I mean, *yes*, you'll be in your proper grade, and *no*, this bit of fourth class in Germany isn't going to do you any permanent harm. I had to move around a million times when I was younger, and that didn't damage me. In the end. I graduated just fine."

"In 1973," said Noah.

"Right you are," said his mother. "Only a few months after I showed up at that school in Charlottesburg, by the way! So you see, it can be done."

"Showed up" *was one way to say it,* thought Noah, as he,

almost automatically by now, tucked more data into his "Mom" file.

"Where were you before? Where were you in 1971 or 1972?"

Was it just his imagination, or was there the tiniest pause before she answered? But she answered with one of her hooting laughs.

"Tiny Podunk town with a tiny Podunk school!" she said. "Glad to get out of there, you'd better believe it. And look what we have here: the opposite of tiny."

They were arriving at the station now, out at the edges of Berlin where that brand-new school was just dusting itself off and opening its doors. It might as well have been on the moon, almost, it was so far away.

The moon, that is, after a few hundred years had gone by, and the astronauts—no, *cosmonauts*—had managed to build huge slab-like buildings all over the place. There were thousands and thousands of apartments in those buildings, but they looked like a giant with a strong affection for rectangles had set up a block village on the edge of town.

"Remember what the name of this district is?" said Noah's father, who was also coming along for this big occasion of dropping off Noah for his first day of school. "Hohenschönhausen! Sounds sort of like Tall-Pretty-House-Ville!"

"Tall, yes," said Noah's mother. "Pretty—not so sure about that."

Noah knew exactly what they were doing. They were keeping the banter going so he would forget to be nervous. It wasn't working perfectly, but Noah was determined to be brave.

They took him into one of the new buildings, not very beautiful but recognizably a school.

"Here we are!" said his mother, and she led them into the main office, where Noah's parents and an official-looking woman had a quick chat.

"COME. I WILL TAKE YOU TO YOUR ROOM NOW, JONAH," said the woman, turning back to Noah.

Well, how about that? Some things seemed to be true all around the world.

"He has no trouble hearing," said Noah's mother politely, in German, as she had said in English to other teachers and principals and secretaries a million times before. "And his thinking is completely normal, too—"

"Normal" might be pushing things too far, Noah thought. But he tried to smile like a normal ten-year-old boy with a fully normal brain.

"It just takes him a little longer to speak sometimes. But he likes to participate."

"I see," said the woman, though she looked skeptical. "So. How is your German, young Jonah? You know we

230

are not a school here for the instruction of German as a foreign language. You will be expected to do what all the other children do."

"I can understand. Speaking is harder," said Noah in German. Wow, the amount of rust on his tongue! And he had even chosen just about the simplest sentence he could think of.

"Oh!" said the woman, since this was her introduction to the Astonishing Stutter. "Well! Well! We'll have to see how you do, then, won't we?"

"Good luck, Yo-Yo," said Noah's father. "We'll see you this afternoon. And his mother gave him a hug and waved good-bye, hope and worry fighting to see which would win control of her face.

Secret File #21
THE BRUNO BEATER SCHOOL
If you think back to the schools you have attended over the course of your life, some of them may well have been named after famous people. Martin Luther King? Washington? Lincoln? The person in your small town who was on the school board for thirty years?

Well, names of famous people were also commonly assigned to East German schools.

The teachers at Noah's brand-new school out in Tall-Pretty-House-Ville had been informed at an all-school teachers' meeting the week before that their school was going to be taking part in a contest to earn the honor of naming the school "the Bruno Beater School."

Bruno Beater had been the German Democratic Republic's first deputy minister of state security. His special tasks had been organizing spies in the West and perfecting the state's electronic surveillance systems. Microphones and tape recorders and bugs! It was a very good name for an elementary school, the teachers were told.

The hearts of all the nicer teachers at that school must have sunk when they heard that announcement at the pre-school-opening assembly.

They had mostly decided to become teachers in order to get permission to go to college, and they wanted to go to college for the same reasons most people want to go to college: to read books, to think about history, to study other languages, to find out more about scientific discoveries, to *learn*.

But being a teacher in the German Democratic Republic meant also having to watch your students, always, always, always, for *ideological deviations*. Which means: not thinking right.

In the olden days, long before Noah arrived in Berlin, teachers were supposed to try to trick their students into revealing whether their parents watched the East German or West

German news on TV at night. Story is, the clocks were different shapes on the Eastern and Western editions of the news. You could catch a little kid out by noticing a slip in the way he drew a clock on the news. That sort of thing!

By 1989 they had given up on keeping people in East Berlin from watching the West German news. In fact, they had moved the East German news to a different time slot so it didn't have to compete with the West.

But teachers still had to pay checkup visits to their students' homes, and were still dreaded by some of their students' families, and were still, although Noah had no way of knowing this, largely miserable about it all.

chapter twenty-two

WORLD PEACE DAY

It turned out that the first day of the school year was officially called World Peace Day. The teacher made a little
speech about world peace, and because Noah was in her
class, she improvised by pointing him out and saying,
"This year we have a guest among us, who comes from
a land where many people suffer from homelessness and
unemployment. We must work for world peace right here
in our classroom by showing him how well behaved and
studious children are in the German Democratic Republic,
and how eagerly we are developing our talents and skills to
be of use to our socialist mother country in the future. Are
you prepared?"

And all of the children, standing, chanted together, *"Immer bereit!"* Which means "Always prepared!"

It was the slogan for the Young Pioneers, Noah learned later, the club they all belonged to, like a universal, required scouting association, only with lots more politics and no religion at all.

When the teacher told the class they all had to bring in their dues for the Young Pioneers, she looked over at Noah and hesitated for a moment—she almost actually tripped on her words.

But Noah said, *"Ich auch,"* which means "Me, too," because he wanted to do whatever they all did. He certainly didn't want to spend his school days sticking out like a sore thumb.

Of course, as soon as he opened his mouth, every kid in that room had turned around to stare at him.

You'd think they'd never heard an American accent or an Astonishing Stutter!

Oh, right. They probably hadn't.

Still, all things considered, everything went okay that first day. The kids were the usual mix of nice, neutral, and in-your-face. Most kept away from him, but a few made a point of saying hello. You could tell they weren't sure whether he was really normal in his head, with his stutter, even though the teacher had made a point of saying, "Our guest, Jonah, has a serious speech defect, but I understand his intelligence is normal."

Which was well-meaning but still made Noah feel a little like a freak. However, he had had speeches like that made about him many times, and he knew he could survive it, if he just got through recess without doing something that looked stupid, like tripping over his shoelaces.

When his parents showed up at the end of the school day to take him home, they were, of course, irritatingly interested in how the day had gone. They even asked dumb parental questions like "Any new friends?"

Really! "Any new friends?" on the very first day, when you're the strange outsider with an American accent and a stutter?

"They're all so *young*," said Noah, with more heat than he really intended. He backtracked just a little. "I mean, they're young, and I'm sure they're nice. But it's not really likely we're going to sit around and talk about math or history for fun, or anything. Not anytime soon."

"History all around us!" said his father, taking a pointed sniff of the air. "Do you know how many East Germans are flooding into Hungary these days? You know how much pressure there is on the edges of everything all around? Look at it this way —"

"No," said Noah's mother, and her voice alone was as good as any border. "Honestly. This is a crowded place. Time to hush."

She backed up that warning with one of her no-nonsense smiles.

So they talked about homework instead.

Later on, though, when Noah went into his room after his snack, an amazing thing happened. Even though it was daylight, the floor of his room spoke to him, soft but clear:

Tup! tu-TUP!

And a few minutes after that, he heard the door downstairs close, and when he looked out his window, there was the wild blond head of Cloud-Claudia, heading across the street to the not-park.

Noah instantly understood: that *Tup! tu-TUP!* wasn't just a hello—it was an invitation.

He grabbed his jacket and waved at his parents and went down the steps, too, to find Cloud-Claudia at that ragged fence, waiting for him.

She clapped her hands, *Tup! tu-TUP!* and grinned. "Come outside!"

"Yes!" said Noah. Finally they could work out a proper code. They could make a start, anyway. They learned some message rhythms together and then sat there, feeling like they had accomplished something.

"Hey, Cloud-Claudia!" said Noah. "How was school for you?"

"Boring, very dull, bad," said Cloud-Claudia. "And you?"

"All right, I guess," said Noah. Then he thought of

something. "Listen, can you help me with this thing I have to do?"

"What's that?" she said.

"For the wall newspaper." The German word was *Wandzeitung.*

This was a big display on one of the classroom walls, and it changed periodically. The children were supposed to contribute articles and pictures. The teacher had explained the current topic, and it happened to be—

"Dolphins and whales," said Noah. "I know you are very good at whales. Will you help me cut some out?"

Cloud-Claudia smiled, smiled, smiled. Her smile was the smile of someone finding out that her secret messages have indeed been received.

"Ja," she said. "I'll go get my scissors. In the courtyard on the other side of the building, there are actual steps to sit on."

They made a rhythm that would mean the steps in the courtyard: *tap, taptap, taptaptap.* And, while they were at it, a signal for emergencies—*tap tu-Tap TAP!*—though how a signal would help in an emergency, Noah really had no idea.

Then Cloud-Claudia went home to get scissors, and when she came back, they sat on the steps and cut out whales companionably and talked about crises in the other world. Because there were bad things happening in the

Land of the Changelings. So said Cloud-Claudia, who had been thinking about this a lot, apparently.

"They're forgetting themselves, always more," she said. "They might think to themselves, 'Oh, we had this funny dream once, with a girl named Something-or-Other in it! But what was she like, exactly, that girl? And what did she used to call us?'"

Cloud-Claudia looked at Noah very seriously.

Noah was thinking about the wood in his *Alice* book, the one where things have no names, where Alice doesn't know she's Alice anymore, and the fawn she's walking with (until they reach the end of the wood) doesn't even know it's a fawn. There's a picture in the book of Alice and the fawn, leaning close together: *friends*—until a moment later, when they reach the end of the wood and remember who and what they are, and the fawn takes fright and runs away. Noah could see that forgetting one's name could be a problem—but also that someone finding out you are not who you said you were could be a problem, too.

"They've forgotten even who *they* used to be," she said. "In your name is a little seed of everything that you are."

She cupped her hands to show him, like someone carrying a teeny-tiny baby tree.

"Oh," said Noah, who wasn't even Noah anymore. "So if your name is changed, you are a different person?"

"But yes, of course, Wallfish," said Cloud-Claudia.

He was thinking about that. Did it matter that he wasn't Noah anymore? What was the difference between being Noah and being Jonah?

When he was two years old, his parents had given him the most beautiful wooden ark, with pairs of wooden animals—elephants, giraffes, seals, dogs, lions—to march up the plank and into the boat, two by two.

"This is *Noah*'s Ark," they had told him a thousand times, and they smiled when they said so. It had made him happy to be the sort of Noah who has a wooden boat filled with pairs of wooden animals, all to be sailed around in puddles—when Mom wasn't looking—and to be kept safe from the flood.

He liked to think of himself as the kind of person who kept things from drowning and went off in a boat to look for new land to live on.

But now he was Jonah, and Jonah didn't travel on top of the water, but underneath it, in the belly of a whale. That was darker and stranger and spookier than the Noah story, but all the same it was pretty cool, too. It must have taken a lot of courage to remain yourself when you had been swallowed by a whale.

And he did like the way Cloud-Claudia called him Wallfish. That also felt right, somehow. He would never have known he could be a Wallfish if he hadn't left his old name behind and become a Jonah.

"They should have taken me with them to the Changelings' Land," said Cloud-Claudia. "Why didn't they?" Her voice was so quiet now, but Noah could hear every word she said, and he knew, just knew, knew in his bones, who she must be talking about.

"Your parents didn't mean to leave you here," he said. He had to push right through the awkwardness of saying something like that—not easy, not in any language. "It was an accident. They couldn't help it."

"They're forgetting me there, I guess," said Cloud-Claudia. "They don't have me there to remind them."

"But the Changelings' Land—that's something we made up. You know that, right?"

Cloud-Claudia stared right at Noah, long and hard.

"I can prove to you it exists," she said. "There's a place where the people from the Changelings' Land come and look right in at us here. I found it once. Brunnenstraße. Want me to show you sometime?"

She stared at him again, waiting for an answer.

"*Ja,*" said Noah finally. What else, under the circumstances, could he say?

Secret File #22
THE MISUSE OF TRIPS TO THE
HUNGARIAN PEOPLE'S REPUBLIC

Noah's father was right: more people than ever were flow-
ing through the Hungarian border. Shortly after midnight on
September 11, 1989, buses loaded with East Germans who had
been camping out for ages on the grounds of the West German
embassy in Budapest passed right through the border into
Austria. They didn't have to crash through the border—it was
opened for them.

The East German government understood that things were
getting desperate.

On September 13, the minister of state security issued a
secret internal directive entitled "Actions Taken to Ensure the
Timely Recognition and Prevention of the Misuse of Trips to
and/or Through the Hungarian People's Republic." Here's some
of what that secret directive said:

> Section 1.2. At that frontier crossing point on the border of
> the CSSR [Czechoslovakia] most commonly used for travel
> to the Hungarian People's Republic as well as in all inter-
> national airports of the GDR, the expedient use of screen-
> ing procedures is to be strengthened in collaboration with
> the border and customs personnel . . . in order to identify

suspicious activity suggesting potential for illegal abandonment of the GDR.

"Illegal abandonment" meant "leaving the country without permission."

"Suspicious activity" meant all sorts of things, but it could have meant having too big a suitcase or taking a photo album with you. Anything that made it look like maybe you were thinking you might not come back.

chapter twenty-three

THE BOY FROM OVER THERE

The whales brought in by Noah for the class wall newspaper were reasonably well received and got put up along
with some carefully lettered sentences about how (1) whales
were the largest inhabitants of the oceans, and (2) whales
and dolphins were both mammals, and (3) greed had made
some people, especially under capitalist governments (that
is, people who did not live in the German Democratic
Republic), hunt whales practically to extinction. That
was fairly funny, thought Noah, because of course if you
looked at a map, you would soon see that it was a long way
from Berlin to any possible whale you might want to hunt.
Judging from the coal in the air in Berlin, East Germany

wasn't always the most environmentally conscious country in the world.

Nobody wrote anything for the *Wandzeitung* about old long-ago Jonah and his ride inside the belly of a whale. They didn't seem to know that story. That was okay with Noah, though. As he sat at his classroom desk solving math problems that, to tell the honest truth, were way too easy for someone who should rightly have been starting sixth grade this year, it cheered him up to look over at the wall newspaper from time to time and see the *Walfische/* wallfish there that Cloud-Claudia had made—so much more alive, so much more intricate in their decoration, in their cleverly curling water spouts, in their wise wallfish eyes, than the ones cut out by the other kids in that class.

A wallfish on the classroom wall! It was like a secret message again, cheering him up when life at school threatened to become too dull or difficult.

There were definitely some difficult things, that was for sure, although math wasn't one of them.

For the first couple of weeks, for instance, Noah couldn't figure out whether his teacher, Frau Müller, was a friendly sort of person or not. That puzzled him, because he was used to being able to tell after about five minutes, max, whether or not the teacher in front of his class that year was going to be a good one. And usually he'd been pretty lucky.

But it was surprisingly hard for him to read Frau Müller's intentions.

She had a brisk but pleasant way of telling the class what to do and when to put their notebooks away. Noah appreciated that. And she seemed, as far as Noah could tell, fair in her grading. So that was fine, too. But every time the class was reading a story aloud, she would give him a strange, he might even have said *anxious*, look—and skip him. If he raised his hand in class, she would give him another one of those strange, even *anxious*, looks and then only pick him if it happened to be a math problem—and even then, not often.

After a few days of this, Noah began to get the point. His participation in class was not desired. He was used to teachers back home hemming and hawing sometimes, if they were a bit stumped by the Astonishing Stutter. But usually Noah could just keep talking and talking and raising his hand until it began to seem normal and the teacher relaxed a little. That had been Noah's usual approach. He figured if he just forged ahead, everyone else would eventually come to see how normal—or normally abnormal—the whole thing was. But none of that worked with Frau Müller. It was a stumper.

Then one day Frau Müller said something to the class about the problem of youth unemployment in the United States, and one particularly bold boy, named Axel, had said, "Why don't we just ask Jonah? He comes from *over there*, doesn't he?"

Noah already knew Axel's name because he was always getting himself into trouble and being asked to explain to the class why his behavior had been "unworthy of a student in the Bruno-Beater-Schule."

The word Axel used for "over there" was *drüben*, a word with the flavor of apples, tart and sweet. It's hard for an English speaker to get that *ü* sounding sufficiently puckered up; Noah practiced it in his mind during the hush that followed on the heels of Axel's boldness, his own silent inner voice toggling for a moment between "drooben" and "drewwwben." It was an important word in East Germany, *drüben*, because "over there" actually meant "over there on the other side of the Wall." That made it a dangerous word in classrooms like Noah's.

The effect it had now was magical.

The whole class turned its collective head from Axel to the teacher to Noah, all at the same time, almost as if someone had decided to make a ballet for swiveling heads. They turned their heads and then froze, holding their breath. Waiting to see what would happen to someone who spoke so boldly, using words you did not use at school, like *drüben*. Or to someone, like Noah, who had just been so boldly singled out as coming from Over There.

Frau Müller went pale, then flushed pink, then went pale all over again.

"Axel, stand up. Our guest Jonah is here to see how a socialist classroom collective functions. We do not pester our guests with questions, Axel. I will be writing to your parents. Again! You are delaying our lesson and interfering with the normal progress of education."

That was when Noah began to understand something about his teacher: it was not just about the stutter. When he stopped by her desk at the end of the day to say, "Frau Müller, I don't mind if the other kids ask me questions," her face took on the expression of someone trying not to show that she knows she has been caught in a trap.

"I'm certain, Jonah, you had a very different school experience before coming to visit us here in Berlin," she said stiffly. "This is not really a classroom suited for someone like you. This is not the educational system you come from, and you will have to understand that we cannot allow the education of the other children to be derailed in any way. After all, they are the ones who will grow up to defend the socialist cause with word and deed, so we must not let anything happen in our classroom that might blunt their historical optimism."

"Oh," said Noah, understanding the words but not so much understanding the long, twisty sentences those words combined to make.

The teacher's face softened for the briefest of moments; she was not unkind. Noah could see that she didn't at all mean to be unkind. She was just caught in a trap.

"These are the arrangements that have been decided upon," she said. "So of course we must all take on this task with dedication and consciousness. If you, Jonah, sit quietly and do not respond when the children ask inappropriate questions, then it will be best for everyone. Understand? It is best if you do not speak. You may sit quietly and work on your own."

There! He saw it now. The reason she looked at him all the time the way she might have looked at a boy-shaped ticking alarm clock, ready to go off at any moment and disrupt the universe, had, for once, absolutely nothing to do with the Astonishing Stutter.

It had to do with where he, Noah, came from.

He was from *drüben*. No, worse than that, from Virginia. No, even worse, if only she knew: from the faraway Land of the Changelings. Who knew what terrible things a changeling like him might say?

That thought might make even a very slightly rebellious person want to talk loudly, just to make the point that he, too, was a person, even if he was also a *Wechselbalg*!

But Noah could see that if he opened his mouth in class, it was the other kids who were likely to get into trouble. And not only the kids.

He could see that in the anxious lines around Frau Müller's eyes, the shadows on her face that had already deepened considerably only a few weeks into the year.

Oh, of course. The real question wasn't whether she was "kind" or "unkind." The truth of the matter was that Frau Müller was *afraid*.

Secret File #23
HISTORICAL OPTIMISM! CHEW ON THAT!

Frau Müller was afraid because part of the job of a teacher in East Germany was making sure nothing unexpected ever happened in any classroom, and an American child was bound to be a constant source of the Unexpected. It's not that she disliked this *Jonah Brown* who had landed in her classroom like a meteorite from the outer reaches of space. But look what that foolish Axel had said so thoughtlessly about *drüben*! Life *drüben* was not a topic for the fourth class. If someone said the wrong thing, whether about here or about *drüben* — or said that Frau Müller had said the wrong thing — or made the kind of face that suggested he or she was even *thinking* the wrong thing — about anything — Frau Müller could lose her job.

Noah's teacher had gotten the stuff she said about *historical optimism* out of recent speeches by Margot Honecker, who was the minister of education as well as the wife of Erich Honecker. She set the tone for schoolteachers, and that tone was long-winded and icy. Here's the sort of thing she said when talking to groups of teachers in 1989:

> Our young socialist order had its childhood diseases, and it has had its growing pains. It had and has good friends, and it has always had and still has today strong and dangerous enemies. We are forever forced anew to defend ourselves politically and economically in the international class struggle in direct confrontation with the strongest and most experienced imperialist forces.
>
> Our epoch is a bellicose one and requires youth who can fight, who will help to strengthen socialism, who will take up the socialist cause, who will defend socialism with word and deed and, when necessary, with weapons in their hands.

She had also complained about "so-called 'modern conceptions of literature'" — no "reading for pleasure" for her!— and scolded those teachers who let classroom discussions get out of hand.

If Noah had known these things about Margot Honecker's speeches, which were studied in special meetings by all the unfortunate teachers at the Bruno-Beater-Schule, then he probably would not have bothered to go up to Frau Müller's desk at the end of the day and say he would be glad to participate in class discussions.

As you can imagine, East German schools were not big fans of class discussion. Much less a class discussion led by a child from the capitalist West!

· chapter twenty-four ·

IT COULD ALL EXPLODE

"It could all explode," said his mother with a smile.

She was smiling because they were on a family stroll in the evening, which was when Noah's parents exchanged the news. Even outside, it made sense to be reasonably cautious. Even outside, it was not impossible that someone could be listening. There were special antennas that could pick up things people said from fifty feet away. But that was pretty fancy technology, and probably they wouldn't bother in the case of Noah's family. "Our job is to be boring" was how his mother put it—but she had said that when they were walking around Budapest.

"Explode?" asked Noah. He didn't like the way that word sounded in his brain or felt in his mouth.

"She means it's all getting tenser in this country," said Noah's father. "People aren't as patient as they used to be. Change is happening everywhere else, so they want change here, too. You know what? Every week in Leipzig— you've been to Leipzig, remember?—every week there are protests there, starting in a church. Last week I heard there were hundreds, maybe thousands, of people marching."

"Really?" said Noah. It was so hard to imagine anything like that happening here in Berlin. A big demonstration. People marching and chanting. With all the police everywhere? Seemed impossible.

"It's the pressure from the border opening in Hungary," said his father.

"It's the pressure from everywhere and everything," said his mother with a very sweet smile.

"And guess what they were chanting this week?" said his father, pointing up at a cloud shaped like a frog.

"What?"

"It always used to be 'Let us out! Let us out!' But this week they changed the words—"

"*We're staying here,*" whispered his mother. "Scarier, isn't it?"

"I get it," said Noah after a moment. "If they go, they're gone, but if they stay, then they want things to *change.*"

"Whose child is this, anyway?" said Noah's father with a very long, rumbling chuckle. "He's turned out very clever.

Is it our brilliant parental training or something in the water?"

"Something in the water," said his mother. "I'm afraid we're only so-so as trainers."

"You know where things need to change?" said Noah. "School. I'm in a lot of trouble just being there. And I'm not even chanting and marching. I'm just *there*. . . ."

The faces of Noah's parents fell, both at once. For about a second, they looked a little stricken—and then they seemed to remember their own Rule #4, about looking cheerful. Noah's father put his arm around Noah's shoulders.

"Well, I'm sorry to hear that. Doesn't sound like fun."

"Better than sitting at home," said Noah, to make them feel a little less guilty.

That was true some of the time, but not during PE class, when they did gymnastics routines—like running and jumping off a thick beam thing and then doing a neat somersault on the mat on the other side. Sometimes it seemed to Noah that all the other kids must have been practicing gymnastics routines since they were tiny things.

And then there was the Young Pioneers kerfuffle.

The Young Pioneers—that East German scouting group everyone seemed to belong to—met after school. There was confusion about what they should do with Noah. One week the other kids lent him a red scarf to wear, and they all ran around together. The next week, a teacher said she didn't think that was right, since the guest came from a different place, and they made him sit in an uncomfortable chair in the school principal's office all afternoon. The next week, the grown-ups had changed their minds again, and the "Guest Jonah, from the U.S.A." was allowed to come to the activities but warned not to talk.

What the Young Pioneers at the Bruno Beater School mostly did was prepare for the huge celebration coming up: the party for the fortieth anniversary of the founding of the German Democratic Republic. To judge from the news programs on television, everyone in the whole country was supposed to be preparing for the fortieth anniversary. In school, Noah and his classmates spent hours studying how wonderful the celebration was going to be.

It was like the exact extreme *opposite*, Noah decided, of a surprise party. With a surprise party, you don't expect there to be a celebration, and then something happens and it turns out everyone's been preparing a party for ages that you didn't even know about—unless, as often happens, you sort of guessed, a little bit around the edges.

But there were not supposed to be *any* surprises of any kind at the GDR fortieth-anniversary party.

None at all.

None.

Noah sat quietly all day, whether wearing the borrowed

scarf or not, doing what everyone else was doing, but also trying to remember not to raise his hand when the teacher asked a question.

The other kids noticed how quiet he had become, but they didn't know why.

A girl with brown hair in two pigtails came over to him one day and said, "If you don't know how to talk, why aren't you in the *Sonderschule*?"

Special school.

Her name was Anja, which sounds like "Anya."

"What's that?" said Noah, though his stomach was already sinking.

"I thought they put all the ones who can't talk or do normal stuff in the *Sonderschule*."

He couldn't help it. He broke the teacher's rules a little.

"I can so talk," he said. "I'm talking right now. And I do all the work."

He even showed her his math page, filled with neat rows of solved problems.

"You talk funny, though," said Anja, giving him a suspicious stare.

"*Ja*, sure, I do," said Noah, and then he couldn't help it; he had to ham it up for her, just a little. "But where I come from, everyb-b-b-b-ody talks like this."

"Oh!" said Anja.

Later that day, Frau Müller came by his desk and

said, "I'm surprised and disappointed that I have to remind you, Jonah, about our agreement. You are not going to disrupt the educational program of the Bruno-Beater-Schule in any way."

"*Ja*, Frau Müller," he said. "Of course."

Secret File #24
GOING AROUND THE WALL, GOING ON TRAINS, GOING, GOING, GONE . . .

Despite that new chant—"We're staying here!"—in actual fact, more and more people were still racing to get out of the country. It was an untenable situation, which means it couldn't last. The pressure on the government was enormous. Young people wanted out! Workers were leaving!

In September 1989, about 45,000 East Germans left for the West. A quarter of those had been given official permission. The other 33,000 or so just left—not through the Wall but by going *around* it, through the West German embassies in Poland or Czechoslovakia, or by walking or driving across the Hungarian-Austrian border.

At the end of September, the 3,500 refugees holed up in the West German embassy in Prague, the capital of Czechoslovakia, were given permission, as a "humanitarian gesture," to leave for the West. They got onto special trains that traveled right through the GDR — with their doors sealed so nobody else could get on — to West Germany.

People waved at the trains. A few months before, people might not have waved, but it was almost October now, almost the fortieth anniversary, and everywhere it was beginning to feel like something might just explode, for real.

· chapter twenty-five ·

FIELD TRIP

Tup! tu-TUP!

The floor of Noah's room called him outside, where Cloud-Claudia was waiting again by their fence, with the puzzle box in her hands.

"I did it twice," she said, shaking the puzzle in its box a little. "It's a good one. Did you bring our map, Wallfish? The street called Brunnenstraße—where is it?"

They found that street on the map. It was close to the edge of the printed city—at one end of the street, Claudia had inked in one of those gates she liked to draw.

"If we go look there," she said, "we might be able to see them, the changelings. I'm going to go Wednesday after school, because that's when the *Oma* is going to the doctor. Meet you on the steps, then, Wednesday, soon as I can sneak out."

When Noah told his mother that Cloud-Claudia seemed to think there was a place in Berlin, somewhere on Brunnenstraße, where her parents could look in from . . . (here he got a little stuck, not wanting to say anything about the Changelings' Land, which felt too private for sharing) . . . from another world? like from heaven, sort of? his mother looked very taken aback at first, and then thoughtful.

"I think I know what gave her that idea," said his mother. "Remember we told you about those platforms along the Wall on the other side? People can climb up and peek in at this side of the city. All the peeking over goes one way, of course! That's how it is. Your friend saw people looking once, maybe, and turned that into a story about her parents, poor girl."

"Oh," said Noah.

He was reminded all over again of how terrible it must be for Cloud-Claudia, having lost her parents. Cloud had only her grandmother now to take care of her, and her grandmother wasn't a kind, sweet old granny. But if Noah—if Noah's parents—he couldn't even think the thought through.

He would have absolutely no one left in the world.

"She said she's going there, Wednesday afternoon, when her grandmother's out at an appointment."

His mother thought about that.

"Wandering around the city alone?" she said.

"Not alone if I go, too," said Noah.

"The Rules!" said his mother. "Not sticking out!"

"Walking isn't sticking out," said Noah.

His mother seemed to have another idea. She snapped her mouth shut and looked at him, calculating something.

"Wednesday," she said. "Wednesday, then. Hmm. Well, okay: *yes*."

And that was the strangest, most unexpected *yes* Noah had ever gotten from his mother. It was the kind of yes that is the tip of a great big enormous secret iceberg, but what could Noah do about that? He filed that yes away in the "Mom" file in his brain. She was up to something, but what was she up to?

On Tuesday, his mother went over to West Berlin to visit the library there, as she sometimes did, and that meant they had a nice big salad for dinner, with fresh tomatoes and everything, brought back through the Wall by Noah's mother.

Then it was finally Wednesday afternoon, and Noah went down to the courtyard steps after he got home from school, wondering whether Cloud-Claudia would show up after all.

When he got downstairs, he found Cloud-Claudia already there.

"Hello!" she said. "Let's go!"

She had a ragged grin on her face and was pulling on her jacket.

They started walking, just walking down the street, at first saying nothing.

"How's school going now?" said Noah after a while.

"Bad," said Cloud-Claudia. "Bad, bad, of course, very bad. And you?"

"Sometimes bad, sometimes all right," said Noah. "I am supposed to sit very quietly and not say anything."

"Me, too," said Cloud-Claudia, and she grinned.

"They think changelings shouldn't talk," said Noah.

"Never, ever," agreed Cloud-Claudia. "Because they talk very funny, like you, or they always say bad and wrong things, like me."

"No, you don't!"

"I do. But it's not fair they don't want you to talk. You should write an *Eingabe* about it, that's what you should do."

The word sounded like "Ine-gah-buh."

"What's an *Eingabe*?"

"An *Eingabe*! It's like a question or a complaint. An official complaint. They have to listen, if it's official. It's one of the best things about the whole country, that they have to do something to make things better if there's an official complaint. That's what my papa used to say. When we bought that tent that turned out to be no good — it leaked and leaked, and so he wrote an *Eingabe*, and — oh, never mind. Give me a pen."

She sat down on a stoop, pulled out a piece of paper from her pocket, and right then and there wrote a letter to the principal of Noah's school. She wrote:

> Dear Mrs. Principal,
> I am writing this *Eingabe* to ask to be able to speak
> sometimes in class because I am just a kid like the
> other kids and although I talk funny, they will be able
> to understand me perfectly all right and it is hard to
> learn when you have to be silent all the time.
> Many thanks,
> Jonah

Cloud-Claudia had this funny, small, cramped handwriting. It was like something an elf would write. When she finished writing, she folded the paper into squares very carefully.

"Okay," said Noah. "Now what do I do with this?"

"You give it to the principal of your school, of course," she said. "Just walk into the office and give it to her."

"Hmm," said Noah. He wasn't sure how likely he was to go storming into the principal's office, but he appreciated Cloud-Claudia's letter all the same.

"After all, I can understand you fine, and I don't have magic ears," said Cloud-Claudia, showing him her two, very ordinary, ears. "At your school they just don't want to bother trying."

They walked a few more blocks.

Then Cloud-Claudia said, "Did you bring the map?"

"No," said Noah. "I just . . . remember how the map looks."

He didn't want to have to explain how that worked, that this morning he had filed a picture of the map away in his brain. Fortunately Cloud-Claudia didn't ask what he meant.

"*Ach!* Too bad," she said. "That's foolish. If you come to the edge of the Changelings' Land without a map, it's like you're rattling a locked door with no key. We won't be able to get in."

The thing was, Noah wasn't even so sure anymore about whether she was kidding, whether this was about a pretend door into a pretend place or whether, somehow, she had slipped into the crack between the real and the not-real and gotten stuck there.

"Why do you need a map to get in?" he asked her.

"The map reminds the place it's really there," said Cloud-Claudia. "Otherwise it forgets."

"Okay," said Noah. She had such a strange way of looking at the world!

They walked quite far up the streets that Noah had memorized, all the way to the very end of Brunnenstraße. And then they were there, at the place where the Wall interrupted the street: where there was a blank end to their side of the city.

"This is it," said Cloud-Claudia in a whisper. She seemed almost shy for a moment.

There weren't a lot of people in this odd, blocked-off street. Far away, beyond the Wall, though, yes, there did seem to be people. They were up high, so they must really have been standing on one of those platforms his mother had talked about. Whoever they were, whatever their reasons were, they were looking now over the Wall at Cloud-Claudia and Noah, who were maybe *inside* and maybe *outside,* depending on your point of view. They were rather far away, but he had the impression there were a few men up there, some old and some young, and a woman with pale hair and one shoulder a little higher than the other. You couldn't see details or anything, even if you were Noah, who had extremely sharp eyes.

Noah's strongest wish right then was to turn around

and get away from those staring people, quickly. He didn't like being looked at, like an animal in a zoo. It felt wrong to him, everything about this place.

Cloud-Claudia was looking around; she seemed puzzled, even a little dazed.

"It doesn't look exactly the way we drew it," she said. "Where's the gate?"

And then she, too, saw those tiny shadowy figures peering *in*, or maybe *out*.

"Are those people?" she said, squinting.

"Yes," said Noah. "I think so, yes. Come on, let's go."

She caught him by surprise, however: she took a deep breath, straightened up, and all of a sudden right out of the blue she *waved*.

Right at the Wall.

Noah jumped. In fact, a pulse of anxiety went right through him, like a bolt of lightning. For that one moment, he hadn't been paying close enough attention, and Cloud-Claudia went and broke Rule #3: *Don't call attention to yourself! Don't stick out!*

He felt very keenly that he should have seen that wave coming. He should have stopped it somehow before it happened.

"Oh, don't," he said, and he noticed his voice was sounding frantic. "Come on, Cloud — let's go back home."

"All right, Wallfish," she said. She was calm now; she let

him hurry her out of that street. "But you know what? It's good to remind them we still exist."

"But Cloud," said Noah, and then he was stuck for a moment. He was so rattled by the whole thing that thoughts he had kept carefully hidden inside were now threatening to spill right out.

"You do know—you do know—they can't really be there?" he found himself saying. "Your parents—they can't be there."

The Astonishing Stutter had done its best to hold back those reckless words, but somehow they got through the gates all the same.

Cloud-Claudia's back stiffened some beside him.

"Why not?"

"Because in real life it's a city for—for—*living* people," said Noah. He felt like a skunk, pointing that out. But he was so worried, he couldn't help it.

"It's the Changelings' Land," said Cloud-Claudia.

"On our map, it's for changelings, but in *real life*," said Noah, trying to be gentler now, in the way he said it, "people live over there. Ordinary living people."

Cloud-Claudia spun around to glare at him.

"You think I'm crazy," she said.

"No!" said Noah. That is, he certainly hoped she wasn't.

She looked at him, and her eyes got wider and wider and stranger and stranger.

"But *how can they be dead?*" she said. "How *can* they be? How can that have happened?"

It was like a wild kind of crying, too wild even for tears, right there in the streets of Berlin.

"Shh, shh," said Noah helplessly. "Oh!"

He had messed this up, messed everything up—that was for sure. He put his hand on Cloud's shoulder and found that under his hand, her arm was bony and fiery, both at once, and all that pain that was burning in her— the loss of the mother who loved her, the father who loved her—jumped like a prairie fire right from her to him and ran through everything, burning through all the cautious little walls he had put up everywhere inside him and making him cry, too.

"I'm sorry, I'm sorry, I'm sorry," said Noah. For a while, that was all he could say.

When he had to wipe his tears away on his other sleeve, to see where they needed to be going, he saw she was still dry-eyed and staring, those sobs heaving up from somewhere deep inside her.

"They won't even tell me what day they died," said Cloud-Claudia in a tiny, awful voice. "They won't even tell me the date. What *day*. What day they died."

"But your grandmother—she must know—"

"She won't tell me. I need to know what day they died. They left me all alone, and I don't even know how long I've been all alone. *I need to know what day they died.*"

"You could ask—" said Noah, but he didn't know whom she could ask. "I mean, that's something they keep written down somewhere. Someone knows that."

Cloud-Claudia took a breath and was already more like herself.

"I could write an *Eingabe*," she said. "I could write an *Eingabe* of my own about it, and make them tell."

Secret File #25
PEEKING OVER

In the East German newspapers, they liked to run little interviews with ordinary, happy workers. Propaganda was a big part of every newspaper's job, which meant making East Germany look as good as possible, no matter what. That was getting harder and harder. Other countries in the East Bloc (like the Soviet Union) were loosening some of the controls on their citizens and allowing more travel, but for the East Germans, whose whole country was just about the same size as the U.S. state of Virginia, the world seemed to be shrinking rather than getting bigger.

In June 1989, the newspaper profiled a young woman who had become a model worker.

Here's what the writers said she said about the Wall:

> I'm almost as old as the Wall. Exactly one year younger. That kind of thing sort of makes you think. When I drive along the border, sure I'd like to take a peek at the other side. But live over there? No.
>
> What happens if you've got children and maybe no work, after all? All right, that doesn't have to happen. But it's bad enough that it *could* happen. . . .
>
> The Wall should stay where it is.
>
> I'm certain of everything here. If a brick doesn't fall on my head and I don't do anything myself that's wrong, in principle nothing can happen to me my whole life long.

You can imagine how some people in East Berlin groaned when they read that. Some of them — more and more of them — more and more and *more* of them — really didn't want to live in a place where "in principle nothing could happen" their whole lives long.

Their country was shrinking.

And they were trapped in it.

· chapter twenty-six ·

"BE PREPARED!
ALWAYS PREPARED!"

Noah was still a little shaky when he got home, and from the way his parents shot sidelong glances his way, he could tell that the shakiness was showing. That was all right. He needed them to notice so that they would take him out on a stroll around the block so that he could ask them what to do about Cloud-Claudia's *Eingabe.*

It was his mother who took him on the debriefing walk, as it turned out, while his father did the dishes.

"All right, what's wrong?" she said. "You look like you just witnessed the sinking of the *Titanic,* not that the *Titanic* would fit in Berlin's tiny little river."

Noah felt too worried to laugh.

He explained about the whole idea of the *Eingabe*, how Cloud-Claudia's father had used one to complain about a bad tent and how Cloud-Claudia had written one for his school principal.

"Oh, dear," said his mother. "Very nice of her, of course, but you'll have to tear that right up. The Rules!"

Complaining about not being allowed to speak in class apparently violated the "Be polite! Don't let your worries show!" Rule (#4), not to mention the "Don't stick out!" Rule (#3).

At this point his mother was still smiling, though. She seemed amused, not horrified.

Then Noah tried to explain to her what had happened to him and Cloud-Claudia, there by the Wall, how they had both basically fallen apart for a moment.

"She doesn't know what day her parents died! Her grandmother won't say. Nobody will tell her. Even though they're her parents!" His throat clenched up tight. "That's why she's got this plan, to write this other *Eingabe*, about asking someone official to tell her the date—"

"Good Lord!" said his mother, and now she was clearly shocked, and Noah's mother was never shocked by anything. "You talked her out of that, I hope!"

"No, why?" said Noah. "They must have the date written down in their papers somewhere. Why shouldn't she know when her parents—her parents—"

He got stuck again, but his mother didn't wait for him this time.

"You have to tell her not even to *think* about asking questions like that," she said. "I'm serious. Her whole family could get into terrible trouble."

"But she doesn't have a family anymore, not really," said Noah. He was beginning to feel mad about all of it. "And who cares if that awful Frau März gets into trouble?"

He paused for breath and only felt madder.

"Anyway, why can't she ask what day her parents died? It's only fair for her to know that. I think she should know everything she wants to know. You can't say her family would get into trouble, not when her parents aren't even alive anymore. Nobody can hurt them."

"No, no," said his mother. "Stop. You can't think that way. Trust me. You don't understand."

"Why don't you ever explain anything?" said Noah. "*That's* what I don't understand. And what I *think* is, they should tell Cloud when her poor parents died."

He wasn't smiling. That meant he was breaking the Rules. But maybe sometimes a friend is worth breaking rules for.

"Well," said his mother after a pause, "they can't."

"Why?"

She was gripping his arm, and he could feel her hand

trembling as it held on to him, held a little too hard. She was trying to decide something.

"Because it's not true," she said finally.

"What's not true?"

Here she gave him a quick hug, just so she could say into his ear in one of her quietest voices, "They aren't dead."

"What?" said Noah. "What? What?"

He couldn't find his way past that one shocked word.

"Quiet, now," said his mother, still smiling carefully. "I'm only telling you this so you'll understand how important it is for your friend to *back down*."

"But—the accident," said Noah, and then he got stuck again: *"What?"*

"Do try to smile," said his mother. "There was no accident. Well, there was, but not a car accident. They were trying to get over the border, from Hungary into Austria."

"What?" said Noah. How could any of this be? "Are you sure?"

"Happened back in June," said his mother. "The border wasn't completely dismantled yet. They were climbing a fence, and something went wrong, and her father got caught. Broke his leg and got stuck on the fence. And the Hungarian border guards came—"

"No, really?" said Noah. He was remembering the border guard at the Pan-European Picnic, the long, mysterious conversation that man had had with his mother in Hungarian. What had they been talking about back then?

"Don't look so distressed," said his mother. "It's too noticeable. Anyway, the border guards came, but they were already under instructions not to do things like shoot people anymore, so they waved Claudia's mother away, farther into Austria. And they took Claudia's father back into Hungary, saying he needed medical help for his leg. And then he could go through regular channels to request a visa—that's what they said. Can you imagine how awful that must have been? So the mother ended up going on into Austria without her husband—"

"And without Cloud," said Noah. Why didn't she see the worst part of this whole story? Cloud-Claudia's parents had decided to run away, *leaving their own daughter behind.*

"Yes, without anybody," said his mother. "But it was even worse for the father, I'm afraid. The Hungarians patched him up and then some mucky-muck said the rules required them to return him to his country of residence."

"Here," said Noah.

"That's right. Here. Where he was arrested for breaking the law against 'illegal abandonment of the GDR' and put into prison. Oh, it's awful. So that's the point: they can all still be hurt—badly, badly hurt. Understand? You have to make *sure* she doesn't write that letter."

"Yeah, okay," whispered Noah, but it was hard even to make his tongue move properly to form the words.

They walked another block, and then Noah thought of the most important thing: "Mom, you have to tell Claudia and Frau März. You can't let them keep thinking—"

"Oh, Frau März knows. She knows perfectly well."

His mother's eyes narrowed for a mere moment.

"No, she doesn't," said Noah. "She's the one who told Cloud-Claudia about the car accident."

"It wasn't true, and she knew it. At first she was trying to keep her job, I guess. Someone higher up in the ministry probably put pressure on her: told her she'd better lie to everyone or be fired. Can't have the mother of criminals in a high post."

"Not *criminals*," said Noah.

"Criminals," said his mother. "They broke the law. They tried to abandon their country. They tried to leave. So, in the GDR: criminals."

"How could she lie like that?" said Noah.

"I guess she's afraid," said Noah's mother. "Frau März must figure it's better for her granddaughter to think her parents are dead than for her to know one of them's in prison and one of them is over the border in the West."

"But that's *wrong*," said Noah. He felt so furious that he thought something might just go pop in his brain. "We have to tell Claudia the truth. It's horrible. That's just so wrong, what Frau März is doing."

"There's a lot about all of this that's wrong," said his mother, and her smile brightened itself up again. They were almost back to their own street at this point. "And believe me, you mustn't say a single word to your friend. I'm only telling you this because I had to make you see how serious the situation is. With the fortieth anniversary coming up, there isn't a millimeter of tolerance left anywhere in the system. So I can trust you to be sensible, yes? You mustn't tell her anything. Not a single thing."

Noah sputtered.

"I'm serious. It wouldn't be fair, asking her to keep a big secret like this—and what if she couldn't do it? What if she said something?" His mother, still smiling, shook her head. "No, we shouldn't be messing with this case at all, really. We could all get kicked out, and then I'll never finish my dissertation. I'll never be able to make you call me Dr. Mommy, when I finally get my PhD! And I've been looking forward to that for years!"

Noah had one last horrible thought.

"Oh, Mom," he said. "If her parents had just waited until August, none of this would have happened. If they'd been at the picnic thing we went to. And with Claudia, too."

"They could have just walked through the gate," said his mother. "It's true. But they didn't know. None of us knew that was going to happen. I'm afraid that's how history works in real life. You don't know what the future's really going to bring until it's already the past."

Noah was not as good at keeping a fake smile on his face as his mother was. He leaned his head against her coat for a moment as they came around the corner, trying to make sense of a world where such awful things could happen to a kid like Cloud-Claudia.

"That seam is going to come loose soon," his mother added suddenly, poking at Noah's jacket. "I'll sew it up when we get back home."

Every seam everywhere is loose, thought Noah.

He got home and hung another couple of clouds in the window. Cutting paper and hanging things up is usually another good way not to think about things. Projects. Projects help.

But his mind kept circling around Cloud-Claudia's family, and every time he looked at the details of the story, something new and terrible jumped out at him.

It was awful, what had happened to her parents. But the whole thing was awful. What would make parents so desperate to leave a place that they would even leave their own daughter behind—and not just anywhere, but under the thumb of Frau März? How could they have thought that was okay?

Oh, Cloud! Oh, Cloud!

And then he thought about his mother telling him he absolutely must not tell Cloud-Claudia the truth, and he had the strangest feeling.

He thought that his mother, who was almost always right about things, might this time be *wrong*.

How would Noah feel if he had been told a lie about his parents, and a friend had known the truth and *hadn't told him*?

He guessed he would feel pretty bad. That friend wouldn't have been a true friend; that's how Noah would feel—once he found out the truth, of course. And people always find out the truth in the end. That was something Noah had noticed over and over, in books and movies and sometimes in real life, too. Someone always lets the secret out. Faces have guilty looks. Evidence turns up.

Someday, surely, Cloud-Claudia would find out.

Her mother might finally be able to send a letter, maybe, once the border people had calmed down. All right, that would probably be a long time from now. But eventually.

And her poor father would get out of prison at some point, right? They'd have to explain it all to her then.

But that might be years from now. She could be thinking for years that her parents were dead when they really weren't.

But if it wasn't safe for her to know? He didn't want her hurt more than she already was.

His mind was running in circles now. How was he going to be able to face Cloud-Claudia after this? He kept thinking, *I've got to decide what to do.*

Because he didn't know what to do, he ended up opening the puzzle box that Cloud-Claudia had given back to him not that long ago. All those tiny pieces! He was impressed that she had done that puzzle on her own. Twice.

He ran his hands through the little pieces—there was something comforting about that, almost like playing with sand at the beach. He thought vaguely about starting the puzzle again himself, but he was really too restless for puzzles.

Then he noticed something on the back of one of the pieces. He looked closer.

In little, precise handwriting, someone had written a name: *Sonja.*

He started sifting through all the pieces, looking at the blank sides now, not the picture sides.

He found another one: *Matthias.*

And, after a lot of searching, another: *Claudia.*

Names!

And when he flipped those three pieces over, he saw that they went together, of course. They made the picture of a little house to the left of the tower.

He could see how it would feel good to put those pieces together that way.

If the world he and Cloud-Claudia were living in was a kind of jigsaw puzzle, it was one that had been shaken up into a thousand pieces, for sure. No, not a thousand pieces—a million pieces.

A million pieces, and no picture on the box to help them get it right.

Secret File #26
FORTIETH-ANNIVERSARY PLANS

Here are some of the things that were planned for October 7, 1989, the fortieth anniversary of the founding of the German Democratic Republic:

- On the night of October 6, a parade of 100,000 young people carrying torches was to pass through Berlin to demonstrate the loyalty of the Free German Youth to their motherland.

- On Saturday morning, October 7, along the Karl-Marx-Allee, there would be a grand honor parade of the National People's Army of the GDR and of Troops of the Border Patrol, passing for review before Erich Honecker, general secretary of the Central Committee of the Socialist Unity

Party and leader of the State Council of the German Democratic Republic, and before "eminent guests from the entire world." The most eminent guests, including Mikhail Gorbachev, leader of the Soviet Union, where democratic reforms were already well under way, were to stand with Honecker before an absolutely enormous red banner that said 40 YEARS GDR above a copy of the GDR seal, which combined a hammer and a compass within a wreath of rye. Many tanks and jeeps would roll down the street.

· There would be musical entertainment for the masses.

· Sausage and bratwurst stands were to be set up all over town.

· There would be plenty of places where you could buy souvenirs to take back home with you when you left Berlin.

· Feasts and banquets would be held for the honored guests.

Not all guests were to be honored, however. Some were not desired. It became harder and harder that week to cross into East Berlin from the West, and on the actual Saturday of the anniversary, the border was closed up tight.

chapter twenty-seven

OUT INTO THE DARK

Like everywhere else in East Germany, the fourth class of the Bruno-Beater-Schule had been filled for weeks and weeks with reminders that soon, soon, East Germany would be forty years old. The wall newspaper, no longer populated by friendly wallfish, displayed pictures the teacher was sure would be appropriate for the fortieth birthday of the GDR. Erich Honecker, the head of state, had been staring out from the wall of Noah's classroom for ages, looking very earnest and making Noah nervous.

Noah spent the week sending stern, silent messages back in the direction of that self-satisfied face:

Did you really put Cloud-Claudia's father in prison just because he broke his leg at the Hungarian border?

And then he'd remember that he had to decide what to do, and the ball of ice in his stomach would roll around, making him feel slightly sick.

The whole first half of that week, he only saw Cloud-Claudia for about forty-five seconds, out in the non-park. He said to her then, "No *Eingabe!* I've been thinking—it might be a problem—don't send that *Eingabe!*" and then, fortunately, he had to run back inside for dinner before she could ask any really difficult questions, like "Why?"

He had no idea how to answer a question like "Why?" He spent days going over and over the whole thing in his head: Was breaking the Rules and telling her what had happened to her parents the right and good thing to do— or a stupid and silly thing to do—or even a terribly wrong and dangerous thing to do?

He simply did not know. And it bothered him so much that for a couple of days he was as perfectly quiet at school as even Frau Müller could want him to be. She gave him an approving look at the end of his third completely silent day; that was irritating. But on the other hand, by the end of the third day of silence, he had figured out a possible solution. A fix. A possible way around the problem.

He tapped the signal on the floor for the back courtyard steps and then waited there for what felt like ages, his nervous fingers pulling at a loose thread in his jacket where his mother had tried to mend the seam—but nothing wanted to be mended anymore, and his fingers seemed to be rebelling against all of his mother's projects, anyway.

"Cloud!" he said when she finally arrived. He had almost lost hope by then.

"I was thinking about something," said Noah. "When we went up to the edge of the city and you waved—do you remember you waved?"

"*Ja,*" said Cloud-Claudia.

Noah pressed his hands tightly together, trying not to mess this up. He was remembering the distant ghostly figures on that platform, in particular the woman with the uneven shoulders, too far away to be seen clearly. *Keep it vague and you're not technically lying,* he told himself. *Keep it as close as you can to the possible truth.*

"Well, I thought *maybe* I saw someone there, looking over at us. A woman, you know. I'm pretty sure, anyway. A woman who looked like you, sort of. With hair maybe a little like yours. Did you see her?"

Cloud-Claudia just stared at him for the longest time. Noah felt like a building with a huge elevator in it, and the elevator was sinking and rising, sinking and rising.

"*Ja,*" said Cloud-Claudia in a whisper. "I think I did. Yes. I'm sure I did. Because it's a magic place, the Land of the Changelings. In a magic place, she could still be alive."

"Cloud! What I'm thinking is maybe—" said Noah, though the Astonishing Stutter had risen up like a tidal

286

wave and was trying to drown every one of these words, "maybe your grandmother doesn't always tell the exact truth."

Of course, when it comes to *lying* and *telling the truth*— sometimes there's a pretty complicated edge between those two. Sometimes you have to lie because you're trying, as hard as you can, to find a way to tell the truth.

Cloud-Claudia's face was beginning to shine. It was the sky when the sun finally is about to rise. It was the ocean with a great white bird soaring above it and an island just coming into view. It was a girl whose mother may not be gone forever after all.

I'm trying! Noah told the universe. *I'm really trying, as best as I can.*

Noah and his parents ended up watching the parade for the fortieth anniversary of the founding of the German Democratic Republic on television. His parents were uncharacteristically nervous about wandering the town on such a momentous day. The security forces were jumpy, they said. Everyone was on alert.

"They don't want trouble," said Noah's father. "What's more, they'll go to any length necessary to avoid trouble. So we definitely, definitely do not want to be seen as causing even one iota of trouble."

Eventually Noah talked them into going out on a

sausage-finding expedition, and what he discovered then was that it really felt like any big parade day. The weather was gray, and some adults looked bored, but most people were very much enjoying their bratwursts, and the kids had little flags in their hands, which made them happy, too.

Noah's parents weren't in the right mood for celebrations, however, and to be honest, Noah wasn't, either. After their bratwursts and a few attempts to listen to bands playing, they wandered back home.

"Well, we'll see how it all turns out," said Noah's mother, her hands doing some kind of nervous little dance against her sides. "It's a pain that the embassy's closed, though. I wouldn't mind seeing if we have any mail. You guys can go Monday."

Noah would have liked to see the thousands of tanks rolling down the Karl-Marx-Allee in person, rather than on television, but he didn't mind all that much. The kids on television, waving their flags, looked more cold than thrilled, partly because every new military group had to stop so the leader could shout a long greeting to Mr. Honecker.

All in all, bratwurst plus watching things on television seemed like a fine option.

So the day lumbered to its conclusion. They had supper early.

Noah went to his room to work on the puzzle—in

theory, anyway. He just mumbled excuses and left the living room, and then for a while he sat on his bed, pulling at the loose thread in his jacket seam and worrying. He still felt uncomfortable around his parents, since he wasn't sure yet whether he had done the right thing, not leaving Cloud-Claudia, as his parents had insisted, in the dark. The dark was so dark for her; that was the thing.

And he hadn't said *everything*. He had kind of led her to a break in the trees and told her to *look, look*. Maybe that didn't count as telling.

Maybe, though, it did.

Finally he pulled that thread too hard, and the seam of his jacket came just very slightly undone. Oops! He hadn't meant to do that, and after his mother had sewn it up and everything—

Then his mind turned an unexpected corner, because his finger ran into something strange inside that seam. He pulled it out—just a thin, thin piece of paper, covered with two columns of words.

Names.

A list of names hidden in his jacket.

Click.

Then he realized his hands were shaking: *Names hidden in his jacket!*

His mother must have hidden them in there. *A safe hiding place,* she must have thought. Who would bother about a kid's clothes? But that meant—what exactly did that mean?

Put it back, put it back, hide it away and pretend you never saw it—that was what his brain had to say.

As his fingers were stuffing that thin scrap of paper back through the weak spot in his jacket seam, his muddled-up thoughts were interrupted by shouting from the apartment below. It sounded like Frau März was furious at poor Cloud-Claudia for some reason, and Claudia, uncharacteristically, wasn't mustering up the shouting skills to be furious back. She said something loud and wobbly. A door was slammed. Then she must have been in her room, the twin room to the one Noah was in, each on his or her side of the horizontal Wall.

Something was definitely, definitely wrong.

Cloud-Claudia cried for a long time, and then the crying stopped.

It stopped all at once, as if she had had some sort of very clever idea and decided that crying would not be helpful.

And then the floor said to Noah, *Tap, tu-Tap TAP!*

The emergency signal.

Noah stood up in the dark. What do you do when there's an emergency? You respond somehow. You do what needs to be done.

Outside his window, over by the construction site that was supposed to be a park, across the street there, a small shadowy figure had just appeared—a small shadowy figure in Cloud-Claudia's coat. She looked up and down the street, and then she started pacing up and down the street.

What was she doing, out this late? He couldn't let her actually run away, at night and everything, could he? Emergency!

Noah was already grabbing his scarf and the map. It was surprisingly easy to sneak out of the apartment, for the simple reason that his parents had absolutely no reason to think he would ever do such a thing, so their ears were not pointed toward the front door, listening for every possible creak. Of course, he did try not to make very many creaks or to pound his way down the stairs. He went fast and quiet. When he got out onto the street, he looked right and saw the small back of Cloud-Claudia's coat, just about to turn right at the corner. He ran after her, not shouting, of course, because he certainly didn't want to draw anyone's attention to the girl who seemed to be running away, but moving as fast as he could.

"Cloud!" he half whispered when he was finally close enough. "What are you doing? Wait up!"

She wheeled around when she heard him begin to speak. There were streaks of tears shining on her cheeks, her eyes were puffy, her nose was running. She was in pretty miserable shape.

"What's wrong?" asked Noah.

"Had a fight with the *Oma*," said Cloud-Claudia. "It was a real stinker, too. She was mad because I don't care about school, and my grades are bad. And she's in a bad mood anyway, because watching all the TV reports makes her mad. Also, apparently it's all my fault my parents are gone. *Ja*. That's what she said."

And she turned around with a shudder and started walking again.

"No, no," said Noah, trotting after her. "It wasn't your fault, Cloud. How can she say that?"

"I'll tell you a secret," said Cloud-Claudia.

She turned her head to look at Noah, her puffy eyes on a slight sideward slant.

"My *Oma* has been drinking a lot, all this week. She hides the bottles, but I know where she hides them. She says she doesn't know where my mother and I came from, that we have to cause such trouble. She says why couldn't she have a normal child and a normal grandchild? She would still have a job; she'd be celebrating the fortieth birthday with everyone. She says the whole country could have been normal if people like me and my mother and my father hadn't messed everything up."

"That's not true."

"She says"—Cloud-Claudia pulled herself up very tall, just daring Noah to laugh or make fun of her, though what Noah really felt like doing was throwing things or screaming or crying or something—"she says my parents couldn't stand me, either, the way I behave, so abnormal all the time. She says—they were running *away from me.*"

She shot a very sharp-edged glance in Noah's direction.

"Oh, Cloud, no," said Noah, though the ice was rolling all around his stomach. "No, no, no. Why would they do that?"

"I was too difficult. I disgusted them. So finally they ran away and died. *And good riddance to all of you*—that's what my *Oma* just said."

"That's awful," said Noah. "She doesn't mean it. Slow down, Cloud! You said yourself she's been drinking a lot recently. It's mixed up her thinking—that's what's happened."

"Don't make silly excuses, like I'm a baby who can't take the heat or something. Anyway, my mother isn't dead. They aren't dead. I'm sure we saw my mother. They're there."

"*There,*" echoed Noah.

"The Land of the Changelings," said Cloud-Claudia patiently, and she started moving faster along the sidewalk. "I'm tired of waiting for them to remember their names and remember me. I'm going over there."

"Cloud, listen. You know you can't do this," said Noah, feeling that guilt in his belly again. If he'd kept his mouth shut, maybe they wouldn't be out in the dark streets of Berlin right now, heading God knows where. "You can't just go over there — it doesn't work that way."

Cloud-Claudia wasn't listening to him, though.

"And now they're still not thinking," she was saying, "and soon they'll forget I ever existed, and I can't stand that."

She wiped the back of her hand across her eyes.

"I saw her. She's there. I know she's there. You coming with me?"

Noah looked around, feeling helpless. What to do? He couldn't drag her back home, and anyway, did he want to drag her back to that awful grandmother of hers? He knew they shouldn't be running around Berlin on their own after dark, but it would be worse for Cloud-Claudia to be on her own, clinging to those crazy ideas of hers.

And whose fault was it, anyway, that she had all these crazy ideas?

"*Ja,*" he said. "Of course I'm coming with you. Which way are you going?"

"Back where the edge is, maybe?" said Cloud-Claudia. "Where we saw her looking at us. Anyway, you've got the map."

Noah jumped. He had forgotten about the map in his hand.

"Good," she said. "Then the changelings will have to let

us in this time. The whole country will know it's supposed to be there if we've got the map with us."

It was all so surreal. She turned around and kept walking, and Noah kept up with her, walking fast enough that it would have been hard to say anything. Not that he really knew what to say to her!

Also, he was thinking again about that day they had walked to the edge of East Berlin and Claudia had waved. His mother had thought that was a good idea, for the two of them to go to the Wall that day. Why? And she had known a lot about what had happened on the Hungarian border. He was beginning to have very tangled thoughts about all of these things. Could it be that—?

"Listen," said Cloud-Claudia. They stopped in the dark, listening.

"Sounds like a bunch of people shouting."

"Chanting all together," she said. "Do you hear them? 'Come out and join us.' Hear that? Maybe they're wanting to get through to the other side, too."

She started running again, toward the chanting and the shouting.

"Oh, Cloud, be careful! What are you doing? Stop it— please stop."

He was becoming desperate from being so worried and from so much not knowing what he actually should be doing or trying to do.

She paused to look back at him.

"*You* can go home if you want, Wallfish. I'm not stopping you."

"But Cloud! You can't just run up to some strange crowd of people. What if they're dangerous?"

Dangerous in German starts with a *g*: *g-g-g-gefährlich*. He could have slaughtered that word, with its foolish *g* trying to trip him up.

Cloud-Claudia was already gone, though. So Noah had no choice but to follow.

They were going north, north, north on cold, dark streets, following the noise of that crowd. When at last they spilled out onto the big street, suddenly there was chaos all around. Hundreds of people marching and chanting— and following along beside them, what must have been policemen.

"Do you hear that, Wallfish? 'We're staying here.' Do you know why they're saying that?"

"Because they want things to change," said Noah. "They won't go away."

"Because if you go away, you forget," said Cloud-Claudia. "Maybe you remember something at first, just a little, enough to go to the edge and peek, but already then you're forgetting, probably. 'Waving? Who is that waving at me?'"

"Cloud, please—we'd better go home!"

"These people here are trying to remind us all of our names," said Cloud-Claudia, and her voice was so fierce that Noah fell back a step. "Like we have to do for the changelings!"

Noah was feeling little prickles of fear running along his backbone. He felt very out of place here—like an alien changeling person, lost in a strange city at a strange time.

Behind them someone shrieked suddenly. The sound of someone being hit by something. What was going on? What was going on?

"Please, Cloud?" said Noah. "Please? Can we go now? I'm worried about all the police."

"I want to see where the people are going. We'll be careful."

She pulled him farther along the street. They kept away from the loudest shouting, darting like shadows along the side of the crowd. There were other people doing the same thing, and they kept away from them, too.

"Look up ahead there!" said Cloud-Claudia. "The candle church! That must be where they're headed."

It was kitty-corner across the street from them, a church with candles burning on the porch in front. A group of people stood behind those candles, and above them, hanging in the doorway of the church, was a hand-painted sign, dark letters against the white background, hard to see. Noah tried to read it aloud, with his stop-and-start German: *"Wachet und betet. Mahnwache für die zu Unrecht Inhaftierten."*

He recognized *haft* hiding in that long last word, but that was pretty much all. It made him nervous.

"What does that mean?"

"No idea," she said. "Something about prisoners and it being unfair. Don't know what a *Mahnwache* is. Let's sneak across the street that way, with all of them."

"Cloud, wait," said Noah, but she wasn't waiting. He didn't want to leave her on her own in that crowd, where something huge was happening, or had already happened, or was about to happen—so he jumped out into the street, following her as best he could.

Secret File #27
FOR THOSE UNFAIRLY IMPRISONED

A *Mahnwache* is a vigil. The candle church was called the Gethsemane Church, and so it was a good place to hold a vigil involving praying and waiting, since in the story in the Bible, Jesus prayed and waited in the Gethsemane garden in Jerusalem, under the olive trees.

The sign hanging in the church's doorway said this: "Keep watch and pray. Vigil for those unfairly imprisoned."

Those were some of the bravest words anyone had ever painted on a sheet on the eastern side of the Wall.

Cloud-Claudia's father, of course, was one of *those unfairly imprisoned.*

But Cloud didn't know that yet.

· chapter twenty-eight ·

AND THEN BAD
THINGS HAPPENED

Cloud and Noah were in front of the church, below the
porch with the candles on it, when the police charged the
crowd. They seemed to come from everywhere, all at once.

Noah grabbed Cloud's coat, and they tried to hide from
the swinging batons and shouting voices in the middle of
the crowd.

"What are they doing? What are they doing?" said Cloud-
Claudia.

And she wasn't the only one saying that. There were
cries of dismay from all around them.

"Stop! Stop! We're peaceful!" people were saying. "Stop
hitting!"

But the shouting and thwacking sounds didn't stop.

"Stay with me," said Noah to Cloud, but he wasn't sure she could hear him. "Don't let go!"

Somewhere in the chaos of the last minute, they had grabbed each other's hands, the way you hang on to a railing when the waves get so high the boat seems about to pitch right over.

They hung on to each other, and the sea of people around them rolled and bobbed and shouted.

That whole group of people was being moved over to one side, closer to a row of police vans. Sometimes the police would drag one or two of the people in that crowd away from the rest and throw them into a van.

Noah and Cloud shrank back, hanging on to each other like crazy, but the crowd and the line of policemen with their batons and their crazy-angry voices kept moving, and so they had to move with them.

Suddenly there was a gloved hand on Noah's shoulder, yanking him out of the crowd. He yelped in surprise—*a policeman was pulling him toward one of those vans!*—but he didn't lose hold of Cloud.

A woman right nearby made an upset sound, an outraged gulp.

"What are you doing, you people? These are *children!*" she said. Noah saw she had taken Cloud's other hand and was trying to keep her own body between Cloud's face and those awful batons, and he felt so grateful to this woman he had never seen before, he could almost have cried.

But the policeman pulling on Noah just got angry.

"Bringing children to your riots?" he shouted at her. "Idiots! Then you all come along. Come!"

And a few other policemen came over their way, too, pulling on that trio of Noah and Cloud and the woman they didn't know, who was still holding on to Cloud's other hand. On the woman's face was a mix of shock and distress and horror.

"What are you *doing*?" she kept saying.

Now the crowd was shouting at the policemen, too. Like Noah himself, they seemed to have trouble believing this, that the police would be dragging a couple of kids toward their dark police vans.

"Mouths shut!" said the police. "Silence! Come! You're under arrest."

And they shoved them right through the door of a van, into a dark space that already seemed full of people. Hands reached out to steady Noah and catch Cloud.

"Children!" they were saying. "Treating children like this!"

The door banged shut. The van leaped forward, throwing Noah and Cloud against all those people perched on benches along the sides of the van.

The woman who had helped Cloud leaned closer to them.

"You kids, where are your parents?"

The van was bouncing along; Noah's chest was zipped up tight with anxiety, and he saw that Cloud was gasping a little as she breathed. It had all happened so suddenly!

"I don't know," said Cloud-Claudia to the woman. "They disappeared. Why did they put everyone in this truck?"

There were murmurs from all the other people in the van. Things like "Poor kids" and "Shameful, grabbing children like that!"

The kind woman put her arm around Cloud's shoulders.

"Stick with me," she said. "I'll try to look out for you."

"Where are they taking us?" said Cloud-Claudia. That was Noah's chief question, too.

"Police station, I guess," said a man leaning against the other wall of the van. "They shouldn't be picking up kids, though."

"They thought these were mine," said the kind woman. "Brutes."

Noah's head was spinning. The police station! He was being arrested by the East German police! What would his parents say? How could he have let this happen? And *what would happen now to Cloud?* Or to her father, already locked up in some prison somewhere?

Those were all very unpleasant thoughts. But then he remembered yet another terrible thing: that thin sheet of paper, that list of names hidden in his jacket. What if the police found that? He had the feeling that would be worse than unpleasant: that would be a disaster.

"We've got to get out," he said while his hand pulled at the seam of his jacket. The bouncing of the van made the Astonishing Stutter more astonishing than it had ever been. Heads turned to stare at him through the gloom of the van.

Cloud gave his other hand, his left hand, a firm squeeze.

"He can't speak," she told the people in the van. "He can't say anything, not at all."

Then another squeeze of the hand, like she was signaling something.

What was that about, telling people he couldn't talk? But then he realized with a kind of shock that she was trying to do for Noah what he had wanted to do for her: protect him. Shield him.

She didn't know how much more she had to lose than he did.

He squeezed Cloud's hand back. She was trying to take care of him. All right. He was determined to take care of her, too. They were changelings, both of them. That had to count for something.

He had the tiny sheet of paper scrunched up in his

right hand now, pulled out through the weak spot in the seam of his jacket. He rubbed it into a few pieces and then sank his head down into his hand, as if everything had just become too much for him. And, really, honestly, it sort of had.

But he also got the little shreds of paper into his mouth. Just like a spy in the movies! His throat was so dry from nervousness, he thought he might choke on those little pills of paper — but he didn't. He gulped them down, and the gulp sounded amazingly like a sob. Good. Good.

"Mein Gott," said someone in that van. "Taking children!"

That was when the van lurched to a halt, and the doors were yanked open. There was a bright artificial light everywhere that made your eyes blink.

"Hurry, hurry!" said the policemen, pulling people out through those doors. "You want to stay up all night causing trouble? Making your country look bad? Be our guest."

Noah hung on to Cloud-Claudia, and she hung on to him, and there on the far side of Cloud-Claudia, the kind woman was still holding her other hand. They stood blinking on the pavement, on the cement surface of some large garage. And then the whole group in that van was trot-marched through a door, down a big hall, and through other doors, and down another hall, and there were policemen everywhere. It was all very surreal, unbelievable, strange. The last doorway led into a big bare room, a kind of cellar-garage, ugly as could be and with fluorescent lights that made your head ache and filled with shouting. Other people were in here, too—from other vans, Noah guessed.

They moved into that big cellar room cautiously at first, but then the policemen started shouting at everyone to *hurry up, hurry up, you worthless slugs,* and there were more of those awful thwacking sounds.

Noah felt a whimper rise up in his throat. He swallowed it down as best he could. No time for that now! He had to be very strong and alert if he was going to keep Cloud safe.

The policemen were shouting, shouting, shouting.

"Schnell! Schnell!"

They wanted everyone to stand against the wall, hands on the wall above shoulder height, legs slightly spread.

There were shouts from the other side of the room, where, out of the corner of his eye, Noah could see a police-man whacking someone's legs with his baton because he didn't like how the man was standing.

They'd better obey, then.

That meant letting go of Cloud-Claudia's hand. He tried to stay very close to her, though.

Cloud was staying close to him, too.

"Why did they take us?" she said. "We were just walking by."

There was a chorus of complaint from their side of the cellar.

Noah kept hearing the word *Kinder*, which means "children." The other prisoners clearly thought that Noah and Cloud shouldn't be there in that awful cellar. They were calling out to the guards, trying to get them to come over and do something for the children, to get the children out of this place.

The guards barked back and thwacked some more people on the legs, trying to shut everyone up, but eventually somebody who seemed perhaps slightly more senior than the others came up to where Noah and Cloud-Claudia and the kind woman were standing.

"Na ja," he said to the woman. "Bringing children along to your riots and your vandal parades! Not very clever, you hooligans! What kind of mother are you, putting a child through something like this?"

The kind woman took a deep, shaky breath. Noah could see that she was frightened and angry, and that she was another person, like Noah, trying to do the right thing and not sure what the right thing to do was, exactly.

"You've made a mistake, officer," she said. "These children aren't mine. They were playing near the church. They weren't in any protest. I'm just trying to keep them safe from your batons. They shouldn't be here."

The policemen's eyes bugged out.

"Nice try!" he said to her. And to the whole cellar, he shouted, "Who here is the parent of these children?"

And there was silence, of course.

"Let them go," said some young man standing not too far away. "It's not right, frightening children this way."

"Yes, yes!" said other voices from all around that bald, cold room. "Let the kids go!"

The guards shouted again. *Stand properly and shut your mouths.* That's what the guards kept shouting. The wall was cold and slippery under Noah's fingers. And his legs kept trembling, which made it hard to stand the way the policemen wanted everyone to stand. And he could see, on his right, Cloud-Claudia's hands on the wall, too. She had her head turned to look at him. Her eyes were large and tired, and her hands were beginning to slide down the wall.

She said something to Noah.

"What?" he whispered. "What?"

Cloud-Claudia scooted a few inches closer to him.

"Now we'll never get there in time," she said. "It's already almost too late. They'll forget us for good."

Noah stared at her, not understanding a thing for a second.

Then he realized—it was the Land of the Changelings

she was talking about. Nobody but Cloud could be in a police cellar and worry about an imaginary country!

"We've got to get out of here," she said. "We really do."

Well, Noah certainly agreed with that. He wasn't at all sure what to do, though.

The policeman nearest Noah and Cloud-Claudia, the one who had said all those nasty things to the kind woman, was consulting with another officer at the door at the far right of the room. Noah could tell they were talking about them, about him and Cloud, because they kept looking over in their direction. They seemed to be having an argument of some kind. Then the man in the door vanished into the hallway.

"Don't be afraid, children," said the woman next to Cloud-Claudia. "They can't possibly keep you here. They'll have to let you go."

The next part of the night lasted forever. They just stood there and waited. Their hands would get tired of pressing against the cold wall and start slipping, and then some guard would shout, and they would try to put their hands up higher again.

Finally, Cloud-Claudia just sighed, *"Nein,"* and she let her hands fall right down to her sides and rested with her head against the wall, and the guards didn't do anything about it, so Noah let his hands slip down, too.

It was like a bad dream.

And he was so tired. Fear and tiredness were kind of wrestling to control his brain.

He wondered whether his parents had even noticed he wasn't in the apartment anymore. Perhaps they hadn't! They might just peek into his room in the dark and not notice nobody was in there anymore.

Of course, even if they found out he was missing, what could they do?

And so on and so on. After a long bad stint of these thoughts, Noah saw a couple of officers coming toward him. One of them was a woman.

"Come with me, you two," she said. Her voice was very curt, no nonsense, the kind of voice that makes people line up and start marching.

Cloud-Claudia darted close to Noah and slipped her hand into his. Her fingers were cold but comforting.

Around the room, tired people were saying things like "Finally!" and "Those poor kids, having to wait here so long. You won't get away with this!" and, to Noah and Cloud-Claudia as they passed by: "Finally letting you go. You'll be all right now, children."

"Silence!" said the woman guard, and she hustled Noah and Cloud out of that cellar, moving them along so fast that Noah didn't even have time to say *Danke* to the woman who had been so kind. He had to settle for sending grateful thoughts back in her direction from the hall: *Thank you, thank you, thank you.* And then the door of that awful cellar clicked shut behind them.

They went farther down the hall. A second guard had joined them. Noah was wondering what time it was now. Some impossibly late hour, he guessed. He was so tired. His thoughts were just one big confused tangle. His parents were going to be mad. How were he and Cloud going to get home, anyway? He didn't know where the van had taken them. He didn't know what street they were on, or even what part of Berlin they were in. He had a feeling it would be a very long, cold walk home.

Then the woman stopped.

"You," she said to Noah. "In here. We have a few questions for you. The girl comes with me."

"No," said Noah, but it didn't come out as a word you could understand.

Cloud-Claudia was gripping his hand so tightly, he couldn't feel the tips of his fingers. She shook her head. Shook her head again.

"*Nein, nein!*" she said. "Don't take him. He can't even speak right. You have to leave him alone. Let us go home. He can't talk."

"Be quiet, I tell you," said the woman guard. "You

311

both have gotten yourselves and your parents into a huge amount of trouble. You come with me. The boy goes in here."

And before Noah could think what he should do now, she had peeled Cloud-Claudia's fingers loose from Noah's hand and started leading her away. And at the same moment, the second guard pulled a key out of his pocket, unlocked the door on the left, and pushed Noah into that little room.

"Sit down," said a man behind a desk.

The room was very small and very plain, but there was a bright light spilling over everything. The chair the man wanted him to sit on was practically swimming in light. It made his eyes water. He was so tired. His eyes just wanted to close. He wanted to close his eyes and rest.

He sat down in that chair.

"So," said the man, "what is your name?"

Noah, however, was too distracted to answer right away. He had just noticed what was on the wall to his right: a blank rectangle of glass, pretending to be a mirror.

Even though he was so tired that he just wanted to curl up in a heap in the corner, he still knew right away what that was.

Secret File #28
MIRROR, MIRROR, ON THE WALL

Here is why Noah recognized that mirror: When he was very little, he had gone to a funny sort of nursery school, a school run by the local college. That nursery school had had a few of those mirrors — Noah had called them the ghost windows because he saw flickering shadows in them sometimes.

"Good eye, Noah!" his mother had said. His name had been Noah then, of course. Noah's mother was always proud when he noticed things. "You're right about the shadows. The shadows are students doing research. They watch the children playing and take notes."

He had been only four years old, but it had shocked him.

"You mean there are people *spying* on us?"

"Observing," said his mother. "*Observing* you. For their research. It's completely normal. The parents all signed a release form at the beginning of the year."

But Noah hadn't liked the idea of being spied on, no matter how ordinary his mother said it was.

For a whole two weeks, he went on strike at that nursery school. He sat in a corner and wouldn't do anything that might be interesting to the ghosts behind the mirror.

The first day, the teachers said, "Oh, it won't last."

The third day, the teachers said, "He can't possibly keep it up."

By the end of the second week, however, they had explained to Noah's parents that Noah was disrupting the normal function of the school and suggested they might want to find another place for him. So they did.

That was long ago, but he had never forgotten it — and he always checked mirrors for ghosts.

chapter twenty-nine

DOING THE RIGHT THING

In the little room with the desk and too much light, Noah gripped his hands tightly together to steady himself.

Remember Cloud-Claudia, he told himself. *Remember her father, in prison somewhere.*

He was determined that from now on he was not going to mess up. Somehow he was going to figure out what the right thing to do was.

But he was so tired. Just sitting down in that chair had made him break out into a huge yawn.

"Boy!" said the man behind the desk. "I asked you your name! What's your name, and why were you rioting in the streets of Berlin?"

"I wasn't," said Noah, though his tongue stumbled through the words. He was *so* tired.

"What's that?" said the man, looking taken aback. "Speak up clearly, please. Your name."

So despite his good intentions, Noah already had no idea what the right thing was to say. He thought it over. In thrillers, you're not supposed to let the other side know what your name is. But this was real life. And he couldn't see how his parents were going to be able to come rescue him unless these people knew his name—his Berlin name.

"Jonah," said Noah. "Jonah Brown."

Of course, there were about a million extra syllables there. He was so tired! The Astonishing Stutter always got worse when he was tired and stressed out.

"What?" said the man. "Say that again." Then there was a pause, and Noah realized that the man must be listening to someone talking into some small machine hidden in his ear, the way the policemen on the streets of Berlin paused to listen when they stopped you to ask for your papers seven minutes after you'd left the American embassy.

"You can't talk?" said the man. "The little girl—your sister?—said you can't talk. We can ask your sister these questions, then."

"No, no," said Noah. "Please, you have to leave her alone."

"What did you say your name was again?"

"Jonah Brown," said Noah.

"What?"

"Jonah Brown."

"Stay here for a moment. You are under surveillance. Do not move."

The man came out from behind his desk and went right out into the hall. Even before he had fully gone through the door, he had started arguing with somebody on the other side.

All Noah heard was "What? He's whose? What a mess. And who's the girl, then?"

And then the door slammed shut, and Noah couldn't hear anything anymore.

Noah sat in his chair. The man didn't come back. Time dribbled on.

It felt like it had been a million hours — no, years — since he had looked out his window and seen Cloud-Claudia out there with her coat on, walking away into the night. Could he have done something different, something clever that would have kept her safe? Where was she now, and what were they doing to her?

He would fret, and then doze off, and then go back to fretting, and then find himself half asleep again. It was all a nightmare that wouldn't stop.

But every time his head nodded forward because sleep was rising like a puddle all around him, a guard banged on the door.

When his head sank forward to rest on the desk, the door behind him actually flew open, and a guard came in to shout at him in person.

"No going to sleep!" said the guard. "You must stay awake here. You have not been given permission to sleep."

"Where is—?" But he wasn't sure whether Cloud-Claudia had already told them her name. *Cloud-Claudia,* he thought, wondering what was happening to her. He remembered her father, in prison. He even remembered her mother, who must surely be worrying all the time, wherever she now was on the other side of the Wall, about Cloud-Claudia and Cloud's father.

The guard slapped the desk with his hand to wake Noah up.

He jumped in his chair, and tears blurred his vision for a moment.

"I'm so tired," he said. "I'm so, so tired."

And at that moment, two more people came into the tiny space, the man who had been asking him questions earlier and another quite different man, with gray hair and serious brown eyes.

"Here, now, you can't do that," he said to the guard who had slapped the desk. "We don't frighten children needlessly. Out with you."

Noah blinked a few times, to see whether maybe he was dreaming now. It wasn't just that the gray-haired man had made the guard back off a bit. It was that the gray-haired man was speaking English.

"Yes, yes," said the man, seeing Noah's surprise. "As you see, we know who you are."

"Then will you call my parents, please?" said Noah. "This is all a mistake. We just got caught by mistake."

That was what he meant to say. What it came out sounding like was much more mysterious and choppy.

The English-speaking man went around to the chair behind the desk and sat down, while the German-speaking questioner stayed standing at the side of the room. Between them and the ghosts behind the mirror, Noah had perhaps never felt so stared-at in his life.

"Now, now, now," said the English-speaking man. His hands were hiding inside thin black gloves. "First we have some little mysteries to clear up, of course. For one thing, you have been lying to us, Jonah. That's not acceptable at all. That girl out there isn't your sister."

"Is she okay?" said Noah. "And I didn't—didn't say she was my sister!"

"What? Didn't you?" said the gray-haired man. "I think you did. You certainly gave that impression. It really looks quite a bit like you have been trying to mislead us, Jonah."

His dark eyes were miniature versions of the ghostly mirror on the walls: something was going on in them that was hard, from where Noah was sitting, to see clearly.

"It's no good lying to us," said the gray-haired man. "We know all about it. I think you have to show us we can trust you."

The man who was standing said something worried in German. It was a little too fast for Noah to understand. The gray-haired man said something, also in German, about how this was too good a chance to pass up, and that they couldn't be faulted, could they, because the boy's handicap made it very difficult for them to understand the name he was giving.

"Your friend, the little girl who is not your sister, has already explained the situation quite clearly to us," said the gray-haired man to Noah. He had switched back into English again to say it. "She has told us the whole story — how you were sent out to reconnoiter with the trouble-causing elements."

"What? No!" said Noah. What a story this man was telling! "That's not true. We just accidentally bumped into those people. No one sent us."

The man smiled.

"You expect us to believe that? You really do? No, Jonah. We aren't idiots here. It is shocking that parents would send children into such danger, but that's part of the *little secret* about your parents, isn't it? Not a very nice little secret, I'm afraid."

He leaned forward.

"They've been using you, using you all the time, your parents. Haven't they, Jonah? Using you and, I'm afraid, using that poor young Claudia as well. To tell you the truth, I'm a little shocked by such reckless behavior."

Noah just looked at him. He really had no idea what this man was getting at. And he was so, so tired. . . .

Another one of those watchful smiles.

"You, Jonah. You were their ticket into this country, weren't you? You were their perfect cover story, the boy with trouble speaking to show that his dear mother must really be dedicated to her research on that topic. They dragged you here so that we would be distracted, so that we wouldn't notice what they were really up to. And we both know what that was, don't we?"

"No," Noah said. It was the most he could do at that moment. That one "no" was meant to negate absolutely everything the man was saying. One flimsy little word trying to hold back a flood of awful news.

There was ice forming in his belly again.

The man said, "I'm afraid, young man, that we both know the truth here: your mother is not just a nice researcher who cares about handicapped children, and your father is certainly no novelist on vacation in East Berlin. Your parents are *spies*, Jonah, American imperialist spies. Their chief goal is the destruction of the German Democratic Republic, and you, young man, are just part of their disguise. You are nothing more than a fake mustache or a clever wig."

"No," said Noah again. But of course some stunned and horrified part of him was also thinking, *What if it's true?*

"But *yes*," said the English-speaking man. "We have plenty of proof, Jonah. What's all this, for instance?"

And almost like a magician pulling a rabbit out of a hat, he brought an envelope out of a briefcase and dumped its contents onto the table: a hundred little blank scraps of paper. A rubbish heap of paper.

"Jonah Brown, what is this?" he said again, but Noah was just gaping at the mess of paper there.

He shook his head, puzzled. That didn't please the English-speaking man very much.

"Every one of these pieces of evidence, Jonah, came out of the pockets of your father, Sam Brown."

Trash from his father's pockets! All this time, they had been *picking up all that trash that bumbled from his dad's pockets to the ground and filing it away in envelopes*. It was like the people who follow horses on parade, scooping up all the horse poop. It was nonsensical. It was —

Noah felt the tickle of a laugh rising up in his throat, but he forced it back down.

"This is hardly a laughing matter, boy," said the man, even though Noah had swallowed that laugh. "Your father, Sam Brown, has been distributing suspicious message-like

322

items all over Berlin. But our people are alert; you can be sure of that. A gross violation of the laws of the German Democratic Republic will not be allowed to occur without notice. What do you have to say about these messages, Jonah?"

"They're not messages," said Noah. "They're blank. They're . . . garbage."

The word "garbage" took him a while. During that time the English-speaking man frowned and brought out another piece of rumpled paper from another envelope.

This one was a page torn out of a book. Noah had a first brief impression of checkerboard squares and formulae and penciled numbers down the sides of the page, and then recognition flooded him, and once again he felt that ghost of an urge to laugh, only it was too much work to laugh.

"That's the page he tore out! That awful boy Ingo! That's the chessboard from *Alice*!"

The whole face of the English-speaking man lit up, as if Noah had said what he most wanted to hear.

"He admits it," said the English-speaking man to the German-speaking one. Then he repeated the phrase again, probably for the benefit of whatever shadowy onlookers were standing behind the mirror. "*He admits it*. This evidence of illegal activity belongs to the American citizens currently resident in the German Democratic Republic,

Sam and Linda Brown," said the man. Noah couldn't help noticing that when he spoke, all his consonants and vowels obediently lined up *just so*. "You see, now you don't have to keep lying so carefully, Jonah. Now it is all out in the open, finally."

"It's a page from my book," said Noah. "Only someone else wrote on it."

"Who wrote on it, Jonah?" said the man. "Who wrote that? And that?"

"*That's* just about chess," said Noah. "My father was trying to explain it to me—but where all those other numbers came from, *there*, I don't know."

"Of course you don't know," agreed the English-speaking man. "He wouldn't have told you what any of those meant, I shouldn't think. You were just a pawn."

"What? No," said Noah. "I just told you: those numbers weren't there when Ingo tore the page out of my book."

"Calm yourself, Jonah Brown," said the man. "It's too late for lies. You already admitted that your father wrote on this page. That's enough. That's sufficient. That will do."

Now Noah didn't know what to say at all.

The English-speaking man smiled and picked up the poor torn and number-covered page with great care, to slip it back into its envelope and set it to one side. He swept the scraps of paper, with a little less care, into their envelope, too. And then he folded his hands and looked at Noah again.

"So we will have no more fooling around," he said, a new edge to his syllables. "The girl Claudia has given us other interesting pieces of information as well. Please empty your pockets."

The German-speaking guard (Noah had almost forgotten about him, he was so quiet) took a step forward.

Noah put a cold hand in his jacket pocket. His fingers found the apartment key and the five marks that were his allowance for the week. He put those things on the table.

"Don't waste our time," said the English-speaking man. "The other pocket."

Where the map was.

He pulled the map out and put it on the table, next to the five marks and the key.

"Exactly," said the English-speaking man, pulling another pair of gloves out of a drawer in the desk and handing them to the other guard. "Very interesting. A map of Berlin. My colleague and I are quite interested in maps, young man. Did you know that? Put your jacket over here, now, please."

The German-speaking man put the other pair of gloves on and opened the map, spreading it out over the desk. When he unfolded it, the German speaker gave a hiss of triumph. It wasn't the streets of East Berlin he was looking at. It was the little inked-in houses and fountains and people and trees of the *Wechselbalgland*.

"Carrying around secret maps of West Berlin! Who made this map for you?" said the English-speaking man.

"We were pretending," said Noah. His own voice sounded especially weak and jittery to him. He doubted that these men spreading out his map with their gloved hands could understand anything he was saying. He almost didn't care. It was so hopeless, and he was so very, very tired and worried and mad. "It was a *game*."

The German-speaking man had actually brought out a magnifying glass from somewhere and was peering closely at the Land of the Changelings, making quick, excited comments to the other man, who answered in nimble German sentences. However well he spoke English, he seemed to speak German even better.

For a moment Noah dozed off, right there in that uncomfortable chair. He just winked out from sheer exhaustion. It was such a relief to close his eyes and let go.

A shout from the men looking at the map woke him right back up again.

The men were there again, shaking him and pointing at the map. Asking some sort of excited question. Shouting something that sounded very German but awfully familiar.

"Sonja Bauer! Matthias Bauer!"

"What? What?" said Noah stupidly.

"Why do you have criminals' names inscribed onto your illegal map of West Berlin?"

The English-speaking man was pointing at something on the map.

"Stand up!" he said to Noah. "Right there! You are trying to smuggle classified information into West Berlin! You are working with your parents, whose project was to pay bribes to *these people,* to corrupt citizens of the German Democratic Republic and turn them into spies for the West!"

Noah stood up reluctantly to see what they were pointing at. It was a tiny little pair of people, added by Cloud-Claudia when she had last had custody of the map. And above their heads she had inked in names, in the teeniest print imaginable: *Sonja Bauer* and *Matthias Bauer.*

He hadn't even seen that she'd done that, until these awful men in their uniforms started shouting at him and tapping on the surface of the map with their magnifying glass.

Somehow, despite everything, Noah managed at that awful moment to remember what the story was about Cloud-Claudia's parents. He managed somehow to say to the men with their gloved hands: "But those are just the names of her parents who died. They were in a car accident."

The men stared at him. The people behind the one-way mirror undoubtedly stared at him, too. Noah didn't care anymore about any of that staring.

"Car accident, you say?" said the English-speaking man. "Then why have you drawn them on the other side of the border? Why have you drawn pictures of GDR citizens *Sonja Bauer* and *Matthias Bauer* standing in West Berlin? There's no point in pretending. Your little friend has already told us all about your parents' secret mission here. She was recruited, like her parents, GDR citizens *Sonja Bauer* and *Matthias Bauer,* to engage in activities that would damage the German Democratic Republic. And your pictures here are the *proof.*"

He remembered not to correct them about who had done the drawing.

He shook his head.

"But I keep telling you: it's not really West Berlin. That's the *Wechselbalgland.* It's where changelings come from. And maybe go back to. We made it up! It's not real. Look at the little castles! Look at the flying horses! Look at the candy-cane trees!"

Noah couldn't help himself. He pointed to those crooked little Pegasi, and some tiny little border fence snapped inside him, and he began to laugh the horrible exhausted laugh of someone who has been kept up for seven hours in garages and cellar rooms in a police station in East Berlin,

328

who has been asked nonsensical questions a thousand times, and who can see that those nonsensical questions are simply never going to end. . . .

"C-c-c-candy-cane trees!" he said again, choking on fatigue, on misery, on fear, on laughter, and on those hard consonants, which fed the Astonishing Stutter and made it something huger than life, larger than any words he might possibly have been trying to say. And then that made him laugh again, and then there were tears splashing on his hands for some reason, and then he just couldn't even speak or think a coherent thought anymore, he was so worn out.

He had the vague impression that the men were talking to each other; one of them actually started shouting at the other one of them in German; some dim part of his brain registered the door of the cell opening as one of them left. But he did not care anymore.

Finally somebody took his arms and lifted him out of the chair so that he was standing—wobbling on his own two feet.

"Come!" said the woman who had led Cloud-Claudia down the hall so long before—how long had it been? Long!

Noah followed her out the door. At the last minute, he remembered the map and turned around for it, but the woman gave him a pull forward.

"Quick, now," she said. "Faster!"

They went down various halls and through various doors. Noah could not have said whether these were halls he had been in before or not. They came into a sort of waiting room, and there at the end of it was Cloud-Claudia, asleep on a bench. There were great smeary tracks down her face. She had been crying before she fell asleep.

"Oh, Cloud," said Noah, more for himself than for her, because she was so solidly asleep.

"Quiet, you," said someone he hadn't noticed before, filling out papers on a table.

It was Cloud-Claudia's horrible grandmother.

She looked like she had been crying, too. Her hand was shaking as she wrote on those sheets of paper.

The guard who was leading Noah grabbed his shoulder and turned him forcibly away, so that he was facing the other side of the room.

"Sit still and mind your own business," said the guard.

He fully meant to do that—sit still and mind his own business—because he was practically asleep himself, and he didn't want to cause any more trouble. But there was a noise from behind him, where Cloud-Claudia's grandmother was struggling with those papers.

"You!" she hissed. "Why were you dragging an innocent child out through the streets at night? Telling her such lies? Now you've ruined her life. A child, and you've *ruined her life*."

That made him angry enough that he turned to glare at her, despite all the guards around.

"It wasn't—wasn't—wasn't—me telling the worst lies," said Noah, feeling the warm tide of anger spreading over his face.

"Silence!" barked a guard.

Noah and Frau März glared at each other for what felt like a very long time. But she looked away first, wiping tears from her eyes with a handkerchief. All of Noah's anger turned immediately into an ickier feeling, something like shame and miserableness. And he was shivering, maybe because they had taken his jacket away and maybe because he was so tired. Being very tired can feel like standing outside on a day when the temperature is sinking and sinking.

Noah studied his scuffed-up shoes for a while and tried to think about nothing, while his shivers continued.

That was when an indignant bustling whirlwind came breaking through the far doors.

"There you are! There you are! Oh, my God, there you are!" said the whirlwind, gathering Noah up in all of its four arms.

Because the whirlwind, of course, was Noah's parents.

Secret File #29
WHAT THE NEWSPAPERS WERE SAYING

This sort of thing was also happening in other East German cities: Leipzig, Jena, Potsdam, and Dresden.

Marchers chanted, "Freedom!" and "Gorbi, Gorbi!"— hoping for help from the reform-minded Russian leader Mikhail Gorbachev. He was in town, remember, for the fortieth-anniversary celebrations, as one of the "eminent guests." He looked rather disgusted by Honecker's crowd. He made ambiguously ominous comments about *life passing by those who come too late.*

Western news teams were blocked that day when they tried to make their way to the eastern side of the Brandenburg Gate, the most famous monument on the border between the two Berlins. They had to make do with footage of milling crowds of plainclothes security people wandering down the sidewalks with their hands tucked into their standard-issue "ordinary person" jackets. There were so many of them on the streets, it looked like one of those alien invasions where the aliens dress up in human disguise but haven't quite figured out how to blend in with actual people yet.

While Noah was sitting on that bench, so very early on Sunday morning, the East Berlin newspapers were printing up the official description of what had happened the night before:

In the evening hours of the 7th of October, hooligans attempted to disturb the festival celebrating the 40th anniversary of the GDR. In cooperation with Western media, they roamed in packs through the area around the Alexanderplatz and shouted out slogans hostile to the Republic. Thanks to the levelheadedness of the defense and security forces, as well as of the festival participants, the intended provocations could not unfold as planned. The ringleaders were taken into custody.

Most of the people the government called "hooligans" and "ringleaders" were not as young as Cloud-Claudia and Noah — but then again, some of them were.

chapter thirty

OUT

"Stand up," said the guard when Noah's parents came into the waiting room, but he was already in their arms by then.

"Grab your things, kiddo," said his father. "We're getting you out of here."

He didn't have any things, so he just stood there, feeling wobbly.

His mother looked at him and then said angrily, "They've kept him up all this time. Look at him! Were they *questioning* you? How dare they!"

And then she turned to the guards and started raking them over the coals in very good German. She kept gesturing at a third man who had come with them. Noah hadn't noticed him at first, but apparently he was from the American embassy. She pointed at him and pointed at Noah and said angry, angry things about human rights and worldwide conventions on the treatment of children.

Noah stared at her. Of course they had been asking questions. Isn't that what police did when they took you into their garages and their cellars and their tiny little offices? The questions hadn't been the worst part. The worst part had been the standing.

No, he took that back.

The worst part had been when they took Cloud-Claudia in one direction and Noah in another.

That made him look over at Cloud-Claudia, who was no longer asleep. She was sitting up on her bench now, woken up by all the commotion, looking over at Noah.

"Hey," he called out to her while the grown-ups argued all around.

She looked distressed by everything she was hearing.

"They're taking you away?" she said.

"Just going home," he said. "Just going home to sleep."

His father gave his shoulders a big squeeze.

"Afraid not, kiddo," he said. "We're leaving the country. They're sending us out, to West Berlin."

"Quiet!" said the various guards. They were already moving to hustle Cloud-Claudia and her grandmother through a door into some different space. *"The agents hostile to the*

German Democratic Republic will not continue to disrupt this essential post as it upholds our collective security."

"Wait! What? You're going away?" said Cloud-Claudia while her grandmother tried desperately to hush her. She actually managed to break loose from her grandmother's hands and come running over to Noah, miserable wildness all over her face. "You're leaving? Why are you leaving? They all always leave. My mom and dad—they didn't die—they *left me behind on purpose.* They told me, the ones here. *They chose to leave me behind!* And now you, Wallfish! And the ones here took the names away from me. They took them. Now you'll forget, and they'll forget. Nobody will remember anything."

She was hugging him now, and all the grown-ups were already pulling at her, peeling her away. Noah tried to hold on, but the guards and the grandmother were stronger than he was.

Everything had been awful, that whole night long, but this was by far the worst.

They were carrying Cloud-Claudia right out of the room.

"I'll remember everything!" shouted Noah after her. "Everything! *Every*thing! Cloud! Every single thing! And *they* haven't forgotten you. I'm sure they haven't. I won't, either!"

Then she was gone, and his parents were holding him up or holding him back or some combination of the two.

"Shocking," said the man from the embassy. "Really shocking. Well, we should be on our way now."

"Jonah, where's your jacket?" asked his mother. "It's chilly outside."

"They took it away," said Noah.

"Please bring him his jacket and scarf," said his mother to the guards. She was still hanging on to him tightly. "Then we'll go."

They brought Noah his jacket and scarf.

He checked, but of course the map of the Changelings' Land wasn't in his pocket anymore. Or the five marks or the key. He was only sad about the map, though. All of Cloud's wonderful little pictures, locked up in some evidence file in this awful building forever.

He was hustled out into the dark, chilly night and put into the backseat of a car with his mother and father.

The man from the embassy sat in the front with another man, the driver.

"Out we go!" said the man from the embassy. And to Noah, he said, "You've caused a lot of trouble here, young man."

"I didn't mean to," said Noah. "I didn't mean to at all. She was running away—all alone at night—I—"

"Shhh," said his mother. "No discussion here—they'll be listening, sweetheart. We'll talk about it all once we're well away from here."

There were headlights shining through the back window the whole way. The East Germans had sent police cars to shepherd them, one ahead and one behind, to make sure their car went right to the border and through. It was like being a criminal, for sure.

The streets were empty now. It was still night, though the date must now be the eighth of October instead of the seventh. Noah caught glimpses of buildings and streets and more buildings and lampposts. When he lowered his head, he could see the television tower, high, hovering above everything else, looking down at them, looking and watching as the three cars drove toward the checkpoint: the police car, the embassy's car, and the other police car.

They were the only people going in that direction through the checkpoint. Actually, there was nobody going in the other direction, either.

"They've shut the border, you know," said the embassy man. "That's why it's so quiet here. All the troubles this weekend; they don't want newspeople or tourists with cameras or what-have-you. They can't keep us diplomats out, of course, but everyone else — *verboten*."

At the checkpoint, a policeman jumped out of the car in front and talked to the soldiers there, pointing at the car Noah's family was in and saluting.

They looked at the passports of everyone in Noah's car, but that was it.

Thwap! Thwap! Thwap!

That was the border guard stamping their passports with some vicious-looking red stamp.

"Well, that's it. You've been kicked out of a country now," said Noah's father. "And before the age of eleven! Kicked out and told never to come back."

Noah was still so tired, he almost didn't care. "What about our stuff?"

"Most of it's in suitcases in the back," said his mother, giving him a squeeze. "Don't worry about it. It's only stuff."

And then he was asleep, dreaming that he was awake and standing and being shouted at, dreaming that he had gotten lost on the way into the Changelings' Land and had ended up in that terrible, horrible police building instead, dreaming above all that he wasn't asleep and would never be allowed to sleep again.

And then they were leading him from the car into a building, through the bite of cold air.

No brushing teeth. No changing clothes. No nothing. He just flung himself down onto the cot they led him to and slept.

Oh, there was one strange moment, before he fell completely asleep. Somebody was taking his shoes off, and then his jacket. His mother, he thought. Then he opened his eyes, although he was really still mostly asleep, and saw his mother ripping open the seam of his jacket.

"Oh, no," she was saying under her breath. "Oh, no. Oh, no!"

Her hands were tense fists, hiding her eyes.

"Pointless!" she said to herself. "All pointless, after all!"

It was frightening to see her that upset. Noah's mother was so good at not letting anything show.

"Mom?" said Noah.

She took the fists from her eyes immediately. Tried to put one of her normal expressions on.

"Are you okay?" he asked.

"Of course," she said. "Completely fine. Lost something—that's all."

"Not lost," he said, the Astonishing Stutter becoming an extraordinary mumble, he was so tired. "I've got it."

She smiled then, though her hands stayed tense.

"Sweet boy. Jonah. You should be asleep."

Jonah? Was he still Jonah, even here on the western side of the Wall?

Apparently so.

Apparently the listening just went on and on, no matter which side of the Wall you happened to be on.

The Wall! When would they ever be far enough away from it?

"I *am* asleep," said Noah.

And a moment later, he was.

Secret File #30
THE DEVIL'S MOUNTAIN

Not so terribly far from where Noah was sleeping was a mountain with a sinister name: the Teufelsberg — the Devil's Mountain. It was a mountain made of rubble, from all the buildings in Berlin that had been destroyed during the Second World War. Grass grew over this mountain of crumbled ruins, and on the top were funny buildings that looked a bit like planetariums.

They were actually secret American ears, those buildings. Inside them, soldiers listened and listened to the secret conversations buzzing about Berlin.

It helped to have your mechanical "ears" perched on top of a hill.

Everyone was listening to everyone, always, in both sides of Berlin, West and East. Remember that West Berlin was still technically an occupied city. That was one reason why Noah remained "Jonah" even after crossing back through the Wall.

· chapter thirty-one ·

CLOUD AND WALLFISH

Over the next few days, official people asked him questions in a nicer, warmer, comfier room. They let him sleep a lot, but Noah was tired of questions. And he had questions of his own, which he knew he couldn't ask.

Questions like these:

When could his name go back to being Noah?

How much of what that English-speaking man at the police station had said about Noah's parents was true? Were his parents really spies? Had they really been using Noah like a disguise? Like a pawn?

And was he ever going to see Cloud-Claudia again?

Part of getting older is realizing that sometimes you

have to be the person who answers your own questions. Noah watched and listened carefully, and he got as far as this:

1. Since they all called him Jonah in that place, he figured he was stuck being Jonah for the time being, maybe until they got back to safe and quiet Oasis, Virginia. On the other hand, he discovered he didn't mind being Jonah so much anymore. If he hadn't been Jonah, he wouldn't have ever known he was a wallfish!

That was the first question, more or less answered.

2. The second question had only dark tunnels for answers. He didn't think much of the *East Germans'* evidence for his parents' being spies — the page from *Alice*, the blank scraps of paper — but neither could he forget those file folders in his brain, the ones labeled "Mom" and "Dad" and growing thicker by the day. And what about the other part of this question: Had his parents been using him that way? As their *cover story?*

And then everything got very dark-tunnelly again in his brain, and he tried to turn his mind around and walk away from this whole question, which was so dangerous and seemed possibly about to hurt way too much.

3. The THIRD question, though!
To that one, Noah got an official answer from his mother: "See Cloud-Claudia again? Oh, sweetie, probably not—I'm so sorry about that."

But the more he thought about it, the less acceptable that answer was.

There were still things people wanted to ask Noah and his parents, and forms for them to fill out because they really were filing protests about the way Noah had been treated in that police station, and also there were some arrangements that had to be made concerning what they did next, so they were staying in a little apartment that belonged to the U.S. Army in West Berlin.

The television in it was, ironically, much smaller and plainer than the one they had had in Communist East Berlin. They were not much of a television-watching family ordinarily, but these days the television seemed always to be tuned to the news: seventy thousand people marching in Leipzig! Thousands of people protesting in East Berlin, just on the other side of the Wall! Noah kept his eyes peeled for Cloud-Claudia, but she never showed up.

Finally, he lost patience with merely watching and hoping. He took a very large cardboard box and cut it into the right shape; then he borrowed white paint from a very nice soldier who was touching up a wall downstairs.

"Take me to that place we were waving to from the other side," he said to his parents. "Back when Cloud-Claudia and I went close to the Wall—so close we could see the people looking in from the West. Take me there."

His mother gave him a look, but his father said, "All right, then. Tomorrow."

They went on the S-Bahn with Noah's huge slab of white cardboard balanced between his knees. He got a lot of funny looks from the West Berliners! But he absolutely didn't care.

Right next to the Wall, which on this side was covered with graffiti and paintings and slogans and all sorts of things that were forbidden on the other side, there stood a kind of platform with steps up, and from the top of it, Noah could see that very street he and Cloud-Claudia had been on all those many weeks ago. He was looking into the other world.

"How long are you going to be?" asked his dad.

"A while," said Noah.

"Okay," said his dad. "I'm down there waiting when your arms get tired."

And Noah turned toward the other world and hoisted his cardboard sign, his bright-white-painted cloud, right over his head.

I remember everything! said that cloud. *I'm not forgetting you.* Never.

He stood there for more than an hour, with other people, mostly tourists coming and going, looking at him with kind, puzzled expressions on their faces and sometimes asking him what he was doing.

"It's for my friend," he said to them, and he could see them trying very hard to figure out what he was saying, trying to follow the choppy start-and-stop path of the Astonishing Stutter. "So she knows I'm not forgetting her."

Sometimes the other people helped him hold his sign up for a while when they heard that.

When he came back down the stairs, his arms and fingers were very cold and stiff, but he felt alive inside.

"Can we come back again tomorrow?" he asked his dad.

His father thought about it.

"If you really want to."

"I do," said Noah with total certainty. "I want to come back every single day."

"Hmm," said his dad, but they did. They came back the next day, the next day, and the day after that.

The people on the S-Bahn and in the neighborhood of

the viewing platform started calling him, in a friendly way, the "Cloud Boy" when he walked by.

"Cloud's my friend," he told them. "I'm the Wallfish."

"What? what?"

"Wallfish!"

If he sang it, it came out more smoothly, but it was an odd sort of song: "Wallfish, Wallfish, my nickname is the Wallfish. . . ."

"Kinda small for a *Walfisch*, aren't you?!"

(Because they heard it as the German word, of course. The *Walfisch* that meant "whale.")

He held up his bright-white cloud for Cloud-Claudia and stared at the little people in the street on the other side of the Wall, just stared and stared, wondering whether it was even possible to recognize particular people from this far away. The better-prepared visitors brought binoculars with them, and sometimes they would let him take a look while they took a turn holding up his cloud for a few minutes.

In the mornings, he answered the questions of the U.S. diplomatic people and the U.S. Army people, and then in the afternoon one of his parents—usually his father, since his mother was salvaging what she could of her thesis— would take him and his cloud-sign to the Wall.

"They're shutting the gates," said his father, only a couple of days into Noah's cloud project. "They've changed the rules so East Germans can't travel to Czechoslovakia anymore—unless they're already old enough to be retired. No more Czech Center for German-German relations!"

Noah's father shook his head.

"More history happening," he said, but he didn't even have the heart to sniff the air.

"Do they think they can keep everybody locked up tight forever?" said his mother.

Her voice was indignant and glum, both at once. You could tell she thought maybe they *could* just keep everybody locked up tight forever. Noah was less concerned about "everybody" than he was about Cloud-Claudia, who was probably still locked up tight in the evil grandmother's apartment.

But then again, maybe not. He didn't think Cloud-Claudia was the sort of person to stay locked up forever. Someday she would find a way to get out, and then maybe she would wander back toward Brunnenstraße, or she would be walking around East Berlin, happy to be back out of doors, breathing in the lovely coal-smoky air, when she'd overhear whispers about how some crazy-person *drüben* was holding up some crazy crazy sign at the Wall, shaped like a—and then she would *know*:

Noah had not forgotten her.

He would never, ever forget her, no matter where he was: West Berlin, Virginia, or across the many rivers of the *Wechselbalgland*.

She should not think she was so easily forgettable. Nobody should have to feel that way, and especially not Cloud-Claudia.

Secret File #31
MORE HISTORY HAPPENING

On Wednesday, October 18, three very big things happened.

Noah's family woke up to the news that there had been a big earthquake in California. Bridges knocked down! Freeways collapsing! It sounded awful. Noah had never lived in a place that had earthquakes, but sometimes he had nightmares where things started falling down all around him, like the Tower of Babel when it was being destroyed.

That same day, Erich Honecker, chairman, general secretary, et cetera, resigned "for health reasons."

"Ah!" said Noah's mother.

The following Monday, the regular protest march in Leipzig was absolutely enormous: more than three hundred thousand people walked through the streets, chanting their discontent.

"We'll see!" said Noah's mother. Noah's father perked up and took a whiff of the air, right there in front of their little television.

"Smell it now?" he said to Noah. "Smell that history now?"

chapter thirty-two

NO NAMES

That next Monday, October 23, Noah had a visitor, but not in his family's own little apartment. An American official showed up to lead Noah to the place where the visitor was waiting.

In the U.S. headquarters in West Berlin, there were a lot of rooms Noah had never seen, and then on top of those, there were probably many secret rooms he would never see in a million years, so he followed the man closely, thinking about what time it was and wondering how long this would take. He always left for the Wall at about one p.m., after lunch.

They led him into another room, with windows looking out onto the courtyard and a number of dark chairs. The woman in that room wasn't sitting in any of those chairs. She was facing outside and picking at the curtain with a nervous hand.

It seemed like the sort of hand that would be good at drawing pictures of rocks that looked like magicians.

Her hair was the hair of someone who had been worried for a very long time about things more important than haircuts or even brushes. It was a nondescript pale color, but her eyes weren't nondescript at all. They were the deepest brown imaginable. They had worlds in them. He would have known those eyes anywhere.

Her lips curled up higher on the right side than on the left, just as they had in that photograph Cloud-Claudia had shown him months ago.

Sonja Bauer, said his mind confidently, reading that name off the lost map and the lost puzzle piece and the lost slip of paper in the lost pocket of Cloud-Claudia, who was also lost.

Sonja Bauer, Sonja Bauer, Sonja Bauer.

"You're the boy who knows Claudia!" she said, coming over to take his hands. "Claudia's friend! Is she all right? Is she okay? You know they won't let me see her —"

A sob hiccupped its way out of her, but she took a quick breath to disguise it.

"— or even write to her. Or anything. My own daughter! She must be so unhappy."

For a moment Noah was stumped. What could he say?

"Yes," he said. "She's pretty unhappy, I guess. First they told her you were dead, and then they told her at the police station that you ran away without her."

If he had been speaking English, and if the Astonishing Stutter hadn't been blocking his path with special stubbornness, who knows? He might have been able to say all of that more gently. But on the other hand, there was nothing gentle about the plain *facts*. So maybe it didn't matter so much, how cleverly you packaged everything up in words.

Claudia's mother was on the edge of tears, but she was rather tough, all the same. They were all tough in that family, Noah realized: the grandmother in a harsh way, but the mother and Claudia more like plants that keep stretching bent limbs toward the sun no matter how many times they get trampled on.

"There's so much I don't understand," she said. "Why did poor Claudia think I was dead? Didn't she see me, that day at the Wall? I think she must have seen me. I saw her wave!"

"That was you?" said Noah. Even as he said that, he noticed that one of her shoulders was a little higher than the other. "That was really you?"

"Of course!" said Cloud-Claudia's mother. "They had

told me she might come, that Wednesday, and there she was, just like they said—"

The official American man stepped forward, one brisk step.

"No details, please, about the arrangements."

"Yes, of course," she said, flustered. "Never mind. As long as she knew I was there."

"Well," said Noah, feeling a little flustered himself, "I did sort of hint you might have been watching. I—I thought I was lying." He remembered, all at once, his mother saying something about his taking Claudia to the edge of the Wall, on the Brunnenstraße: *Wednesday—hmm; okay; yes.* Something like that. His mental gears went clickety-clack as he filed that away in the "Mom" file.

"Tell me about her," said Cloud-Claudia's mother.

So Noah told her everything he remembered: about the puzzle, about the photos Claudia had shown them from the camping trip, about the paper whales for the *Wandzeitung*, about the map. Claudia's mother listened with hungry eyes.

"She was lucky to find a good friend like you. Thank you, thank you for being such a friend. She must have felt so very alone—"

But she stopped short there, almost as if she had been about to hit an astonishing stutter of her own. It was the

353

loneliness she had run into. Now even Noah was gone, and Cloud-Claudia must be as alone as she had ever been.

"You have to believe me: we didn't mean to leave her, not really," she said, all in a rush. "We heard they weren't shooting anymore, on the Hungarian border, and we were just drawn like moths. Like stupid moths. Guess we thought they'd let us send for her if we were both on the other side. Every day I wake up and remember and am sorry all over again. Poor Claudia and poor Matthias!"

She was beginning to lose her calm, Noah could tell. The man from the U.S. Mission was watching her with his eyes slightly narrowed. He was being very carefully sympathetic, Noah thought, as if this woman might unexpectedly burst into tears or flames. "Poor Claudia, who thinks I abandoned her! *Because I did!*"

Noah could tell how much that thought must have been scorching her, from the inside out. Noah didn't have the slightest clue what you said to someone being eaten alive by a terrible thought like that. She trembled there for a moment, and then repeated the question that seemed to be haunting her most:

"But I don't understand why she would think I was *dead*."

Noah blinked. "That's what Frau März told her. Your mother. She said you were both dead, killed in a car accident in Hungary. So that's what we all thought."

Except maybe my parents—but he didn't say that, of course.

"Oh, no!" said Sonja Bauer, putting a hand to her mouth, as if it could hardly believe her face was still there. The hand was shaking like a leaf. "No, no, no, no! How could she do that? How could she?"

And then she just crumpled.

Literally: she crumpled to the ground.

The U.S. official jumped to help her. He must have pressed a secret button or something, too, because there were steps in the corridor outside the room almost immediately.

"Oh, Claudia," the woman said, but she was more crying than speaking now. "*Oh,* Claudia! Oh, my poor girl!"

Noah didn't know what to say, but it didn't matter: he didn't have time to say anything, anyway. Another official was already steering him out of the room, a no-nonsense hand on his shoulder, guiding him away, away from the misery that had welled up there.

The Wall did not just slice across Berlin: it sliced right into the hearts of the people who lived there.

Secret File #32
MORE TROUBLES WITH NAMES

An embassy is the place where you find the official representatives of one country in a different country's capital. In East Berlin, capital of the German Democratic Republic, there was a U.S. embassy.

So what could the Americans call their administration and their buildings in West Berlin? It was a problem.

Remember that West Berlin was not officially a part of the Federal Republic of Germany, but rather an occupied city. The Americans did have an embassy in West Germany, in the faraway town of Bonn. In West Berlin they could not, technically, have another "embassy." And yet they did have many people to house and lots of business to transact — and, of course, lots of codes to listen to.

What the Americans ended up calling the non-embassy embassy in West Berlin was the U.S. Mission Berlin.

It was — like everything about Berlin in those years — a most peculiar situation.

· chapter thirty-three ·

A WALK IN THE WOODS

"Let's go on a walk in the woods this morning!" said Noah's mother cheerfully in early November.

That was code.

It meant: *Noah, it's really getting to be time for us all to leave Berlin, since they've asked you all their questions and we can't go back over the Wall, so let's take the bus to the Grunewald forest and walk among late-autumn trees while I try to talk you out of your adorable but hopeless cloud-at-the-Wall project. Wear your scarf and mittens.*

They went through the gate into the woods, and Noah thought how peculiar it was that West Berlin, which was just a tiny island in the middle of East Germany, some-times felt so large! The trees of the Grunewald went on and on and on and on, almost as if they'd never heard of borders, edges, or Walls. You could get lost in there, he bet, if you weren't careful.

It was cold that day. Even in all his layers, Noah was a little chilled in those cold, still woods.

They were totally sympathetic toward Noah and Cloud. That's how Noah's mother started: *Completely sympathetic.*

But very soon, it would be time for them to go home.

"But I don't know whether she's seen me there yet," he said. "I can't leave until she knows I was there. That I didn't forget."

"I think we have to be more realistic, sweetie. She's most likely never going to see you," said his mother. "I wish that weren't true, but you know it is. We've wanted to support you in this thing, but I'm just telling you that soon, very soon, it's going to be time to leave Berlin and go home."

"You're saying that because they've asked us all their questions."

His mother gave one of her hooting laughs.

"That's one reason," she said. "Also they're tired of putting us up, and my usefulness here is running out, too. Aren't you ready to go home?"

Noah shook his head because he didn't want to be distracted by thinking about *home,* not yet.

"See, I've been wondering some things, too," he said.

"Oh, dear," said his mother with a half laugh. "All right. I guess you have."

"I mean, I've been thinking a lot. About everything."

"And?" said his mother.

"And one thing I've been thinking is that Dad must have been dropping those bits of paper on purpose. He wanted to keep them all guessing, on the other side of the Wall. It was like being a decoy, I think."

"Hmm," said his mother. "Are you done?"

"Not exactly," said Noah. He didn't add his other thought about his father, how if he was a *decoy*, then he must have been distracting the police from *something*, and how that *something* seemed like it might have to be *what Noah's mother might be up to*. But he left that thought alone. Instead, he said, "And I think I know when you learned Hungarian. It was during those extra five years."

His mother stopped short, right in the middle of the path. Turned and looked at him. Just stared. She didn't even say, *What are you talking about?* or something like that. She just stared.

In his mind he had opened up the "Mom" file; he picked up those imaginary notes and looked at them, in his mind, and the words to explain what he thought tumbled out into the quiet woods in stops and starts and pauses and floods:

"You told me I'm six months younger than I always thought I was, though now I don't know what's right, actually. But I think *you* are five years older than you say. Or maybe even six. That picture of you and Grandpa—that was from 1953. From the time of Queen Elizabeth's coronation. I figured that out. And you said that was your fourth birthday. *So*—"

He paused only long enough to take a deep, cold breath. Forest air! No coal smoke anywhere! It was a treat to breathe in these woods.

"So what I've figured out is, I think you must have been born in 1949 and then did something else after high school—after your *first* run through high school. I think you studied somewhere and learned all these languages. And then they sent you to Charlottesburg, to kind of pretend to be a senior in high school all over again. Like I've been pretending to be in the fourth class here. And maybe you even had a different name to get used to. Like you and Dad said, people change their names all the time, right? And then you just went on through college and everything, but with those extra secret years. And I don't know what you were doing in East Berlin exactly, but I figure it's got something to do with the names you sewed into my jacket—"

"Names!" said his mother. Her eyes had secrets in them. Curtains and more curtains. "What are you talking about?"

"The list of names you put in my jacket," said Noah. "I found it."

"You found it," said his mother. Echoing is safer than saying anything outright.

"That awful night, when the police got us. I found it hidden in my jacket. I didn't know what those names were, but I figured you didn't want the East Germans to get them."

"No," said his mother. She was really staring at him now. "Are you saying the East German police didn't take anything out of your jacket that night?"

"Well, they took our map—Cloud's map—and some money and stuff. But there wasn't any list inside my jacket by the time they were looking."

"No?" said his mother. "Why? Where did it go?"

"I—I ate it," said Noah, not sure whether he was mostly proud or mostly embarrassed.

His mother looked entirely surprised and then threw her head back and laughed.

"Oh!" she said. "You're amazing! Really, you are! Well, it's gone, then, one way or another."

Noah shifted his weight from foot to foot. He was nervous about this next part, too.

"What were those names?" Noah asked.

"Nothing that matters to you," said his mother. "Nothing that matters now. That list is gone."

"No," he said. "It's not really gone."

"What do you mean?" asked his mother.

"I took a picture of it," he said. "Is it important?"

"You did what?" said his mother. She sounded shocked, which was very seldom the case, when it came to Noah's mother. "You took a *picture*? That's not possible. Where in the world did you get a camera?"

Noah sucked in his breath.

"Not with a camera," he said. "It's in my head. I can keep pictures in my head."

"You can't keep a picture of a long list of words," said his mother, but she wasn't entirely confident now, Noah could tell.

Noah looked at her and started reading out names from the picture in his mind. Probably his pronunciation was pretty terrible!

His mother went pale and put her hand over his mouth for a moment, to stop him.

"Shh," she said. "Wait one second—here's a pen."

Noah's mother never went anywhere without a pen. And she always had a notebook, too.

While Noah wrote down the names he could see on the list in his mind, his mother stood there quietly, rubbing her arms because she was cold or because she couldn't believe what was happening, or perhaps for both reasons. Noah had to focus very hard to get the names on the paper to match exactly the names in his mind.

As he finished, his mother plucked the notebook out of his hands and examined the list he had written there with a look that Noah had never seen on her face before: surprise and delight and awe, all mixed together.

"You did it," she said, a few times in a row. "You really did do it. And I had no idea!"

That moment was very sweet: golden-rosy and brimming with satisfaction, like the best peach you ever tasted.

And then Noah thought of something:

"Who are they?" he said. The golden moment dimmed very slightly.

"That's nothing for you to worry about," said his mother.

"But what will happen to them now?" said Noah.

"We can't know that," said his mother.

"But are they going to get in trouble, now that I wrote their names down?"

"Why are you asking such wild questions?" said his mother with a quick lightning bolt of a smile. "Come on, notice how cold it's gotten? It's time to go home."

"But if you won't tell me whose names those are, then how do I know whether it was the right thing to do, writing them down?"

It was truly like an itch he couldn't keep from scratching. His mother was looking at him in surprise, and he was almost as surprised by himself as she was.

"Of course it's right. What else could it be?" said Noah's

mother, tilting her head to one side before pulling Noah back onto the path that led out of the wood and back into ordinary life. "Anyway, it's cold out here, and I promise you those people have been doing bad things."

"But do they have kids?"

"Oh, now, really!" said his mother, but her voice was quieter.

"It's just—What if your names were on somebody's list? Yours and Dad's? What if someone arrested *you*? *What would I do then?*"

It was Cloud-Claudia he was thinking of, of course. Someone had thought her parents were bad people—and look what had happened to them and to her!

"I need to know what the right thing is."

His mother studied his face and shook her head.

"Sorry, but we never get to know everything," she said. "Not even us grown-ups. We just do the best we can."

Noah held out his hand.

"Then maybe you should give it back to me, that page with the names."

His mother shook her head with a smile that was just the slightest bit rueful around the edges.

"Can't do that, sorry!" she said.

"Then it's like what that man said," said Noah.

Noah could feel his mother go instantly and completely still, studying him; she had a real talent for sudden focus.

"What?" she asked. "What man? Said what?"

This next part was especially hard:

"The East German officer, the one who spoke English, he told me you and Dad were just using me. To get into the GDR. He said I was your disguise. A kid with a bad, bad stutter. Like a mustache or a wig!"

"Oh, now. What a dumb thing to say."

"I don't want to be somebody's *wig!*" said Noah. He really was mad about it.

"Shh, shh," said his mother. "That stupid man must not have kids, that's for sure. Not ones he loves, anyway. A wig is something you could wear or not wear. You could leave a wig in a drawer and put on a hat instead or decide to have red hair instead of brown hair for a while, am I right?"

Noah was surprised to find he was holding his breath. He looked up at his mom and nodded once, very tightly, just hanging on hard to see what was coming next.

"So that's ridiculous. That's got nothing to do with the way I feel about you," said his mother. "Wherever we are, whatever our names happen to be, you aren't something I could take off or set aside. Ever. You, Jonah-Noah Keller-Brown, are the center of the known universe as far as I'm concerned. And that's true no matter what side of the Wall we happen to be on, and no matter what you do or don't do. That's always and everywhere true."

She was smiling. Noah couldn't find the words to

speak. It was like the curtains in her eyes had opened for a moment, and he could see all the way in, to where all the walls were turning out to be windows, and where his mother's heart turned out to echo his own.

His mother gave him a hug. "You've been amazing. Really, you have. No one would ever believe you could do all that. Keeping pictures of lists in your head! Eating secrets!"

Then all of a sudden she straightened back up and grinned at him.

"Here's something I can say for sure: it would have been bad if those East Germans had seen that paper. So you're a hero as far as I'm concerned, for eating that list. And then you're my hero a second time for writing it down. And finally, here's a secret."

She bent down, gave him another hug, and murmured very quietly, secret-like, into his ear: "All those questions you like to ask? Just because I can't answer them doesn't mean they're not good questions. You keep asking them. It takes courage to ask why! And now, hero-times-three, it's time to go home, don't you think?"

Time to go home, yes. But to tell the truth, Noah had never felt as much at *home* as he was feeling right at that moment, out there in the chilly Berlin woods. It turns out that *home* is not mostly a place. *Home* is someone putting her arms around you and saying the words your heart longs to hear: *always and everywhere.*

Secret File #33
WALLS AND WINDOWS, WINDOWS AND WALLS

On Saturday, November 4, 1989, half a million people came out to the Alexanderplatz in East Berlin to demand reform, change, democracy. Noah and his parents watched on television — so many people! So many hopeful and determined faces! All those thousands of slogans on the handwritten banners and signs!

> PLURALISM INSTEAD OF PARTY MONARCHY!
> WE DEMAND FREE ELECTIONS!

A writer took the podium and said, "It's as if someone has pushed open a window. . . ."

Noah's father said, "How will all this end?"

Noah's mother said, "A window isn't enough."

Noah thought, *Oh, Cloud!*

Even More Secret File #33
THE NAMES IN THE JACKET

About those names: they were a small part of a list of people in West Germany who were spying for East Germany. Noah didn't figure this out for years, but I'm telling you now. Don't say anything out loud. Don't make faces. Keep smiling and turn the page.

chapter thirty-four

CRAZY KID WITH A CLOUD

It was November 8, a Wednesday. Noah had been given one more week by his parents, and this was nearly the end of that week.

The cardboard clouds did not do well in bad weather, and sometimes got banged up on their way to the Wall, so Noah was on his fourth cloud. Fourth and probably last.

"It's amazing that you're still doing this," said his father. "It's not just making the disappointment worse for you, is it?"

"No," said Noah. How did you measure such things, anyway?

He lugged his cloud up the steps. He was telling himself that someday someone would notice—perhaps already had noticed. A rumor might start. *Crazy guy with a cloud* . . . And someday, maybe, she would hear about it, right? Even if it was years and years from now, and they were both all grown up.

In other words, he was grasping at straws that day, because when time is running out, grasping at straws is the best we can do.

Once again he hoisted the cloud, up as high above his head as he could reach. And he looked out over that so-completely-familiar street and tried not to feel impatient or disappointed or even cold and tired. He had said he wouldn't forget her. And he needed her to know he had not forgotten.

That was when the miraculous thing happened.

One of those little figures walking across the street turned and waved at him. Sometimes a brave person did wave. That wasn't entirely unheard of, especially these days. But this one waved and waved and waved, and even jumped up and down a little. And when it took off its hat to wave harder, it turned out to have what looked like short, misbehaving blond hair on the top of its head.

Noah pointed and shouted and made his cloud bounce up and down some, and before he knew it, one of the other on lookers was handing him a pair of binoculars and holding his cloud up for a moment so that he could focus.

"Hey, kid, is that her? Is that your friend over there?"

Some of these people had been up here with Noah and his cloud before.

The image was blurry. The image kept jumping up and down. But the image was absolutely certainly and amazingly Cloud-Claudia.

He cheered! And you know what? Everyone on that platform cheered with him! Everyone cheered and waved. Noah's father came up the steps to see what was happening.

And Noah made the cloud go up and down, back and forth, sending its message over the Wall as surely as if it had been spelled out in great big ordinary words:

I HAVE NOT FORGOTTEN YOU, CLOUD!!

They waved at each other for a very long time, seemed like, before some larger person appeared—some grandmother-like person—and took her away from that street.

"Wow," said Noah. His arms were more tired now than they'd ever been in his whole life. He felt completely and abruptly worn out, and all the cheering and handshaking that was still going on around him on the platform suddenly felt like too much, somehow.

Fortunately his dad was there to help haul the cloud back down the stairs.

"Well, how about that, kiddo?" said his dad. His voice

tripped up in the middle of the last word, almost as if he had caught a very tiny case of the stutters. "You did it. You had more faith than the rest of us."

"I hope she's not in terrible trouble now," said Noah.

"I don't think so," said his father. "All she did was wave at you! What's so terrible about that?"

Noah just looked at him.

"No, really," said his father. "Even that grandmother of hers must feel that things are changing. Anyway, there's something I've been wanting to say to you, Noah."

Noah!

Noah's eyes caught him by surprise by filling with tears. He had been like a stretched rubber band forever, and now suddenly the tension had evaporated, and that was a kind of shock, too.

"Do I get to be Noah again?" he said, keeping his voice very quiet, as if saying it out loud might frighten his old name away.

"Soon you do," said his father. "Very soon. And you know what? The truth is, you've always been who you are. You're better than the rest of us that way. You've stayed Noah on the inside, deep down, haven't you?"

Noah thought about it.

He had.

It was true.

Though he had learned a lot from being the Wallfish, too.

"So here's our promise to you: When we go home, which is going to be very soon, you'll go back to being Noah. All the Jonah stuff will be put away."

Noah thought about that for a moment.

"When I was born—was Jonah the name I had then? I mean, for real. Or Noah?"

"For real?" said his father. "For real, your name was Baby Boy."

He was laughing now.

"What?" said Noah.

"We couldn't choose a name. We had too many good ideas. So your first birth certificate just says Baby Boy—"

"Baby Boy *what*?" said Noah. "What was my last name?"

"That would be telling," said his father, as if he were making a joke. "But it wasn't Brown. Think of it this way: you've been Jonah Brown for a while; it was the disguise you needed to wear. Maybe you'll want to dress up in another name someday, who knows? Or maybe you'll go back to your Oasis name and never want that to change ever again."

"Can I have my birthday back, too?"

"Yep. Everything can go back to the way it was. There'll be some very boring story about where we all went to, some small boring town in the middle of boring nowhere for boring business reasons."

"Without any boring Wall," said Noah, rubbing his eyes

372

with his mittens. "Mom will make a picture album about all the boring things we did there."

"Right," said his dad.

They were silent for a moment.

"Now Cloud knows I didn't forget her," said Noah.

"You certainly didn't. You are the truest of the true," said his father.

"And I won't forget. I won't ever forget. Can I write her letters?"

His father didn't say anything. The bus was coming, anyway.

"Because I'd like to write her letters sometimes. I bet she'd like getting a letter."

"Now you're getting carried away!" said his father. It was supposed to sound cheerful, but mostly it sounded sad. "A letter! How would you sign it? What address would you give? Not to mention that it would never get through."

Secret File #34
EVERY SINGLE LETTER

Here's why Noah's father was right, as things stood at the beginning of November 1989, about letters having trouble getting through. The Stasi—the East German secret police—didn't just plant bugs in walls and listen to people's secrets.

They opened and copied every single letter that went between the GDR and the outside world. Every. Single. One. And Noah had been expelled! There really was no chance at all that a letter from him — if his cautious and clandestine parents, with all those secrets they were keeping, would even let him write such a letter — a letter that traveled through ordinary mailboxes and in ordinary mailbags, would ever reach Cloud-Claudia on the other side of the Wall.

· chapter thirty-five ·

CRUMBLING WALLS

"So!" said his mother the next morning. "This is it. We're going home!"

She had been happy about the Cloud message finally getting through, too. But they had been told it was high time for them to leave. Thank you for your service, but enough is enough—that is what Noah gathered someone must have been saying to his mother.

Noah wasn't surprised that all the talk now was about leaving. What did surprise him was the news that they had tickets on a predawn flight out of Berlin *the very next day.*

Well, they didn't have all that much stuff to organize. They walked around town one last time—it still felt to Noah like a completely different city, with its burned-out church steeple and its glittering stores, from the *other* Berlin—and then packed up their bags and had one last spaghetti dinner cooked up by Noah's father on the hot plate. They would have to get up so early the next day to catch their flight, it was practically going to be the middle of the night.

"Wait," said Noah's mother. She had been listening to something on the radio. "Turn on the news."

A bunch of men sitting behind a long wooden desk.

"Press conference," said Noah's mother. "Just an hour or so ago. That's Günter Schabowski right there—listen to what he said!"

"Who's Günter Schabowski?" asked Noah.

"Party Politburo guy," said Noah's father. "Government official. The horse's mouth."

The Schabowski person said a bunch of stuff, of which Noah understood bits and pieces. Something about a change in visa requirements?

"It's because of Czechoslovakia—they closed the border, they opened the border, everyone started leaving again—"

That was Noah's father, trying to give helpful explanations, but his mother said, "Shhhhhhh!"

She was standing up now.

A man in ordinary TV news clothes was reading an ordinary summary of news from a piece of paper on his desk. Behind him was a map Noah had seen a hundred times already this year: the two Germanies colored green, with a special yellow teardrop labeled "East Berlin." And under the map, three tight-lipped words:

"*DDR öffnet Grenze.*"

The GDR is opening the border.

That was a sentence Noah could understand the words of perfectly well, but still he had no idea what it actually meant. His father was standing up now, too, watching the man on the TV.

"Wait—what does that mean?" he asked. "Opening the border? What border?"

His parents were looking at each other, looks zipping back and forth between them like electricity running through cables, like lightning leaping from tower to tower.

"Don't know," said his mother. "Schabowski just said the new visa rules would take effect right away. *Right away?* Oh, Lord, now they've gone on to insurance for old people. Where's the real news?"

She turned the channel dial, but there wasn't anything else there.

"Well, tomorrow's going to be an interesting day!" said Noah's father.

"What's going to happen?"

"I don't know," said his father. "We'll see what that Schabowski really meant, I guess."

"*We* won't see," said Noah, feeling bitter about it. All that talk of smelling history in the air, and they were going to get on a plane and fly away. "We're leaving!"

His father looked at his watch.

"In six hours. You, young sprout, need to go to bed and pretend to sleep a little before they take our parent license away. Car's coming for us at four a.m."

"Bed" had been a euphemism in this place; Noah had been sleeping on the sofa. But this last night he was supposed to have his parents' bed, while they got everything ready out in the living room. He stared at the walls and the shadows, wondering what would happen now. Wondering whether Cloud-Claudia's grandmother was relenting. Wondering whether the news meant that someday Cloud-Claudia would see her parents again, and what that would be like—whether they could all forget how she had been left behind, sort of like how he was leaving Berlin behind and Jonah behind and . . .

So he did doze off, after all, despite thinking that couldn't possibly happen.

He was asleep for what felt like about twelve seconds—then his father was shaking him awake.

"Up you get! Sorry, kiddo!"

"Is it four already?" asked Noah. Four a.m. in November feels like the middle of the night. Because it *is* the middle of the night.

But his father was shaking his head.

"Change of plan, change of plan," he said. "It's just about midnight, but we've got to see this. Come now, quickly. The driver will be here any second."

What?

"Things are happening," said his father. "We're leaving a little earlier for the airport—we're going to make a detour. Driver's up for it, so off we go."

Noah stumbled into his clothes, into his jacket, down the stairs, with his suitcase always threatening to topple into his ankles and trip him up.

It was cold outside, and so dark, and there was a car there with a guy standing next to it, smoking. He put their suitcases into the trunk and started chatting with Noah's parents in German.

It was like something that might happen on another planet.

"Started coming through around eleven or so," the driver was saying. "All right! Everyone in? How do you want to do this?"

"Get as close as you can," said Noah's father. "We'll just see what we can see, and then head off to the airport."

"Eyes open," said Noah's mother, giving him a bracing squeeze. She was in the backseat with Noah; his father was riding up front with the driver.

They drove up the big street into the center of West

Berlin. Usually at this time of night on a weekday it would be quiet on these streets in Berlin. But there was a surprising number of people around, more and more as they got closer to the eastern side of the city.

And then it was entirely crowded, filled with people and cars—a huge party taking shape in the street. Like New Year's Eve, sort of, only this was November.

"Bornholmer Straße," said the driver, slowing to a crawl in all that crowd. "God in heaven. Looks like it's all true, doesn't it?"

"What's going on?" said Noah, pressing his nose to the glass. "What's all true?"

"We're at the border now," said his father. "This is the Wall. Those people there are coming through the Wall. It's coming down. It's coming down!"

"What?" said Noah. "Those are people from East Berlin?"

"*Trabis!*" said Noah's mother, pointing at the little cars parading through the crowd. That was the name of those cars, *Trabis*. They were East Berlin cars, not West Berlin cars. They shouldn't have been here, certainly not a whole parade of them, inching along. "Here they come!"

"Want to get out for a minute?" said the driver. "Just a minute, though. Don't want to get lost in this crowd."

They opened the doors and stepped out.

It was cold and bright and the middle of the night, and everybody was shouting and cheering and crying and thumping on the roofs of the cars coming through. There was a crowd of West Berliners cheering on the people coming through. And the bright lights of television cameras. And so much noise! It was the Pan-European Picnic all over again, but at night in a city in cold weather—and so much huger. You had the feeling that this might be the hugest thing you ever saw in your whole life.

Even Noah's parents were crying. They were grinning like fools and waving and crying, which was just not what they ordinarily would ever do.

Noah's eyes had gone right to work from the moment he had stepped out of the car: searching the crowd, searching the crowd.

He was looking for someone medium small, with crazy yellow hair that needed brushing. He looked for that person with as much concentration as he had used all those weeks before when he was hoisting his cloud up over the Wall.

Come on, Cloud-Claudia!

His fists were tense with the effort of that looking.

It wasn't until his parents made some small noise that he remembered them and looked over their way. Their faces had changed. They were watching him, Noah, more than they were watching all the jubilant people.

"She won't be here, kiddo," said his dad. "You know that. That grandmother's not the type to go running to the Wall the moment the gates open."

Come on! thought Noah anyway.

He wanted to prove them wrong.

She had waved, just yesterday.

She knew he remembered her.

She had to be there.

They watched for an hour, and then the driver said they'd better start trying to get out of the neighborhood if they were ever going to get to the airport.

"She's going to be okay now," said his mother. "You know that. Her parents will find her. This has got to be the beginning of the end for all of those walls. Her father will get out of prison. Her mother will be able to come back home. Soon she'll be okay again, whichever side of the border she ends up on."

Noah leaned his head against the window of the car, beaming a good-bye back through all those happy crowds.

Good-bye!

He had never told her his real name, never once. And he never could: those were the Rules.

Well, then, part of him would have to stay Wallfish forever and ever.

Even in the land of the *Wechselbalgen,* some names will
never be forgotten:
Cloud and Wallfish,
Wallfish
and
Cloud.

EPILOGUE

Some years have gone by. In Germany somewhere, there's a teenager with slightly disobedient blond hair and a pile of postcards, mailed to her from all sorts of different places, from all over the world (but never from Virginia).

The postcards have been arriving ever since she was very young, back in the sad old days when she lived in Berlin without either one of her parents. She has made an arrangement with the people who moved into the apartment her grandmother used to live in: they save the postcards for her, and she brings them chocolates or something whenever she comes by to pick them up.

"Not much to those cards, honestly!" says the woman who lives in the apartment. She is a little embarrassed about taking presents in exchange for such a small favor. "But there's no accounting for tastes."

Every one of those postcards has a cloud drawn on the back.

Someday, Claudia knows, someone is going to come to that apartment, following the pull of all those clouds he sent on ahead to her. A true friend—truest of the true. She has told the people living there: *When a guy shows up at your door one day and calls himself Wallfish, go ahead and give him this envelope with my address.*

Her address, a puzzle piece with an inky whale drawn on its back, and a map of Berlin.

AUTHOR'S NOTE

Some books live on the history shelves, and other books are fiction—but *Cloud and Wallfish* has deep roots in both places. Noah and his parents are entirely fictional, as are all the characters in the story. But the world they are living in—even the apartment Noah lives in in East Berlin—is as scrupulously close to the historical truth as I could possibly make it.

I first got to know East Berlin in 1987, when I spent a summer there, working on my German. I made some good friends that summer, and found East Germany such a fascinating place that I decided to devote part of my PhD dissertation to East German literature. That meant coming back to the German Democratic Republic in 1989 to do research. My husband and I had to get married so that he could come along, so I know something about changing your personal life in order to get a visa. We arrived in January 1989 and left in July; we watched the Wall fall from the other side of the world (California) and then returned to East Berlin in the spring of 1990, during that fascinating period when no one really seemed to be in charge of the place and anarchists held parties in ruined buildings.

Every day in 1989, I would walk from our apartment in the Max-Beer-Straße, across the Museum Island (where a statue really did lie on her back behind a fence, waiting for better days), to the old library on Unter den Linden, where I read newspapers and journals from the 1940s. Our local supermarket was the one near the Alexanderplatz that Noah and his father visit. Our apartment really did have a "children's room"—we used it as a study.

Everything that claims to be a historical document in this book—the speeches of Margot Honecker; the decrees of the East German government; quotes from the local newspaper, the *Berliner Zeitung*—is real. I have translated those passages from the German, but I haven't changed what they say. As well as newspapers and books from the period, I also had the journals we kept, the notes I was always taking, the photographs taken at that time by us and by our friends.

One way in which my own experience in East Berlin was very different from that of Noah in this story is that I wasn't as lonely. Eric and I had wonderful friends in East Germany, and with them we went on walks in the woods, attended concerts and plays, and talked endlessly about the future of the world.

In this book, the fictional parts—the story—are mostly to be found in the regular chapters, and the nonfictional historical material in the Secret Files at the end of each chapter. But of course there is a lot of history in the fictional parts of the book, and of course every account of history always has some fiction mixed up in it. When you read a nonfiction book, or nonfiction parts of fictional books, you have to stay as alert as any researcher (or spy). Truth and fiction are tangled together in everything human beings do and in every story they tell. Whenever a book claims to be telling the truth, it is wise (as Noah's mother says at one point) to *keep asking questions.*

ACKNOWLEDGMENTS

Thank you from the bottom of my heart to the two people without whom this book would still be nothing more than a secret file: Ammi-Joan Paquette and Kaylan Adair.

The people of Candlewick are fiercely creative and intelligent. Kaylan Adair's amazing ability to ask the right questions about every page turned revision into a fine adventure. Allison Cole made the book better in countless ways. Maryellen Hanley designed the strikingly beautiful cover. My thanks also to John Mendelson, Kathleen Rourke, and Phoebe Kosman, for everything they do to get books into children's hands. Betsy Uhrig did a valiant job with the copyedits, and Hannah Mahoney checked everything twice.

The wonderful Rosemary Brosnan gave me the great gift of encouragement at a crucial moment: thank you! Jenn Reese and Jayne Williams were catalysts for all sorts of small and large miracles, and I am so lucky to know them.

I have explored Berlin with many extraordinary people over the years. My parents, Robert Nesbet and Helen MacPherson Nesbet, dragged me to (West) Germany when I was a teenager. I wasn't grateful then, but I am now. Susan Nesbet and Barbara Nesbet and Will Waters kept me reasonably sane that year and continue to do so.

Eric Naiman has been asking for a book about Berlin ever since the German Democratic Republic forced us to get married so that he could come East with me in 1989. It took a long time, but here it finally is! With Lee Naiman and Bob Naiman, we explored some remote East German corners in search of a really lovely dinner.

Above all, of course, are the people we came to know and love in East Berlin: my gratitude and affection go to Thomas Bachmann, Silke and Matthias Bugge, Annette Rauh, Grit Heiduk, Meike Bischoff, and Ines Kumanoff. This story would not exist without their stories.

The book about Berlin was drafted in Paris, where I was lucky to be surrounded by the energy and encouragement of Eleanor Naiman, Ada Naiman, and Hannah Konkel, not to mention Soushka. We all rejoiced when Thera Naiman visited. Thank you also to Yuri Slezkine and Lisa Little, who welcomed me back to Berlin on the pleasantest of research trips.

This book is dedicated to Ines, whose friendship melted the Wall.